Aces Wild

Stephanie Renee

Copyright © 2020 Stephanie Renee

All rights reserved

The characters and events portrayed in this book are fictitious. Any similarity to real persons, living or dead, is coincidental and not intended by the author.

No part of this book may be reproduced, or stored in a retrieval system, or transmitted in any form or by any means, electronic, mechanical, photocopying, recording, or otherwise, without express written permission of the publisher.

Cover design by: BookCover4U

This one goes out to my husband. Thank you for being the ultimate inspiration for all of the wonderful guys I write about. I couldn't ask for a better man to call mine. Xoxo. Love you, D.

Chapter One
TESS

"So, where did you say you were going?" The sound of my brother's voice comes through the other end of my cell phone.

I didn't say. Honestly, it's not really any of his business.

"Out." I respond, hoping he will get the message.

"Right. I got that part. But where?"

Apparently not.

"Let me remind you that you are my *little* brother, Ty," I say, my tone warning him to drop it.

Despite the fact that Tyler Wendell is taller than me and far larger, I'm still older than him by about eighteen months… and I'll never let him forget it.

"Little or not, I can still worry about my sister leaving her New York apartment at nine o'clock at night to go roaming the city. Stop…don't put that in your mouth." The last words are directed at one of his twin daughters.

"Which one is giving you grief tonight?" I ask.

"Which one is always giving me grief?"

"Lilah," we both answer in unison.

Tyler and his wife Sam have beautiful twin daughters, Lilah and Abby, who are close to turning two.

"What have my little angels been up to today?" I ask, hoping to distract him from our previous subject.

"Well, Abby has been playing dolls most of the day, and Lilah has been trying to get into everything she possibly can. Earlier, Sam and I walked in the garage for one minute and came back to our kitchen covered in flour. It was everywhere. Looked like a freaking cocaine den. And there was Lilah right in the middle of it, laughing her little ass off," he says.

"Ass!" I hear a tiny voice say in the background.

"Sam is going to kill me," he groans.

My lips pull up into a huge smile. My nieces tend to have that effect on me. Although they look similar, they are absolutely night and day. Abby is the shy and quiet one who never seems to get into any trouble, and Lilah is the passionate, fiery one who always seems to be *in* trouble. I can definitely see her being a little hellion when she enters her teenage years...not that I'm going to tell my brother that. He's got enough to deal with.

"But don't try to change the subject, Tess. You're seriously not going to tell me where you're going?"

I'm really not. He will have some sort of lecture to give me, and I'm not in the mood.

"You know, you didn't worry nearly this much when I was in the Congo working with Doctors without Borders. Why the worry now? You know you and I both grew up in this city, right?"

"Number one, I did worry about you when you were in Africa, but it's not like I could ever get you on the phone to tell you that. And yes, we grew up in New York, but it's not like we were roaming the streets in the middle of the night," he says.

Maybe YOU weren't.

In attempt to get him off my back, I blurt, "Ty, I'm just going out dancing with a couple girlfriends. That's it."

Liar.

"Oh," he pauses. "Why not just tell me that?"

"Because I don't have to explain myself to you," I snap.

"True. I just miss you, Tess. You're always working or traveling. Come to Boston for the weekend," he pleads. "The girls and I would love to see you."

"I miss all of you too, but I have to work this weekend. Trauma in the ER doesn't stop because I'd like a weekend away. But I promise to come back soon." I hope my promise is enough to stop this line of inquiry.

"Okay, fine. Just be careful tonight, okay?"

I agree, and we exchange a few last-minute words before Lilah emptied a whole bottle of toothpaste and smeared it on the dog, and Tyler has to go.

I really do miss him. I miss all of them. Maybe he's right. I do work all the time, and although I don't travel like I used to, I still don't make the time for family like I should. Any free time I have tends to go toward going out to different clubs on my nights off. With the stress of my job, dancing and drinking seems to be the only thing keeping me sane these days.

But I wasn't about to tell my brother that. He would just worry even more. Becoming a father made Tyler Wendell about as paternal as you could get, and it crept into all areas of his life, not just his daughters. When he met Sam, he gave up his partying man-whore ways, and I'm extremely happy for him. But let's just say that I haven't gotten the partying itch out of my system just yet…especially since the past ten years of my life had been taken up with medical school, internship, residency, and then a few trips to war-torn countries assisting with combat injuries. Needless to say, I'm due for some fun in my life.

I finish applying mascara to my already smokey eyes and finish off the look with some lip gloss. Leaning back, I took inventory of myself in the mirror.

Tight black sparkly tank top that clings to my barely-there chest? Check.

Equally tight straight-legged jeans that accentuate my long legs? Check.

Makeup that makes my eyes look sexy yet will probably make me look like a racoon by the end of the night? Check.

Hair down, but still have a hair tie with me for when it gets too hot? Check.

Leather ankle boots that make me look taller than I already am? Check.

I'm not some woman who thinks the world of herself, but I have confidence. Hell, I bust my ass going for a run every day to get the body I have, and I love showing it off.

But I don't get all dolled up in hopes of bringing someone home with me. In fact, I almost never do random hookups. There better be something damn special about him if I'm taking him to bed.

Maybe that's why I haven't been laid in so long…my standards are just too high.

Usually when I go out, it's with my best friend, Chris. He and I have known each other for years but just recently started getting close again after running into each other at a nightclub. Chris is gay, so he never hits on me, which makes him the perfect wingman.

Glancing at my phone, I see a photo from Tyler with their large Labrador mix, Mason, covered in toothpaste.

Poor dog.

With a couple of quick emoji's as a response, I throw my phone in my purse and head out the door, excited for what the night might bring.

Chapter Two

TESS

CLUB ROCK.

That is what the sign reads above the entrance to the club. All of the windows are blacked out so it's impossible to see inside.

Honestly, I know nothing about this place, but Chris bar tends here and said I should check it out. The only thing he really told me was that it was a lot different than most of the places we frequent.

As I open the front door into the dimly lit entryway, I walk up to the bouncer and hand him my ID. His eyes glance back and forth between the photo and my face a few times before he gruffly says, "You here alone?"

I nod. "Why? Is that a problem?"

"No. Just don't see a lot of women going to clubs by themselves anymore. The whole 'safer to travel in packs' thing."

My lip curls into a slight grin. "Guess I'm just a lone wolf. I don't need anyone around to protect me."

The words sound almost arrogant, but they are 100% true. Between my time working in the Congo and my job at the hospital in a bad part of town, I have been taking self-defense classes for years. Not much could scare me anymore. Not after what I had seen.

The large bouncer locks eyes with me, and I cross my arms over my chest, waiting. When he sees me not backing down, he takes a final glance at my ID and holds it under some sort of UV light to make sure it's authentic. When he sees it is, he steps aside and lets me pass.

About damn time, Lars.

Excitement flutters in my stomach as I push past the large double doors leading into the club itself. I get what the bouncer said about women wanting to go places together. Most women I knew would hate to go to a club by themselves. I, on the other hand, seem to thrive on being alone.

As I step inside, my eyes glance around the room, trying to take in my surroundings. Music was thumping but not enough to hurt my ears. I can still hear conversations of people as I walk toward the bar. It's way more low-key than I'm used to.

Instead of the flashy neon lights of some clubs, the lighting in Club Rock is dim yet warm. It's just enough to cast a slight glow on everything it touched.

A dancefloor sits in the middle of the large area, and it's scattered with people grinding on each other. A few of them are going at it so hard, they are practically fucking right there in front of everyone.

When I finally get to the bar, Chris grins when he sees me. "There you are, gorgeous! I was beginning to think you were never going to show."

"Tyler called and wouldn't stop interrogating me," I respond.

He simply nods knowing how my brother can be.

"Vodka?" He asks, already pulling out the bottle before I have time to respond.

He knows me so well.

We catch up about our days for a minute before he steps away to pour a drink for someone else who has just sat down.

While he's gone, my eyes glance around the space. It's a nice place...a bit more upscale than I've been going to lately.

Now, I come from money so I've seen the swanky, fancy bars too, but usually, I opt for the ones that are a bit more mainstream. The whole chandelier, black-tie-affair thing isn't really my gig.

This place though seems to fall somewhere in the middle.

Chris finally returns and I ask, "So, what's the deal with Club Rock?"

His brow furrows, so I continue. "I mean it's not like the typical bars we go to. Where's the techno music and the strobe lights?"

Chris laughs. "Let's just say the owner is a sophisticated guy. You know the kind, dark and brooding. He wanted a place people could go when they got tired of the typical club scene. I like it because it's not quite so rowdy. Yeah, you still have people dancing and sweating all over each other, but you don't usually have the 'just turned 21' crowd who are loud and end up throwing up everywhere."

Looking around, I can definitely see the sophistication factor. Around the entire outside of the large room are large leather chairs and couches, and dark cherry coffee tables and end tables are scattered throughout the seating.

And the place is clean…at least from what I can see. I had been in some seedy clubs where it looked like you might get Hepatitis if you sat down on anything. Club Rock though doesn't have that 'everything needs sanitized' feel to it.

"So, what's to stop all of the 21-year-old's from coming in here and messing up everyone's good time?" I ask.

"Well, I assume you saw Vince when you came in?"

"You mean Lars? The one who was blocking the door?"

He laughs. "Yeah, him. He will turn away anyone who he thinks might cause problems. And if he happens to miss one, and they start causing shit, he will throw them out immediately."

Good to know.

We talk for a few more minutes before I gulp the rest of my drink. "I'm going to go dance, Chris, but I'll be back for more," I wink, and he nods.

"Go get it, baby girl!" He calls after me.

I make my way into the middle of the crowd of people and start dancing. The music is still thumping, and I swear I can feel the vibrations through every inch of me as my body moves.

Every worry I have is suddenly eased away as I am in my own element. A couple of guys come over and try to dance with me, but when they see I'm not giving them the time of day, they quickly lose interest and move on.

Good. I didn't come here for them. I came here for me.

My eyes are suddenly pulled to something in the corner. Or should I say *someone* in the corner. A man is walking down a corner staircase, and the second his feet hit the floor, I swear the air in the room changes. It is as if his presence demands to be felt. He radiates sheer power and authority.

He walks over to the bar, and I can't take my eyes off him. He has dark brown hair which is pushed back from his face and perfectly styled. My mind immediately wonders what he would look like with that hair all messy with a just-fucked look.

Where did that come from?

But my fantasies don't stop there. Seeing his tall, rock hard frame, I wondered what it would be like to straddle and ride him. To climb him like a fucking tree.

It usually took a lot for me to really take an interest in a man, but this one has me all hot and bothered and hasn't even spoken a single word.

When he gets to the bar, he says something to Chris and takes a seat on the same stool I had just been sitting in. He and Chris talked, and I catch a hint of a smile on his handsome face, but it's gone just as quickly as it appeared.

I keep dancing, trying to take my attention off the sexy man in the three piece suit. It's no use though because when my eyes flick up again, I see him once more, but this time, his eyes are staring straight at me.

I wonder if he's looking at someone else, but the intensity in his gaze is unmistakable as his eyes pierce mine. He looks as if he wants to devour me whole.

I figure, since he's staring, I might as well put on a good show. My hips sway to the music, and my hands move seductively along my skin. I turn so I can give him a good shot of my ass.

Okay, who am I?

When I finally get the courage to look back, he is sipping what looks like whiskey, but his eyes are still firmly locked on me. My mouth goes dry as I feel his stare on my every move.

I push my long hair out of my face and begin to make my way to the bar. When I reach it, I say, "Hey, Chris. Can I get another vodka?"

"Sure thing, doll," he says, and I have a drink in front of me in seconds.

I try to pretend not to notice his eyes still fixed on me, but I have goosebumps so big he can probably see them. I expect him so say something to me or to move in closer.

But instead, he sets his drink back on the bar and gets up to walk away. My heart sinks a little until I see him slide a napkin toward me with something written on it.

I wait until he is walking away before I dare glance at it. One word. That's all it says.

UPSTAIRS.

My eyes look up to see him climbing the stairs he descended from earlier. As he takes them two at a time, I can see his muscular thighs about to rip through his suit pants. Jesus, the man is built.

"Who..." I began before Chris cut me off.

"*That* is Alexander Rockford. The guy who owns the place," he said while wiping down a glass.

"What's his story?" I ask.

He shrugs. "No one really knows. Remember...dark and brooding. Most people around here are terrified of him. He's usually nice to me, and we make some small talk, but I couldn't tell you anything personal about him. All I know is he sure is fun to look at."

"He sure is," I mutter, taking another sip.

Chris' eyes caught the napkin. "Seems he's taken a liking to you. Are you going to go?" He nods at the stairs.

Boy, that's certainly a loaded question. One hand, it has been so long since I've gotten laid that I barely remember what it feels like. On the other hand, I don't do hookups with random guys.

But Alexander Rockford isn't just some random guy. Well, he sort of is, but he is also quite possibly the most gorgeous man I've ever seen in my life. This whole clubbing experience was a way for me to have some fun and forget about my problems. And it's probably about damn time I hop back in the metaphorical saddle. Who better to help me with that than Mr. Dark and Brooding himself?

In the middle of my mental war, Chris said, "Well? Are you going to go?"

"Should I?"

"You do whatever you want to honey, but if I had a chance with that, I sure as shit wouldn't pass it up. But I will tell you one thing though…if you're going to do it, I'd hurry up because the one thing I do know about Alexander Rockford, is that he doesn't like to be kept waiting."

Chapter Three
ALEXANDER

I lean back in my chair as I watch her on my computer screen. My club has cameras everywhere, and she certainly stands out in a crowd. She's talking to Chris at the bar, and her eyes keep focusing on the staircase in the middle of the room...the staircase I just came up.

I'm hoping my little note was enough to get her up here. If she lets me, I'll have her bent over my desk screaming my name in no time flat. My dick has been pitching a tent in my pants ever since I laid eyes on her.

The way her body swayed on the dance floor was mesmerizing. Most women danced by doing nothing more than shaking their tits and ass. And don't get me wrong, I love tits and ass, but this woman is more than that.

I study her in the monitor. I can see her long, straight black hair which hangs down to the middle of her back. She's tall...not as tall as I am at six and half feet, but with her heels on, she's only a couple inches off. Her legs are long and slender. She's got a thin frame, but she looks fit. Her cute little sculpted ass and perky tits just round out the whole picture.

My attraction for her somewhat surprises me. I tend to go for petite women...woman who are significantly shorter than me. Woman I can manhandle in the bedroom…if she's into that sort of thing.

No, women like the beauty on the screen are not my type. Yet here I am, eyes glued and completely in awe like it was first time I'd ever seen a gorgeous woman.

After all of her deliberating, I see her step off her barstool, finish her drink, and head toward the stairs.

This should be fun.

My hand flips off my computer monitor so she doesn't see my extensive camera views right as she knocks on the door.

"Come in," I say.

She opens the door slowly yet enters as if she owns the place. This woman oozes confidence. And it's hot as hell.

Without a word, she comes over and takes a seat on the opposite side of my large desk. With her arms on either side of the chair, she crosses one leg over the other.

"You rang?" She said with a smirk.

"I'm Alexander," I say, anxious to get the pleasantries out of the way.

"I know," she replies.

"Did you know who I was when you caught me watching you dance?"

She shakes her head. "No. Chris just told me after you left your mysterious note."

"What else did Chris tell you," I curiously ask.

Her shoulders shrug. "Not much. Said you're dark and brooding, so he doesn't really know much."

My chuckle fills the air between us. "Dark and brooding, huh? I guess I get that. You still haven't told me your name."

She sits pensively for a moment as if trying to decide whether or not to give me the real one.

Finally, she says, "Tess."

Standing up, she begins to pace around my large office. She's taking everything in as if trying to figure me out. I can't stop sneaking glimpses at her ass in those tight, black jeans.

"So, what exactly do you do, Alexander?" She says my

name slowly, and it drips off her tongue. "I mean besides owning this club."

"I do a lot of things," I answer, trying to be as vague as possible.

She giggles. "That usually means you don't really do anything."

I laugh but get out of my chair to stand in front of her so that her back is now pressed up against the wall.

"Oh, Tess, believe me when I say I *do* a lot of things. And I'm *good* at a lot of things."

Although she tries to keep her demeanor calm and cool, I see her pulse strumming in her neck. She softly inhales as I step closer to her, and I can see she wants this as badly as I do.

Before she has time to think another thought, I crash my mouth down on hers. Most women would want to start slowly, but Tess is right there with me, matching passion for passion.

Our tongues dance, and I attempt to pin her against the wall and take control, but her hands are everywhere as she pulls off my suit jacket and turns me so my back is against the wall. As much as I fight for dominance, she battles me for it. Her tongue explores my mouth just as I explore hers. Her hands roam over me as I yearn to pin them above her head. Her fingers grip my cock through my pants at the same time as I am palming her ass.

I pull back, breaking our kiss, and we are both panting.

"You should go," I say, and the look of confusion and hurt on her face is quickly replaced with one of anger.

"What the fuck?" She asks.

But I don't answer. In fact, I don't even look at her, worried that my resolve will quickly fade.

I turn away from her, picking up my jacket off the ground and walking over to place it on the back of my desk chair. Before I can turn back around, I hear the door slam.

As much as I want her, I know better. Women I tend to go after are more on the submissive side and not just in the bedroom. And they know what they're getting into. No strings attached. I fuck them. They leave. No questions asked.

And the number one rule…

I'm in charge.

I don't care how sexy a woman is. That's not going to change.

But that isn't Tess. I could tell from the moment I kissed her. She is all passion, and she craves control as badly as I do.

Not going to happen, sweetheart.

Chapter Four
TESS

What the fuck?!
Alexander Rockford couldn't take his eyes off me all fucking night, and the second we start getting hot and heavy, he kicks me out?

I have no idea what I could have possibly done wrong.

Fuck that. I didn't do shit wrong. Maybe he just couldn't get it up.

No, that definitely wasn't it. I could feel his very, very, large member pressed up against me while his mouth explored mine. Him getting it up definitely wasn't the issue.

I walk back into my apartment and collapse on my bed. I kick off my heels and stare at the ceiling still picturing that kiss. The way his tongue expertly plunged into my mouth…the electricity between us as our hands roamed each other's bodies…the fire ignited between us.

I can't lie…it was hot.

Or maybe it's just been too long since I have been fucked. I count on my fingers trying to figure out how many months it had been and let out a groan when I ran out of fingers.

Damn.

When I was in Africa, I had a short fling with Mark, who

was one of the other doctors. Although we worked damn near 20 hours a day, we still were hot for each other. It was like saving lives all day made us eager to rip each other's clothes off every evening.

Mark was great. And he was a good lay. But we both decided a long time ago that when we left the Congo, we were done. Neither one of us wanted more, and we were leaving that part of ourselves in the jungle. Last I heard, he got called to South America to set up a new clinic, and I came back to New York.

I haven't heard from him since.

After him, there was one drunken night with one of the ER doctors at the hospital, but after he couldn't stay hard due to all the booze, our night was cut short. Thankfully, he was so drunk, he barely remembers any of it. Even though I do, I keep it to myself. No need to make things between us any more awkward than they already are.

Tonight was a heavy reminder of how wonderful that passion and heat between two people could be. I guess trying to find that a little more often couldn't hurt.

It definitely beats sitting in my apartment thinking about my cobweb covered vagina.

I kick off my pants and get under the covers, realizing that my panties are soaked from my little make out session earlier.

Well, at least it still works.

I try to close my eyes, but every time I do, images of him flood my mind. Up close, he was even more gorgeous. His brown chestnut colored hair. His perfect teeth when he gave that rare crooked smile. His chiseled face which has the slightest bit of stubble that rubbed against me when I kissed him.

And those eyes. From far away, they looked dark, almost black. But up close, I could see they were a deep metallic blue. I'm sure just one look from him could bring a million women to their knees.

Am I one of them?

I'd like to think not, but damn, they were sexy.

I remember his body against mine. It was thick and muscular, and even with his suit on, I could feel every single ridge of muscle as my hands explored him.

No. Stop it.

I try to force the images out, determined to get some sleep. Finally, I begin to drift off, but all that occupies my dreams is Alexander Rockford.

Chapter Five
ALEXANDER

The next day, I sit in my office chair listening to my financial advisor babble on and on over speaker phone. Chet is an alright guy, I suppose, but truth be told, I don't listen to him much. It's my money, and I handle it however I see fit. I should probably cut the poor guy loose because I'm sure he's tired of dealing with someone who won't listen to him…but I also know I'm his biggest client, and I'd feel bad leaving him high and dry.

I might be a dick, but I'm clinging to whatever soul I still have left.

So, I listen while he drones on. Every once in a while, he says, "Are you even listening?"

And I respond with the last three or four words he just uttered and go back to my daydreaming.

Daydreaming of the sexy, long-legged beauty that was in here last night is far more appealing than listening to Chet crunch numbers.

Tess.

She seemed so very different than the usual women that get my engine running. Having money and power like I do, I get a decent amount of pussy. I'm not trying to sound conceited here, but it's true. Once a woman finds out who I am, she is begging to let me do anything I want to her.

And I do. *Anything* and *everything* I want, they freely give. And afterwards, I have no qualms about never calling them again. I always make sure they know what they are getting into. I'm not cut out for relationships, and I make no promises that I don't intend to keep.

It's not that I necessarily enjoy being *that* guy. It's that I know I can be closed off and distant, and most women don't deserve that. Plus, the skeletons in my closet would scare most women off. It's better to just keep it casual. *Casual* means less *casualties* in the long run.

But something tells me that Tess isn't the 'casual fuck' kind of woman. She seems like the type of woman to have a man taste her once and be completely infatuated. She probably has them begging for more once they get inside her. And as much as I want to see what's between those sweet legs of hers, I'm not going to start something I can't finish.

As Chet continues to blather on, I pull up the files from the club last night. At Club Rock, we track everything. Not only do I have over fifty cameras on the premises, but I make sure the bouncer snaps photos of all the ID's when he checks them with the black light. It comes in handy if the cops ever come knocking wanting to know if someone was here on a particular night.

I keep hitting the arrow button to scroll through to who I am looking for.

Blonde. No.

Redhead. No.

Guy. No.

Long black hair. Bingo.

'Tess Wendell' was what was typed on her ID.

Quickly, I do an internet search for a Tess Wendell, and honestly I'm shocked at what I find.

Phrases like **Daughter to the real-estate moguls Theo and Maria Wendell** are scattered among the articles.

But there are also titles like:

Local Dr. Tess Wendell to travel with Doctors Without Borders

Tess Wendell starts charity fund for kids with no healthcare

Dr. Tess Wendell stops on the side of the road to help with accident.

Apparently, not only is this woman attractive, she's smart. She's a damn doctor.

And she also has a heart. A big one.

Something I feared, over the years, had metaphorically stopped beating in my own chest.

I was right to send her away. Even though just the thought of her makes my dick hard enough to cut glass, we would be a terrible match.

Although I might sound like an asshole, I'm not looking for a woman to challenge me at every turn. I'm not looking for someone who will 'make me a better man'. As far as I'm concerned, I'm beyond reproach. What's the point in trying to save the damned?

I'm looking for the same kind of woman I've always been looking for...someone who will let me fuck them and won't ask any questions. Maybe it gets a little boring sometimes, but it's what I know, and I'm not about to change.

For anyone.

Even someone as perfect as Tess Wendell.

Chapter Six
TESS

My feet hit the pavement at a steady pace as I run through the park. I'd just gotten off a twelve-hour shift, and of course, what did I want to do? Take a long run through the crisp morning air. For most, it would help to wake them up. For me, it will wear me out enough for my head to hit the pillow when I get home. I hate my monthly rotation on the night shift; I never seem to get enough sleep.

But I love to run. That feeling that my muscles are going to catch fire is the best high I can get. It also helps me to shake off whatever might have happened during my shift at the hospital. Afterall, I can't save everyone.

Being a perfectionist made that fact extremely hard to deal with. Because I wanted to save them all. Every last one. I'm sure every doctor feels that way, but when I first started at the hospital, I would take every single death extremely personally. The lives lost would weigh on my mind for weeks...until I had complete mental breakdown.

I started to work out as a way to get rid of all that bad energy. An outlet for all my stress, rage, aggression, sadness, and whatever other torrid emotions needed to leave my body. It worked. And now, I'll take any form of exercise I can get...except

Yoga. I tried that shit, and let's just say I can't sit still long enough for it to do any good.

My eyes glance down at my smart watch, and I see that I have already gone about four and a half miles, and I'm not really anywhere near my apartment. Turning around, I begin to head back the direction I just came from.

My mind starts to wander thinking about Alexander Rockford. I have no clue why that asshole is on my mind. Okay, yes I do. He's hotter than sin, and I want to ride him all night long.

Those facts aside though, he's clearly not interested.
Fuck that.

I know he was interested. I could feel it by the giant tree trunk in his pants that was pressing into my stomach while we kissed. There was no way he wasn't turned on by me.

So, what was it? Did I do something that turned him off? Was he scared he wouldn't be able to finish the job? Did he not want to fuck in the middle of his office?

If any of the answers to those questions were yes, it would be a total cop out. I'm sure Alexander Rockford had no trouble rising to the occasion and finishing the job. Judging from the way he used his tongue when he kissed me, I bet he could use that tongue in many other wonderful ways.

Damn him. I had been just fine without sex before I had met him. I hadn't even been thinking about it, and now, it seems to be invading every thought that I have.

I picture him using those large hands to touch every inch of my body. I see his hard torso holding me up against the wall while he slides in and out of me. I think of that tongue going down on me until I scream his name.

Even my running, which usually calms me, is doing nothing to quell the ache between my legs. The wind blowing my hair across my neck gives me goosebumps. The cool morning air is making my nipples protrude out of my sports bra. And I feel like every nerve ending in my body is alive.

Knowing I have another night off, I decide it is time to get back on the horse…or the man I guess. It's time to go back to Club Rock.

Because even if I can't have Alexander Rockford, seeing me with someone else will make damn sure he regrets his decision.

Chapter Seven
TESS

"What's up, Vince?" I ask the man planted in the entryway to Club Rock. I thought about calling him Lars but ultimately decided against it.

A look of surprise that I actually know his name crosses his face but immediately vanishes. "Back for more?" He asks.

"Something like that," I reply while he checks my ID. He spends just as much time eyeing it as he did the first time.

"Did you forget me so soon?" I quip.

He just glares at me for a brief moment. Apparently, Vince isn't much of a joker.

When he finally hands it over, I give him a brief smile and walk into the club. With it being a weeknight, the club isn't very crowded. Just a few people are scattered throughout the booths that line the walls, and there are even fewer on the dance floor.

Immediately, I head for the bar and am thankful to see another familiar face. Chris is working again. I meant to text him earlier and let him know my plans to come back, but I completely forgot.

"Hey, beautiful!" He exclaims. "I didn't know you were coming in tonight."

"Hey, you," I say with a grin. "Yeah, I guess I'm just a glutton for punishment."

He's already pouring me some vodka. Once he has it sitting in front of me, he leans down with his elbows resting on the dark wood bar top.

"So, do you want to tell me what happened the other night when Mr. Dark and Brooding invited you upstairs? You just left and never called me. I need details!" He scolds me in a low voice, only loud enough for us to hear.

I sigh. "Not as much as you might think."

His eyebrows raise almost all the way to his hairline. "Was he not able to get it up?"

A giggle escapes me. If Chris is anything, he is certainly blunt. "No, that definitely wasn't the issue. We started getting all hot and heavy, and then, he just asked me to leave."

"Seriously?"

I nod. "Seriously."

"Hmpf. I would say that any guy who didn't immediately jump on you has to be gay, but I'll tell you right now, if that man were gay, I would know it. So, I guess that just makes him an idiot," he scoffs.

"Oh well. His loss is some other guy's gain tonight," I quip with a wink.

"Girl, you better get you some!" He says while thrusting his pelvis.

I start to giggle and try not to spit my drink out.

While I finish my vodka, he and I make some small talk for a few minutes before I move off the barstool and begin to make my way to the dance floor. I'm wearing a pair of tight jeans and a white tank top that is a little shorter than my one yesterday. It never hurts to show a little skin.

As I begin dancing to the music, my mind completely drifts off. I don't think about work or the stress it causes. I don't think about how Tyler won't stop blowing up my phone because he's worried about his sister. I don't think about the million things I probably should be doing instead of heading off to a club every other night.

No.

I think of nothing at all as my body sways in rhythm. It isn't long before I feel a hard body against mine. The man is tall, but right away, I realize he isn't as large as Alexander.

Stop it. Don't think about him.

I turn around to get a look at mystery man's face, and he is definitely attractive. He has longer, messy blonde hair and a sharp cut jaw. His skin is tan like he spends a lot of time outside. And his eyes are an emerald green color.

We dance together, and his large hands are planted on my hips as we slowly move closer. When I turn around, so my back is facing him once again, my eyes meet a familiar gaze at the bar.

Alexander Rockford.

And he is watching me like a fucking hawk as he sips his drink.

Time to give him a show and let him see what he missed out on.

I ease back into my dancing partner and let my ass grind against him. As he pulls me closer, I can feel his member pressing into me through his jeans.

Another part of him that's not quite as large as Mr. Rockford.

The man's hands wander my body as I continue to dance against him. My body might be moving, but my eyes are firmly locked with Alexander's. His jaw is tight like he is grinding his teeth, and he's clutching his glass so hard I worry it might shatter between his fingers.

I hope he's sorry about what he missed out on, and I hope he feels jealous. As juvenile as that might sound, it would give me a tiny smidge of satisfaction.

Hoping to really knock Alexander down a few pegs, I turn my eyes away from his and back to Mr. Blondie. Grabbing him, I pull him close and press his lips to mine.

Truth be told, I have no idea what I'm doing. I'm not the girl who goes around kissing strangers, yet here I am. I've done it twice in two days.

The man's kiss was hot. His long tongue knew exactly what it was doing as his hands pull me into him deepening our embrace.

But it does nothing for me...or my cobweb covered vagina.

The kiss I shared with Alexander had me panting. Had me wanting more. Had me soaking my panties.

This one is doing none of those things.

And now, I'm irritated. This really good looking guy is kissing me in the middle of the dance floor, and I can't even get excited about it. I'm trying to find someone to rock my world, and all I can think about is the man who gave me the cold shoulder.

You know what? Fuck this.

"Would you excuse me for a minute?" I ask the guy behind me.

He nods, and immediately, I begin to head for the staircase that I walked up last night. I'm going to give Mr. Rockford two choices. He can either explain himself. Or he can finish what he fucking started.

Two men wearing earpieces are standing at the bottom of the stairs, but from the look on their faces, they don't seem surprised to see me. As if parting the Red Sea, they move aside and let me pass.

When I reach the top, my heart is pounding in my ears, and I'm not sure if it's from nervousness or excitement.

Apparently, ignoring all of my manners, I don't knock. Instead, I barge through the door like a gust of wind.

"We need to talk," I say.

Alexander's eyes look me up and down as he tries to analyze me.

Good luck, buddy. I can't even figure myself out.

"And what is it that we need to talk about, Tess?" He asks, still not removing his eyes from mine.

"About what the fuck is wrong with you," I say, sitting in the chair opposite him.

I swear I see a hint of a smile, but it's gone before I can know for sure. "Could you be a bit more specific?"

"Let's start with the fact that you can't keep your eyes off me the other night. I come up here ready to have a little no-strings-attached fun, and you tell me to leave just when we are getting to the good part. Then, I come in here tonight, and you're still looking at me that same way."

He leans his elbows on his desk. "And what way is that, sweetheart?"

"Like you have a mental list of things that you want to do to my body."

He chuckles. "You have no idea."

"Then, what's stopping you?"

He inhales a deep breath before answering. "You're not my type."

"Bullshit. I see how you look at me."

"I mean that I like my woman a certain way, and I'm positive you don't fit that mold."

When I don't say anything, he continues. "I like my woman to know who is in charge. I make the rules, and I don't like being questioned."

"Oh…" I hesitate. "Are you into that whole dominant, submissive thing?"

"No, BDSM isn't really my thing. Unless the woman is into that type of thing." Now, he gives me an actual smile…a cocky one.

"So, you want a 'yes' woman is what you're saying? Someone who will obey your every command?"

"Something like that. But you don't strike me as that type of woman. I like to be in charge…and from the way you kiss, I think you do too. That's not going to work for me." He leans back in his chair once more.

Trying to make things a bit more interesting, I run my tongue across my bottom lip before sinking my teeth into it. Getting up from my chair, I walk over to his side of the desk. My legs are long enough that I can sit my ass on the edge of it and still have my feet firmly planted on the floor. Positioning my legs on either side of his chair, I lean back just a little so that he has an enticing view to stare at.

My fingers rub along my collar bone as I start to speak. "So, you want a woman who will let you do whatever she wants to her? A woman who will say 'yes sir' to your every command?" I lean forward to whisper. "A woman who will get on her knees and beg...Mr. Rockford, please fuck me..."

My eyes glance down at the growing bulge in his pants that is impossible to hide.

"Sweetheart, you are playing with fire," he growls.

Moving even closer, I say, "No, Alexander. I *am* the fire."

For a moment, I think he's going to lose all control and rip my clothes off. But I don't give him the chance.

Instead, I stand up and begin to walk toward the door. "But you're right. I'm not that woman. But for the record, eventually, having someone say yes to your every whim will get old. Life isn't nearly as much fun that way. Goodbye, Mr. Rockford."

And with that, I hold my head high and walk out of the office. I don't go back to the bar to see Chris, and I don't go back to my dancing buddy. Instead, I walk home in the cool night air.

It's a long walk, but I don't mind. As much as I love New York City during the day, this city truly comes to life at night. The bright lights from the buildings light up the skyline like they're forming their own new sunrise.

There are still ample people out and about, walking the streets, and looking for their own fun to have for the evening.

I consider popping into another club to try to get my mind off the events of the night, but ultimately, I decide against it and pop into a cute little bakery instead. Apparently, my love for food trumps my love for sex.

After grabbing a danish and a hot tea, I continue my trek home and try to ignore the slight ache starting to form from my high-heel boots. Pausing for a moment, I look up and down the street, and of course, there's not a single cab in sight. I wrap my danish in the few napkins I grabbed and put it in my purse to enjoy when I get home.

I sip my tea and quicken my pace. Trying not to focus on my feet, I finally let my mind try to process what the hell just happened.

A smirk forms on my lips at the thought that I turned Alexander on as much as he did me.

He's right though. As much as I would love that man to take me to bed, I don't think I would enjoy myself nearly as much if I had to obey his every wish. Don't get me wrong, I love a man who knows what he wants. But I also am a woman who knows what I want, and I need a man who can respect that and give it to me.

Oh well.

It could have been fun. But he and I would mix about as well as gasoline and a match.

Eh, maybe I'll let myself imagine just how big our explosion could have been…just for one more night.

Chapter Eight
ALEXANDER

"Hey, you. I was surprised to get your call," says the tiny blonde standing in my doorway.

After I got done at the club, I came here…to my little fuck pad. The place where I always bring women since I don't want them to see where I live.

"Hi, Angelina," I say with a half-smile.

Ever since Tess Wendell stormed into my office demanding an explanation, I haven't been able to get her out of my head. She was already firmly planted there before that moment, but now, it is starting to become a nuisance. The way she started dirty talking and then left me there high and dry was enough to make me lose my fucking mind.

I have things to do, and I don't need thoughts of a female gumming up the works. I figure I must just be horny, and that's why I'm sporting a hard-on every time I think of Tess. All I need is to bury my cock in someone else for the night.

Cue Angelina.

Angelina and I have had a couple fun nights together, and she knows what I like. Plus, it helps that she is the exact opposite of Tess. Staring at Angelina should have me completely forgetting about the sultry vixen that seems to have taken up a permanent residency in my fantasies.

Where Tess has dark hair, Angelina is blonde. Where Tess is tall and thin, Angelina is petite and curvy. And where Tess is feisty and independent, Angelina will give me what I want without question.

And I'll give her a couple of mind-blowing, toe-curling orgasms to return the favor.

One night with her should get Tess out of my head for good.

"Where do you want me?" Angelina asks.

"Couch," I reply, not wanting her to get too comfortable in the king size bed. I smile at her automatic instinct to comply with whatever I desire.

As she walks to the large sofa, she is already unbuttoning her blouse. Her ample breasts come spilling out as she removes the garment. Angelina is quite well-endowed in the chest area, and even though the size of a woman's chest has never mattered all that much to me, hers are sure fun to play with.

My mind wanders to Tess, and I wonder what her tiny tits look like with no shirt or bra. I wonder how she would whimper when I sucked one of her nipples between my teeth as I slid into her.

Stop it.

When I finally pull out of my daydream, Angelina is lying on my couch. Her soft, petite body looks gorgeous lying there. Her blonde hair fanned around her. Her large breasts with pale pink nipples ready to bounce up and down as I fuck her. Her curvy hips that are great for holding onto when I bend her over.

I look down at the front of my pants…and nothing. My dick isn't even the slightest bit hard.

Unbelievable. The past few days I haven't been able to get it to go down, even with my many attempts to handle the situation myself. And now, it wants to lay there like a limp noodle.

What. The. Fuck.

Angelina must notice because even though she doesn't say a word, she gets down on her knees in front of me and unzips my jeans. She grabs my member and begins working me up and down.

Nothing.

She even tries putting it in her mouth.

Nothing.

"You okay, Alexander?" She says, her big eyes looking up at me.

"Just tired, I guess. How about I call you later?"

The look in her eyes shows sheer disappointment. She thought she was coming here for another fun night, and I can't seem to give it to her. Although she opens her mouth to protest, when she notices the look on my face, she snaps it back shut. She knows she won't get anywhere once I've already made up my mind.

Without a word, she gets dressed as quickly as she can before giving me a kiss on the cheek and heading out the door.

I sit on the couch with my head resting in my hands. None of it makes any sense. I am not some teenage kid who can't control his hormones. I'm the man who takes what I want and doesn't let anything stand in my way. I'm the man who is able to make a woman come on my cock all night long while she screams my name.

So why in the hell am I sitting alone with nothing to show for it?

Angelina is sexy as fuck, and I've had so much fun showing her a good time in the past. What makes this time different?

Although I don't want to admit it, I already know the answer.

Tess.

I seriously shouldn't even be thinking about this woman. If I show up right now, she is going to assume that all I am after is a quick fuck. And as amazing as that sounds, I don't think she will go along with it. A woman like Tess Wendell can say she is okay with casual all she wants, but when it comes down to it, she will want more.

And that's something I cannot give.

Hell, that's something she shouldn't want from me. I'm too damaged to do anything but drag her down with me. There's a reason I don't do relationships. If she finds out what that reason is, she will view me as the monster I view myself.

But if I don't do something to get her out of my thoughts, I'll never be able to get anything done. The past few days all I can think about is getting a taste of that sweet body of hers.

Maybe it's the whole *I want what I can't have* thing. The whole *forbidden fruit* idea. If that's the case, then call me Eve because I just have to taste that damn apple.

My thoughts immediately picture climbing between Tess's legs and tasting every single part of her. Her fingers fisting in my hair as she comes on my face and I lap up everything she has to give. I bet she's sweet as fucking candy.

My eyes glance down…and there, my dick is standing at full attention.

Son of a bitch.

Chapter Nine
TESS

I click my blender on, and the loud sound fills my apartment. Nothing like a good smoothie after a five-mile run.

It has been close to a week since I have been to Club Rock, and although my libido is still aching, my thoughts of Alexander are beginning to dwindle.

Or at least that's what I keep telling myself in hopes that it will actually happen. Besides, if I don't see him, eventually I'll just forget about him, right? I mean…I have to. He can't just live in my fantasies forever.

Glancing at my watch, I figure I should probably go get in the shower. I am finally making good on my promise of going to see Tyler, Sam, and the girls, so I'm driving to Boston. I figure maybe I'll stop on the way and pick the twins up a surprise. I'm thinking something super sugary. After all, what's the point in being the fun aunt if you can't hop them up on sweets and then leave them with their parents?

I start to walk toward the bedroom when there's a knock at the front door. Probably another one of my packages from all the online shopping I do. I'm pretty sure the delivery driver knows me by name these days.

But when I open the door, there's no box.

Instead, there is Alexander Rockford...his large body occupying most of my door frame.

"Alexander?" I ask, a bit more rudely than intended.

"Hello, Tess," he says with a boyish grin.

"What are you doing here? How did you find out where I live?"

"I have my ways," he smiles again.

Despite me thinking he's a creepy stalker, I let him in so the neighbors won't hear our conversation.

"No, don't tell me that you have your ways, Mr. Mysterious. You can't just show up here unannounced."

"You barged into my office unannounced," he retorted.

"That was different. It wasn't hard to find your office. I have no idea how you found out where my home is. Are you following me?" I question.

He chuckles. "No. Nothing quite that intense, I'm afraid. The club scans your ID when you come in. Your address is on there."

"Oh," I reply. "Well, why are you here?"

"I wanted to talk to you."

"About?"

My eyes look him over, and I finally take a moment to really look at him. Instead of the three-piece suits I've always seen him in, he is wearing a fitted t-shirt and jeans. The relaxed attire looks even better on him than the formal stuff.

And that perfect hair? It's not quite so perfect today. It's a little messed up like he's been running his fingers through it.

Most of all, I notice the fact that for once in his life, Alexander Rockford doesn't look like he runs the world. He didn't walk into this room like he owned the place. Replacing his cocky confidence is dare I say...nervousness.

I'm not going to lie. I kind of like it.

"Here's the thing, Tess. I can't seem to stop thinking about you."

The words hit me like a slap in the face. "You're the one who said you thought it was a bad idea for us to start anything."

I cross my arms and lean against the counter.

He begins to pace as he talks, and I swear with every word, he becomes more frazzled. "I know what I said! And I'm not saying it isn't true, but for whatever reason, I can't get you out of my head. You're all I seem to think about. I couldn't even fuck someone else the other night because I was too busy thinking of you. I just couldn't…"

I cut him off. "Is that supposed to make me feel better? You were about to fuck another woman and didn't? Do you want a prize or something?" I'm not entirely sure I believe him. I highly doubt that this man who oozes testosterone out of every one of his pores turned down a chance to get his dick wet.

He walks toward me and leans close. "You're missing my point. My plan was to fuck someone else to forget about you. Didn't work. Didn't even get far enough to try because there was your face."

The admission makes me a little weak in the knees, but I try not to let it show. "So, what exactly is it that you're saying?"

He lays a hand on either side of my face and brings my gaze to his. "I'm saying that I think you can't stop thinking about me either, or you would have gone home with that guy from the club the other night."

"How do you know I didn't hook up with someone else after I left?"

"Did you?" He whispers.

My breath is hitched in my throat, and I can't form words, so I just shake my head back and forth.

He leans in and presses his lips to mine. This time, it's not hard and fiery. It's soft and tender. And I can't decide which I like better.

I can smell the clean smell of his soap and faintly taste a hint of mint like he just brushed his teeth before coming over here.

When he pulls away, a sudden emptiness overtakes me. My body craves more contact. I struggle to remain upright but still have to say something. "I'm still me, Alexander. I'm not going to be a woman you can walk all over to get what you want. I'm not going to get on my knees and beg. I come with a big attitude and a smart mouth, and that's not going to change because you want a piece of arm candy who keeps her mouth shut."

"I know," he says, unblinking. "But I don't care. Maybe I'm ready to try something different."

"Then, what are you waiting for?" I ask, my teeth sinking into my bottom lip.

But he steps back. "Let me take you to dinner."

"Dinner?" I ask.

"Yeah, you know that thing people do where they have a meal every evening? Dinner."

When I still stand there flummoxed, he goes on, "I don't want you to think I just came here to get into your panties. Although believe me, I really, really want to do that. That's not all this is about. Let's have dinner and get to know each other a little better."

"Okay, dinner sounds nice." Those are the words I say, but what I really mean is 'Fuck dinner. Let's get naked instead.'

My mind struggles to process all of this. What's his angle here? Is this all just some elaborate rouse to get me into bed? If it is why is he asking me to dinner when I've made it very clear it's not necessary? What's with the sudden good guy act?

"Can I pick you up tonight?" He asks.

"Sure. How about around eight? I have to go to Boston for a few hours."

His eyebrow quirks up at my plans, but he doesn't ask any questions. "Eight o'clock it is. I'll see you then."

With one more kiss that has me swooning, he is out the door.

What the fuck just happened?

Chapter Ten

TESS

"Aunt Tess, watch this!" Lilah exclaims while jumping from one couch to the other.

"Lilah Nicole, we don't jump on the furniture," Tyler scolds.

Lilah scoffs but gets down anyway. "Daddy, you're just no fun," she mutters before walking into the other room.

"Hear that, sis? I'm no fun," he smiles at me.

"Well, I could have told you that," I say before sipping my coffee.

He kicks me from under the table. "Oh, hush. You're the one who is all work and no play."

If only he knew.

"So, how are things going here?" I ask. "The girls wearing you out?"

He lets out a chortle. "Always. But I wouldn't trade it for anything in the world."

"How did you and Sam manage to have the two most different twins in the entire world? They are nothing alike."

Since I had arrived at their house, Lilah had already almost broken her neck about three times running around, anxious to show me all of her 'cool moves'; whereas, Abby sat at the table and colored me a pretty picture to hang on my fridge when I get home.

Night and day.

Tyler laughs. "You know, they are so different, yet they have this bond like nothing I've ever seen before. It's like they complete each other. They have always had their own beds, yet I don't think either one has ever slept without the other. Even if I put them in separate beds, one of them moves to the other one in the middle of the night. They are best friends despite their differences. A Yin to each other's Yang."

"Who's your favorite?" I ask, jokingly.

"Tyler Wendell, don't you answer that question," Sam says as she walks into the room before giving her husband a quick peck on the cheek.

"So, you *do* have a favorite?" I chortle.

"Depends on which day you ask us on," Sam rolls her eyes and laughs. "They both have their moments."

"Clearly, Abby doesn't give you as much shit as Lilah though, right?"

Tyler replies, "No, but Abby isn't as affectionate as Lilah either. She's fiercely independent; whereas, Lilah is still pretty attached to us most of the time."

"Attached to *you,* maybe," Sam interjects. "Most of the time, she doesn't seem to like me all that much."

Tyler scoffs. "That's because you two are so damn similar. Wild. Crazy. Onry. A little hard to handle."

Sam crosses her arms. "I have no idea what you're talking about."

"Save it, woman. Your dad has told me all sorts of stories about you growing up. I think 'hellion' is the word that he used. I think you and this one were cut from the same cloth." He points at me.

"Hey! Why are you bringing me into this?" I cry.

"Because I grew up with you. And you were just as much of a wild child. Always making me tag along on your little schemes. Don't act so innocent. I'm convinced Lilah gets it from both of you. I mean I'm her favorite person, so that's another thing you guys have in common," he jokes.

Sam and I both start to cackle.

"Baby brother, you barely crack the top five," I say with a wink toward Sam.

The girls choose this moment to come running in begging their parents to come outside to look at the butterfly in the yard. We all walk outside, and I closely watch my brother and his family.

Not too long ago, that man was having keg parties every other weekend and taking a new woman to bed every night. Now, he lives in the suburbs with his wife and daughters. Most would say they have the picture-perfect life.

But not me.

Now, I'm not saying it's not perfect for him. It is. But I can't say I yearn for that life. The idea of kids has never stood out to me. Don't get me wrong, I love kids, but I don't know that I'm exactly the maternal type. The cool aunt role suits me much better, and I'm okay with that. And in the future, whatever man I end up with has to be okay with that too.

Or maybe I'll just die a lonely old spinster. At what age should I start hoarding nicknacks and collecting cats?

Ty pulls me out of my thoughts. "Hey, have you talked to Tristan or Tawna lately?"

Tristan and Tawna are our older twin siblings. They are about ten years older than us, so we have never exceptionally close.

I shrug, "Not really. Tawna and I text sometimes, but not much. Mom said that Tristan has been busy at his clinic in L.A., and Tawna is still working in New York, but I never see her. We've all just been doing our own things I guess."

"Well, I hope everyone can take a break from their busy schedules to come here for the girls' birthday that's coming up in a few weeks," Sam said while pouring her another cup of coffee.

"I don't know about those two, but I know I wouldn't miss it for the world, and isn't that all that really matters?" I joke.

"Well guys, I should really get going."

"You're welcome to stay if you'd like. We have plenty of room," my brother says.

"I know. Maybe next time. I, uh, have a date tonight."

Tyler and Sam both stop what they're doing to look at me. "A date?" Tyler questions.

"Yes, a date. I have been known to share an evening with the male persuasion at times."

"Gross," Tyler says. "But I'm happy for you. You don't get out much."

"Says the guy who never goes out unless it's to Chuck E. Cheez," I laugh.

"True. But I have a whole hell of a lot to come to home to."

I know he didn't mean the words the way they come out. He was just joking around, but it still hurt a little. Everyone assumes that just because I'm alone means that I'm constantly lonely. Just because I miss sex doesn't mean I am pining for a man.

"Shit, Tess. I'm sorry. That sounded a lot worse than I meant it to. You have an awesome, fun life, and I am so proud of everything you've accomplished," Tyler says.

"It's fine," I say in a rather curt tone, not wanting to talk any more about this. "I'll text you later."

We say our goodbyes, and a few minutes later, I'm in my car heading back to New York. It's rare that I get to take my car out of the garage and really open her up. A Ferrari doesn't do well on the crowded New York streets, so I tend to walk everywhere or take a cab.

Most times, I crank the music up and sing in my tremendously off-key voice. Today though, I let my thoughts carry me away. Thoughts of what the night will bring and what Alexander Rockford has in store for me.

I'm still not sure about his motives, but as much as that worries me, excitement is the main force running through my veins. All of my life, I've been somewhat of an adrenaline junkie.

Rollercoasters. Skydiving. Base jumping.

I've done it all.

That's why Doctors Without Borders intrigued me so much. It was an adventure. Something new and exciting (albeit tragic) in a strange, unfamiliar environment.

I've always been looking for my next big thrill. The next thing that is going to get my blood pumping and my heart racing.

And from the butterflies in my stomach, Alexander Rockford might be my biggest thrill yet.

Chapter Eleven
ALEXANDER

I knock on the door of Tess's apartment at 8 o'clock sharp. I actually arrived a few minutes early, but I waited downstairs until it was time. I may be an asshole, but I'm a punctual one.

As I stand at her door, only one thought keeps flashing in my mind.

What the hell am I doing here?

First, I want to fuck this woman. Then, I tell her no. Then, somehow, I end up taking her to dinner.

I don't take women on dates.

Ever.

The only time I even come close is when I need a beautiful woman to be on my arm for the evening at an event. Even then, they know it's not going to be 'fun' for them…at least not until I take them home afterwards.

So, why the fuck am I standing at Tess Wendell's door ready to take her to dinner? If it was just sex that I wanted, I could have already had it. She made that abundantly clear. But it's more than that. She intrigues me in a way that a woman never has before. My curiosity is itching to find out why.

She opens the door, and my breath hitches in my throat.

She's beautiful. Absolutely radiant.

"Mr. Rockford," she says with a grin.

"Miss Wendell, look at you," I say as my eyes slowly roam up and down that sexy body of hers.

A slight blush creeps up her cheeks. You'd think with her confidence, she would know how stunning she is. She should know she's a 10/10…a fucking knockout.

Her long hair is parted to one side yet hangs freely down her back in subtle waves. She wears a short black dress that falls about mid-thigh, showing off her long, lean legs. Hopefully, I'll get to know what those feel like wrapped around me later.

The black heels she is wearing makes her almost eye-level with me.

Almost.

I'm used to women being significantly shorter than me, and I like it that way. This is just another way Tess Wendell is making me step completely out of my comfort zone.

"Are you ready to go?" I ask, hoping to God that she says yes. If she asks me to come in that apartment, I'm not sure we will make it to dinner.

She smiles. "Ready when you are."

When we get downstairs, my driver Barry is standing by the back door of the black luxury sedan. He opens the door for Tess, and I help her in before sliding in next to her.

"You have a driver?" She asks. "Very nice."

After reading about her family's wealth, I'm a little surprised she doesn't have one herself, but I don't bring it up.

"Thanks. I have a Porsche too, but I don't like driving it in the city."

"Me too. Well, it's not a Porsche. It's a Ferrari."

My eyebrows quirk up. "A Ferrari?"

She nods. "Mm-hmm. It's an 812 GTS. I actually took her out today when I drove to Boston. But when I'm in the city, I just keep her garaged. I learned my lesson after she got broken into twice in a single week."

A hint of a smile crosses my lips listening to her call her

car a "she". Most women just don't get the fascination with a good car. Sounds like Tess appreciates one just as much as I do.

"So, you don't drive your fancy car around the city, and you don't have a driver?"

She looks at me like I just grew a third eye. "Yeah…I tend to take cabs or the subway, or I just walk almost everywhere I go."

"You walk? Around this city? That's an awful idea. It's not safe. I'll give you a number for my service, and they'll be happy to get you taken care of."

I'm already pulling out my phone to look at the number when I hear a very distinct, "No."

"No?" I ask.

Did she really just tell me no?

"You heard me. No. I don't need a driver. I've been successfully living in this city for thirty years now without having someone chauffer me around. I am just fine doing what I've been doing. I'm not going to change my whole life just because you have an issue with it." She presses her lips together in a line, and I can tell that she isn't going to budge on this.

I have the sudden urge to bend her over my lap, pull up that tiny dress, and spank her cute little ass cheeks until she agrees with me. But that may be a bit too forward. That doesn't stop me from having to readjust my pants though at the mere thought of it.

"Fine," I grumble.

We are five minutes into this date, and already she is disagreeing with me. Rule number one for me is to do what I say and don't ask questions. I know that makes me sound like a huge jerk, but it's what has always worked for me.

I'm not willing to change.

Yet here I sit, mesmerized by the woman in front of me and unable to tell Barry to turn the car around and take her home. My curiosity is still nudging me to see what else the night will bring.

To try to make the air between us a little less awkward, I change the subject back to her car, and she tells me all about it as we make our way to the restaurant.

When we arrive a few minutes later, I help her out and we head inside. The maitre d calls me by name and immediately shows us to our private table toward the back of the restaurant.

As we sit down, I ask if Tess would like a glass of wine, and her face scrunches up.

"What's wrong?" I ask.

"Just not a big wine drinker. A bit too sweet for me."

"Order whatever you like," I say before opening my menu.

"Vodka on the rocks, please," she says, and I order the same, not wanting to order a whole bottle of wine just for myself.

After we make our food choices, we hand the menus back to the waiter, and he walks off. Tess' eyes peruse the room trying to take in all the details.

"Do you come here a lot?" She inquires.

"Why do you ask?"

"Because the waiters all say hi to you and call you by name. Not to mention, we got the best table in the house without you having to flash your wallet at anyone."

She's observant.

"It's my restaurant."

Her gaze narrows in on me. "Your restaurant?"

I nod. "Yes. I own it. I own about half a dozen restaurants throughout the city and am an investor in a few others."

She leans back and taps her fingertip on the table. "So, you're not just a club owner?"

I set my elbows on the table. "You know I'm a little surprised you didn't Google me after meeting me. Most women do."

"I'm not most women," she says with a deliciously sexy smile.

"No, you really aren't, are you?"

"Besides, I like to get to know someone without any preconceptions. I figure if you want me to know something, you'll tell me. If I Google you, it seems like some sort of invasion of privacy."

Now, I feel rude because I definitely did my research on her. Maybe I won't tell her that just yet.

"What is it that you do for a living, Tess?" I ask trying to seem clueless.

"I'm a doctor," she says. I know a lot of doctors who brag about their choice in careers, but Tess says it without any boast behind it.

"What kind of doctor?" I ask.

"Trauma mostly."

"Trauma? That has to be pretty intense."

She shrugs. "I guess. I like the thrill of it though. It's like you have a split second to decide what to do. Your brain has to move at the speed of lightning, so there's no time to second guess yourself." As she speaks, there is a gleam in her eye showing how much she really does love what she does.

"Do you do most of your work here in town?" I keep asking questions just to listen to her talk with such passion about her work.

"Over the years, I have done some work with Doctors Without Borders, but I've been back in the city for a while now. I work in the ER over at Mercy."

"Mercy? That's a pretty rough part of town."

"It can be, but I'm pretty good at taking care of myself." She says the words with such conviction that it makes me not want to worry about her.

But I still do.

That is a rough neighborhood, and anything could happen. As much as I want to tell her she should find a job in a better part of town, I keep my mouth shut. After our disagreement about the car situation, I don't think now's a good time.

I'd like to get through at least one date with her before she figures out how much of an asshole I am and tells me to hit the pavement.

Chapter Twelve

TESS

God, he's gorgeous.

Alexander Rockford sits across from me, and it's taking a whole hell of a lot of will power to not climb across the table and straddle him in front of all these people.

His sexy three-piece suit hugs every bulging muscle on his large frame, and I keep picturing what he would look like without the layers of fabric.

We are close enough that I can see the gorgeous color of his eyes. And every time, he looks into mine, I get lost. It's as if they are peering directly into my soul searching my entire being for my deep, dark secrets.

When I told him I was a doctor, he didn't seem to be intimidated like some of the men I've gone out with. Men hear that I am a doctor and tend to think one of two things. The first one is that I work too much and won't have time for them… which is sometimes true. Or they don't like the fact that I make more money than them, and their delicate egos get bruised. Either scenario, I don't have time for.

But Alexander seems like he is just as busy as I am…and not to mention pretty flush in the cash, so maybe those things wouldn't be too much of a problem.

He's silent for a moment, so I decide it was my turn to ask him some questions. "So, you own a bar and some restaurants. What is it exactly that you do? Are you just some sort of investor?"

He leans forward, setting his elbows on the table, and I can see his solid arm muscles protruding from the expensive fabric of his jacket. "I guess I'm somewhat of an investor. I try to find properties that are losing money and offer my expertise. To start with, I always offer to just be a shareholder, but sometimes, they'd rather just take the money and sell it outright."

"You don't sell them after you fix them up?" I ask, genuinely curious.

He shakes his head. "Usually, after I put all the work into it, I kind of fall in love with the place, and I just can't bear to part with it. It's like they all have somehow become kind of a piece of me."

I give him a warm smile, and he looks almost taken aback by the fact he just revealed something so personal. I'm guessing sharing intimate details of his life isn't something he does very often.

My eyes glance around the room. "It seems like this place is doing really well. I'm sure that the amount you invest pales in comparison to the money that you eventually get back."

He chuckles, and I realize he has dimples in his cheeks when he smiles.

Heaven help me.

"I do alright for myself, but it's not like I just come in, write a check, and sit back and count my money like Mr. Scrooge." He smiles even bigger now. "I actually enjoy coming in and doing some of the work. Of course, I'm no plumber or electrician, but I help out with a lot of the cosmetic work. I like getting my hands dirty. The more work I personally put into a place, the more I will care about its success."

"Makes sense, I guess," I say as the waiter brings over our dinners.

I take a second to look at the large plate of pasta in front of me. I can't decide which is better the look of it or the smell. Then, I take a bite and realize that the taste trumps all else.

The homemade marinara sauce hits my mouth, and I am in heaven. I let out an involuntary moan which seems to get Alexander's attention.

His eyes are looking at me like he is having the same thought I was about fucking right here in the middle of his restaurant.

Something about that turns me on far more than it should.

"Sorry," I said, feeling my cheeks blush. "With my weird schedule, it seems like I am either eating fast food or a salad with absolutely no flavor. It isn't often that I get a hot meal as delicious as this."

His lip quirks slightly. "No need to apologize. A woman moaning is sexy, no matter what the context. But for the record, I hope that I will get more of a reaction out of you than that."

Goosebumps spring up all over my body, and suddenly, the room seems very warm. There is so much electricity in just our gazes that I wonder if we touched, how big the sparks would be. Would we catch fire or merely fizzle out?

The way his eyes flare when he looks at me makes me think we could set the whole damn world ablaze.

I'm the first one to break our gaze as I go back to stuffing my face with delicious pasta.

"I like a woman who isn't afraid to eat," he says while digging into his own portion.

I finish chewing the bite that's in my mouth before I answer. "Oh, I love to eat. Typically, I'm pretty active and have a high metabolism, so I eat constantly. Like I said though, I don't always eat the healthiest of things. I have a weakness for any kind of baked goods. Pastries, cupcakes, cookies, you name it."

He laughs. "I feel your pain."

I scoff. "Oh, please! I'm sure that with a body like that, you stick to a very strict diet."

"You like my body?" He smiles, but when I roll my eyes,

he continues. "Seriously though, I am not perfect. Yeah, I try to work out and eat somewhat healthy, but I am a candy fiend."

"No way," I giggle.

"I'm serious. I love candy. Any kind. But anything sour really does it for me."

With the look on his face, I can't tell if he's serious or not. The man is an enigma.

I study Alexander's face and his body language. This is a man who is used to being in control, and he loves it.

Problem is…I'm the exact same way. We are both alphas, and I don't think either of us is going to concede on that fact.

Everything about this man screams that I should probably get out while I still can. Something tells me that once I wade in this pond, there's a good chance I'll drown. But damnit, with the way he's looking at me right now, I wouldn't even mind.

"I need to ask you something," I say.

"Okay, shoot," he replies before finishing the last of his drink.

"Why'd you ask me out? You said it yourself…we may be too similar. I know you said that you couldn't stop thinking about me, but is it just another case of a man wanting what he can't have?"

He pauses for a moment as if trying to choose his words carefully. "Honestly, Tess, I don't know what it is. I wish I knew why I can't get you out of my head. Let's just say I've been with a lot of women…I guess I should say I've fucked a lot of women, and never has a woman stayed so firmly planted in my mind. And you and I haven't even fucked. That has to mean something, right?"

"Do you think that you'll have had your fill once you get into my panties?"

He chuckles. "With the way I'm thinking about you, I doubt it."

I lick my lips. "Well, I guess there's only one way for us to find out."

Hunger sparks in his eyes as he calls, "Check, please."

Chapter Thirteen
ALEXANDER

Fuck, this woman is sexy. Everything about her gets my engine going. It took every ounce of energy I had to keep my hands to myself in the backseat of my car. Her hand rubbing up and down my thigh the entire drive tested my self-control beyond belief.

As we walk in her front door, our hands are already roaming all over each other, and our mouths are crashing together. The taste of vodka mixes with her naturally sweet taste, and it's infatuating.

Her tongue dances with mine, and she's not shy about taking exactly what she wants from me. Her fingers tangle in my hair as I back her up against the door. One of my hand holds her head still while I tease her with long, slow swipes of my tongue against hers, and the other reaches around to grope her delicious peach of an ass under her short dress. Her barely-there thong does nothing to hide her exposed skin, and I love how smooth it is under my fingers.

Pulling back for a moment, she looks at me. "Take me to bed, Alexander."

Don't have to tell me twice.

Her mouth widens into a big grin, and without warning,

she jumps into my arms and wraps her legs around my waist. As Tess points the way to the bedroom, I begin to walk that direction as she kisses up and down my neck. When she uses her teeth to inflict a small bite, I want nothing more than to rip off that tiny dress and plow into her.

But teasing each other seems to be so much more fun. As I set her down on her feet, her brown eyes gaze into mine. They are filled with pure passion and desire, showing me she wants this as badly as I do. I reach for my jacket, but her hands grab mine.

"Let me," she whispers. Her hands slowly undo the knot in my tie and pull it from around my neck. Next comes my suit jacket, which she takes her time pulling off my shoulders, running the palms of her hands over every inch of skin.

My heart is beating faster as her long fingers began to unbutton my shirt. Her eyes are fixed on mine the entire time. The lower her fingers travel, the harder I seem to get. I'm like a fucking virgin my cock is so hard.

Her eyes finally leave mine as she pushes the shirt off my shoulders. They roam over my body, and the way she looks at me makes me feel like I'm the luckiest son of a bitch in the whole fucking world. Men would kill to be standing where I am right now.

Her hands move toward the buckle of my pants, but I stop her. "Your turn," I whisper.

There isn't too much material of the dress she is wearing, but I still take my time working the tiny straps off her shoulders and down her arms before pulling the whole thing off her body. When it falls to the floor, she steps out of it, and I take a moment to just look at her.

She stands in front of me wearing nothing more than a black bra, matching thong, and black stiletto heels.

Reaching behind her, she undoes the clasp of her bra and lets it fall to the floor. Her tits are small and perky with the most perfect tiny, rosy nipples I've ever seen.

"Damn woman," I growl. "Take the panties off."

"Hey Ace, I'm a lot more naked than you. Take your pants off."

Although I'm not necessarily a fan of anyone telling me what to do, when a beautiful woman tells me to take my pants off, I listen.

Trying not to seem too eager, I slowly unbuckle my belt and begin to take my pants off, trying to give her a good show. I could leave my boxers on and make her take her underwear off first, but I'm tired of waiting.

When my cock springs free, I see a slight glint of something in Tess' eyes although she tries not to show it. Not trying to brag, but I'm well endowed, and she seems to take notice. Her teeth sink into her bottom lip as she stares at it.

Grabbing the bottom of my shaft, I work myself up and down as she watches with anticipation. "Your turn," I whisper.

Without a word, she steps out of her panties, and I'm in awe. Her body is a goddamned work of art. Every part of her looks toned and beautiful. Her skin is tan, and she has a large tattoo running all the way down her side…a string of black and white flowers. It starts right underneath her arm and travels all the way to her hip. I want to kiss every inch of it.

Before either of us can speak, it's like an invisible switch gets thrown, and we are drawn to each other like magnets. Our long, slow kisses have turned passionate and frenzied. And our light, methodical touches have turned hard and fast. I reach my hands up to massage her breasts, and she moans into my kiss as I gently squeeze one of her pebbled nipples. My mouth quickly replaces my fingers as I gently bite each nipple and then flick my tongue over it to soothe it.

Her head is thrown back, and her fingers run through my hair as she moans my name. "Yes, Alexander, just like that."

While my mouth is occupied, I take my fingers and run it up her thigh before teasing her slit. Under the small patch of hair, I can feel that she's already wet for me. My finger teases for a minute before I began giving my full attention to her clit, rubbing small circles over the swollen nub.

Her heart is beating so fast in her chest, I can feel it against me, and I can tell she's close. Her breathing quickens as I rub faster and take my middle finger and slide it inside.

Holy shit, she's fucking tight.

When I crook my finger inside, that's all it takes. Her arms wrap around my neck as her entire body shutters. Her pussy spasms around my fingers, and I can't wait to feel her do it around my dick.

Her chest is heaving against mine as she comes down off the high of her orgasm. Her beautiful caramel colored eyes look into mine before she presses a kiss to my lips. She moans into my mouth as I continue to tease the sensitive flesh for a few more moments.

My fingers slide out of her, and she sinks to her knees in front of me, grabbing the base of my cock and stroking me up and down. Her hands feel so soft around the sensitive skin. She starts to bring me toward her mouth, but I stop her.

Her eyes glance up at me with confusion.

"Sweetheart, as much as I want your mouth around me, if I don't get inside you soon, I'm going to fucking explode."

A sexy smile crosses her lips as she rises from her knees and climbs onto the bed. She crawls toward the headboard to give me a perfect view of that pretty, pink pussy and tight ass of hers. I want to bury myself in every hole this woman has.

She lays on her back with hunger in her eyes. "Well, what are you waiting for?"

Chapter Fourteen
TESS

Alexander's large body climbs on top of me, and I melt underneath him. For such a large man, his touch is surprisingly sensual. And apparently, he has the ability to play my body like a fiddle since he had me coming faster than I can even get myself off.

Maybe I'm just too pent up from my lack of sex in the recent past. Maybe my body was just releasing what it had been missing for months.

Or maybe the man is a God in the sack and knows exactly what he is doing to make me fall apart.

Before he joins me on the bed, he grabs a condom and rolls it on. I'm glad I didn't have to ask him to do it. I guess Mr. Rockford is also Mr. Responsible.

He positions himself between my legs and notches the tip of his cock at my entrance. I take a deep breath as I wait for him to push inside. I am already tight to begin with but add that to the fact I haven't been laid in a year, and Alexander is freaking huge, he is going to stretch me completely. Now, don't get me wrong, I'm not a prude. I have my drawer full of sex toys that I use to get myself off, but none of them even compare to Alexander's size.

He hooks one of my legs around his waist and slowly begins to push past my threshold. I take a deep breath as he moves in further. He goes slowly and begins to rub my clit to take away any discomfort I might be feeling. There's certainly no discomfort…just the feeling of utter and complete fullness.

When he is completely buried in my channel, I take a moment to just look at him. His bulging arm muscles as he holds himself up. His dark hair which now has strands falling into those gorgeous eyes that are so blue I want to swim in them. His abs that look like they are chiseled out of marble.

As he begins to move, I let out a loud moan. With even the smallest of movements, it is like every one of my nerve endings is electrified. I could feel every detail and ridge of his cock as he moves it in and out, sliding against my walls, stretching me with every thrust.

"Damn, sweetheart, you're so fucking tight," he says through gritted teeth.

The only response I can manage is another moan because now, he is moving faster, and I am flying at light speed toward another orgasm. We've barely gotten started, and already, I'm barreling toward the finish line…again.

A few more circles over my clit, and I'm arching underneath him. I dig my nails into his shoulders as he continues his steady rhythm, taking everything I have to give.

As I start to relax, he gets up on his knees and throws my legs on his shoulders as he begins to move again. This gives me an even better view of his defined abs and chest, and I can't get enough. The man doesn't have a physical flaw. Someone should make a statue out of him.

I gasp as he pumps into me harder and faster, each time making perfect contact with my g-spot.

Holy shit.

His thick fingers grip my hips so hard I wonder if I will have bruises tomorrow. I don't care if I do. The euphoria this man is putting me in is worth a couple of battle wounds.

"Alexander!" I cry out while gripping the sheets around

me.

"Yeah, come for me one more time, sweetheart," he says, his voice low and smooth.

As if he is pressing a magic button, the moment his fingers touch my clit, I'm bucking beneath him once more. I don't think I've ever gotten off so many times during sex before. Hell, I was lucky if I got off once, and even then, it was because I was the one doing all the work.

Alexander, though, seems to know exactly how to make my toes curl.

This time as I tighten around him, I feel him spasm inside me as he fills the condom, finding his own release. He moans my name, and I swear it might be the sexiest thing I've ever heard.

Leaning down, he gives me one more long, tender kiss before pulling out of me.

As he gets up to dispose of the rubber, I am suddenly very empty. And not just in the physical sense.

He comes back and lays down next to me, pulling me against his chest. "Wow," he says with a grin.

"You're telling me," I giggle.

"We should do that again," he winks.

"You won't hear me complaining. But first, I need sleep," I reply, my eyelids suddenly growing very heavy as I lay there listening to his heartbeat.

"Okay, beautiful. How about I take you out again soon?"

"Sure. I have to work the next couple days, but maybe next time I'm off?" I am mumbling the words, and I hope they're coherent enough for him to understand.

"Whenever you want. You text me the date and time, and I'll be here." He leans in to give me a final kiss before getting up.

I watch him throw his clothes back on and head for the front door. He insists I get up and lock the deadbolt behind him, so I do.

Once we've said our goodbyes, and the door is locked, I lean against it and reflect on the evening.

My initial assumption that being with Alexander would

be exciting was spot on. One of the greatest rushes I've ever felt. And just like every roller coaster I've ever been on, I can't wait to take another ride on Mr. Rockford.

Chapter Fifteen
ALEXANDER

The next morning, I am wide awake at five AM. I've barely slept a wink, and it's all because I can't seem to get Tess out of my head.

Sleeping with her has had the opposite effect than I thought. I assumed after one wild night, I would have had my fill and be ready to move on.

Fuck, was I wrong.

I still can't stop thinking about her. I can still feel her soft skin underneath my fingers. I can still smell the flowery scent of her long hair. I can still feel her warm pussy clenched around my hard cock.

Speaking of which, my dick is so hard this morning, it hurts. I get up to go take a shower, hoping it will start to go down. But when it doesn't, I take matters into my own hands, so to speak, and stroke myself. My hand glides up and down under the hot water as I think of Tess writhing underneath me. I pump hard and fast until I'm spurting my load all over the shower floor.

What the hell is wrong with me?

This past week, I have jerked off more than I have in the past five years. Usually, my dick gets hard, and I find a woman to fix the problem. We fuck and go our separate ways.

I don't do relationships.

I don't date.

Monsters shouldn't do those things.

Tess told me she was the fire. She was right. And apparently, I'm anxious to get burned.

In no uncertain terms, does that mean I want a relationship. But I do want to see her again. I want to bury myself in her as she moans my name.

But I also want to get to know her better. I want to listen to her talk about her job and the passion she has for it. I want to know if she has any skeletons in her closet like I do.

Shit. I've never been interested in what a woman has to say before unless it's telling me how she'd like me to make her come. This whole thing is leading down a very dangerous road.

As I step out of the shower, all of these thoughts continue to rattle around in my head. I try to push them away knowing that I have an important deal I'm trying to close on today, and I don't need any distractions. Distractions could cost me a lot more than just money, and I can't risk it.

I begin to throw some clothes on and try to go over my speech in my head. I have my numbers ready to go, and I'm not prepared to give the sellers a lot of wiggle room. I'm already paying far over market-value to ensure the old man has a nice chunk of change to retire with.

His name is Charles, and he is a sweet old man with a sick wife. From the moment I met him, I could tell that selling his restaurant is going to be the hardest thing he's ever done. He's been running the place for forty years, and although the place isn't hurting for business, the building is beginning to fall into disarray, and he doesn't have the time or strength to fix it up.

I offered to be a shareholder and help him with the repairs, but he insisted he was ready to sell. With a warm smile, he said he and his dear wife were going to spend their last few months together traveling the world.

Our previous discussions play back in my head an hour

later as we sit across the table from one another trying to hash out a deal. Surprisingly, he doesn't scoff at my offer and instead signs the papers right away.

"You know, you're free to negotiate," I tell him.

But he shakes his head. "Don't need to, son. Your offer is more than fair. Pretty generous as a matter of fact. I can't tell you how much I appreciate it."

While he is signing his name on the multiple forms in front of him, I look around the room. Gino's is a small Greek restaurant that has certainly seen its share of customers. The walls, which were once brightly painted, have faded with time, but they are still lined with pictures of Charles meeting various celebrities through the years.

The booths need an upgrade since the vinyl is starting to pull apart, and the floors need replaced, but the place is still homey. It has a nice feel to it, and I'm glad I've decided to add it to my portfolio.

After the deal is done, and no one is left besides Charles and myself, he pours us each a small glass of Bourbon.

"To new beginnings," he says as he holds up his drink.

I tap my glass against his, and we each take a sip. "So, are you going to miss it, Charles? Running the restaurant, I mean."

His shoulders shrug. "I mean of course. It's what I've been doing for forty years. But as time has gone on, I have realized there are more important things in life than work. My Betty, for example. I don't want to miss a moment more with her."

"How long have you been married?" I ask.

"Fifty-two years."

"Holy shit," I cough on my drink, and he chuckles.

"Yes, it seems like quite a long time, yet, it hardly seems like that long at all."

"And she never got mad with how much you worked? I definitely know how time consuming running a business can be. What's your secret?"

Leaning forward, he takes another sip. "Honestly?"

I nod, and he sits in silence for a moment thinking about

it.

"To tell the truth, I don't know that there is one particular answer to that question. But I will give you a couple things I have learned over the years. For starters, find a woman who doesn't depend on you for her happiness."

My forehead scrunches, so he goes on. "When I met Betty, she and I both had our own lives...our own jobs...our own hobbies. We didn't depend on each other to be happy. We were already happy, and when we got together, we each brought our own joy into the relationship. If you are solely responsible for making someone else happy, it's easy to forget how to be happy yourself.

"Also, find yourself a good woman. A woman who will stand by you even when times get hard. And in return, be a man worth standing by."

I let his words sink in. The old bastard might just have a point. Hell, he's been married over fifty years, chances are, he knows what he is talking about.

But as much as the idea of having a good woman by my side sounds nice, I don't think I will ever be a man worth standing by.

I am just too broken. My soul is just too damned.

Chapter Sixteen

TESS

"Thanks for walking me out," I say to Elliott, one of my coworkers who insists on walking me out every evening we work together.

Don't get me wrong, the gesture is nice, but I am also not some damsel in distress, and I hate it when people treat me as such.

Nevertheless, I don't say anything except for a simple thank you. Afterall, who am I to make chivalry even more dead than it already is?

When I begin to walk toward the curb to hail a cab, I notice a very familiar black sedan parked not too far away.

Alexander.

A whisper of a smile falls on my lips as I wonder why he's here. It doesn't matter. After he left the other night, I realized I didn't have his number, and I hadn't heard from him in two days. I figured maybe he had just had his fill.

But here he is.

"Hey, Tess, I was wondering if maybe some time you would like to go out and have dinner with me?" Elliott's words pull me out of my thoughts.

"Huh?" I ask.

He repeats the question, and I'm a little shocked. Never has this man expressed even the slightest interest in me…except for my safety by walking me out.

Honestly, I'm not quite sure how to answer. Sure, Elliott seems like a nice enough guy, but definitely not my type. Not wanting to exactly say that, I reply with. "Oh, Elliott, I'm so sorry, but I'm actually already kind of seeing someone."

"Oh, I'm sorry. I didn't know…you just never say…" he is stuttering over his words.

"It's okay. I just don't usually talk about personal stuff at work." At least that part is true. I try to keep my work and home life very separate. It helps me to unplug when I get home at night.

"Okay, well, have a good night," he mumbles, clearly embarrassed, before walking in the direction of the subway.

I wait for him to be out of view before my gaze falls back on the sleek black sedan. Except this time, I notice the window of backseat is cracked a little. Mr. Eavesdropper.

I walk over and tap on the glass. As he rolls it down, I say, "Hey, stud, you looking for a good time?"

"Sweetheart, you have no idea," he quips.

"Why are you here? How'd you find out where I work?"

"You told me where you work."

"Okay, that still doesn't answer why you are here. Or how you knew when I'd be getting off," I lean down, so my head is level with the window.

"I realized I didn't have your number, so I've just been waiting here all day. Been here about seven hours now."

"What? Why would you wait that long?" My words are frantic, but as he starts to laugh, I realize he's kidding. "Haha, very funny."

"I called the hospital earlier, and they told me what time you got off."

"Traitors," I say with a laugh.

"But really, I realized I didn't have your number, and although I probably could have found it through other ways, I figured you'd want to be the one to give it to me."

Man, his voice is so deep and smooth that it's hard to even focus on what he's saying.

"Give me your phone," I say.

He hands it to me, and I enter my number. "But since you're already here, would you like to go ahead and ask me out again? Don't worry, I'll act surprised."

He laughs. Not a chuckle, but a loud, booming laugh that is quite infectious.

"Sure. Tess, would you like to go out with me again?"

I throw my hand over my heart and feign shock. "Well, I thought you'd never ask! I would love to! How about tomorrow?"

"Deal. Text me a time, and I'll be there."

I lean in the window and give him a quick peck. "See you tomorrow, Ace."

"I have to ask. What's with the 'Ace'?"

I smile. "You ever play blackjack?"

"Yes..." he says warily.

"You know how when you have an Ace, it can either be that perfect 1 that you need to make it to 21? Or it can be the crappy 11 that busts you?"

"Yeah. So, which one am I? The 1 or the 11?"

I shrug. "I haven't decided yet."

Chapter Seventeen
TESS

"You look stunning tonight," Alexander says to me from across the table.

Blushing slightly, I take a strand of hair and tuck it behind my ear. "You don't look too bad yourself, Ace."

He grins at me. "You know, I don't think I've ever had a nickname before."

"Seriously? No one has ever called you Alex or Xander or anything?"

"Nope. Always just been Alexander."

I scoff. "Oh come on, I'm sure girlfriends in the past have had pet names for you. Like baby or babe or honey."

"Never really had a girlfriend...outside of high school that is."

Okay, now he has to be shitting me. "What? No girlfriend? I can tell for a fact that you aren't living like a monk... you're way too good with that thing," I say, pointing in the general direction of his manhood.

A deep chuckle escapes his chest. Leaning forward, he whispers, "I never said I didn't fuck. I've done my fair share of that. I said I haven't done the girlfriend thing since high school."

"Why?" It might sound like a loaded question, but I think

it's an important one. Although I don't know why I am acting like it's so scandalous that he hasn't had a girlfriend. When was the last time I had an actual boyfriend? Years. But I don't tell him that.

He takes a deep breath before beginning to speak. "After high school, I went through some rough shit. I really was in no position to give my full attention to anyone, so I broke it off with the girl I was seeing. After that, I got busy trying to make something of myself. It became easier to just keep things casual."

I lay my elbows on the table and look into his eyes, careful not to get lost in them. "Is that what we are doing here? Casual?"

"I don't know. What do you think it is?" His tone says he doesn't have a clue either and is trying to feel me out.

I work my bottom lip between my teeth as I try to think of what to say because honestly, this is all new territory for me too. Certainly, neither one of us seem very well equipped to handle a relationship.

Finally, I say, "I think casual is good."

His eyebrows quirk up. "You do?"

"Mm-hmm. You said yourself that you don't do relationships. And I mean I'm not exactly wanting anything serious either. What's wrong with two people who are highly attracted to each other having some fun without all the emotional bullshit?"

"And you think we can have that?"

"Why not? Not everything has to be some dramatic soap opera where it's all or nothing. I think we could land somewhere in the middle."

He nods. "I like that idea."

"But I think we need to lay down some ground rules," I add, completely making this up as I go.

"Oh, I know all about rules. I have quite a few of my own." He is smiling, but I can tell he's serious. Maybe now isn't a great time to tell him that I enjoy breaking every rule that's laid in front of me.

"Rule one. Yes, this is casual, but I don't like to share. If you're fucking me, you're fucking *only* me. I don't need to be one in a sea of many."

"Does the same rule apply to you?" He asks while crunching an ice cube from his now-empty glass.

"Of course. You'll be the only man that I let into my bed."

"Okay, I can live with that. What else?"

"Although we aren't in a relationship, there isn't anything wrong with hanging out or going to dinner. It's more of a friends with benefits situation as opposed to a booty call."

He nods. "Alright. Anything else?"

"One more. If either one of us starts to 'catch feelings', we end it and look back on this for what it was. Two people blowing off steam having a really great time."

"Deal."

The way he says the word makes me feel as though I've just signed a deal with the devil. And the way he is staring at me is getting my blood pumping. I can't wait to get out of here and have some of that 'casual fun' we've been talking about.

Opting to change the subject, so we can get through dinner, I ask, "So, is this place another one of your business ventures?"

The restaurant we are in tonight is more of an American steakhouse. Being a doctor, I know I should be opposed to eating too much red meat, but I'm a carnivore through and through, so this place is amazing.

He chuckles. "No, not this one. This is just a restaurant I've always liked. I come here a lot."

We are quiet for a few moments before he leans in and begins speaking in a low tone. "Tess, I know we just went over all these ground rules, but I think I need to really make a couple things clear."

I take another sip of my vodka and nod for him to go on.

"When I say I don't do relationships, I mean it. And there's a reason. I'm not a good man, sweetheart. And no matter where this is heading, that's not going to change. I'm never going to be a knight in shining armor who shows up on a white horse to save the day."

I mimic him in leaning forward so our faces are mere inches apart. "Well then, I guess it's a good thing I'm not a princess who needs saving, huh?"

We are both locked in an intense stare for what seems like hours before I finally add. "I'm not looking for a savior. I'm perfectly capable of taking care of myself. This..." I gesture between the two of us. "Is just two people getting to know each other and having some fun. That's it. Let's not turn it into something it isn't."

He agrees, but things seem to be a bit awkward between us for a moment like neither of us know where to go from here.

Now, it's his turn to change the subject. "So, do you have any family?"

I nod. "Yeah, I have three brothers and a sister and my parents are still alive. They live here in New York. Given my last name, I'm sure you've heard of them. They run Wendell Real Estate."

He smiles. "Okay, I did know that one, but tell me about your siblings."

"I have an older brother and an older sister who are twins...Tristan and Tawna. They are about nine years older than me, so we've never been exceptionally close. And then, I have a younger brother, Tyler. He and I are less than two years apart, so we grew up pretty much inseparable."

"Are you still close?" He asks before taking another bite of steak.

"Very. I mean it's a little hard because he lives in Boston, so we don't see each other as much as we used to. Plus, he's married with two twin toddlers of his own."

Alexander's eyes grow big. "That must be quite the handful."

"Yeah, the girls are night and day, so Tyler and Sam are always dealing with one thing or another. But when I can get away from work, I drive to Boston and spend time with them. That's where I was today. It's fun to be the cool aunt who gets them all riled up and then hands them back to their parents."

"Oh, you wouldn't do a thing like that, would you?" He jokes.

A wicked grin crosses my face. "Oh, yes I would. It'll always be fun messing with my brother."

He leans forward. "You're just a naughty little thing, aren't you?"

I mimic his motion, also leaning forward, so our faces are mere inches apart. "You have no idea. Why don't we get out of here, and I'll show you just how naughty I can be?"

Hunger flicks in his eyes, and ten minutes later, we are in the back of his town car as Barry drives us back to my apartment.

This time, I am a bit more brazen with my efforts to tease him and drive him insane. Running my hand up and down his thigh, I let my fingers gently graze over the outline of his hard shaft through his pants. My hand gives it a light squeeze as his breath hitches in his throat.

"You better behave, sweetheart," he says low enough for just me to hear.

"I don't like behaving," I whisper before nipping at his earlobe. " I like being very, *very* bad."

"I can see that. But you forget something."

"What's that?"

"I like being bad too. And I don't play fair."

Before I can ask what he means, I feel his hand slip underneath the hem of my dress. His fingers make quick work of my panties, pushing them to the side as he begins to tease my slit. He pulls me closer so I am practically on his lap as his long, thick fingers plunge inside me. I go to let out a moan, but his hand covers my mouth.

"Shhhh. We wouldn't want Barry to know how bad you're being back here."

His fingers continue to work inside me, pressing my g-spot like it's some magic button while the pad of his thumb rubs over my clit. Sweat breaks out over my skin as I can feel heat rushing through every inch of me. But just when I am about to soak his hand with my orgasm…he stops.

He pulls his fingers from me and takes his time moving them to his mouth and licking them clean.

Panting, I ask, "What the fuck was that?"

"Sweetheart, I told you I don't play fair," he says with a wicked grin.

Oh yes. I definitely made a deal with the devil.

Chapter Eighteen
ALEXANDER

The five minute drive back to Tess's apartment feels like an hour. As much as I enjoy teasing her and getting her nice and wet for me, I am ready to get inside and fuck her all night long.

Can't Barry drive any faster?!

We both sit in silence as our hands lightly rub over one another. There's so much sexual tension between us right now you could cut it with a knife. Her cheeks are flushed, and her chest is rising and falling like she is out of breath. After she didn't get to finish, her body is craving me. It needs me to satisfy it and give it what it needs.

A lot of women wouldn't feel comfortable being brought to the brink of an orgasm in the back of a town car. But Tess didn't seem to mind. In fact, she almost seems to get off on the thrill of it all.

When we finally pull up outside her apartment, I hesitate a moment before stepping out of the car.

"What's wrong?" She asks.

"If I walk in there right now, your doorman is going to get one hell of an eyeful," I reply, my eyes darting to the bulge in the front of my pants.

"Come on. I'll take care of it," she says with a wink.

I have no idea what she means, but I do know I don't want to wait another minute before burying myself inside her, so I step out.

As we begin to walk inside, she pulls my front right against her back and wraps my arms around her as we walk. I look just like a man who can't keep his hands off his extremely attractive date.

Guilty.

The doorman gives us a slight hint of a smile, and I lean down to trail a line of kisses down her neck to keep up appearances.

We step into the elevator, and the moment the doors close, my mouth crashes on hers. She rubs her fingers through my hair and pulls me deeper into our kiss. I back her up against the wall, and planting my hands on her ass, I lift her so her legs wrap around me. I grind myself into her, and she moans into my mouth.

If this elevator doesn't hurry the fuck up.

Finally, the door opens, and an elderly couple is standing there, open-mouthed staring at us. Without putting Tess down, I excuse us and walk to her door.

"Have a good evening," I say as I walk past, holding onto Tess's ass to make sure she isn't flashing the old folks.

We reach her door, and she stops kissing me just long enough to unlock it. But she is still in my arms. We walk through the threshold, and I kick the door closed before heading straight for the bedroom.

When I finally put her down, we rip each other's clothes off. There is no slow and seductive teasing this time. It is all animalistic heat and passion.

As I pull the bra from those perfect tits of hers, she lowers herself to her knees in front of me. Quickly, she undoes my button and zipper, and my cock springs free. I'm so hard it almost hurts, but as Tess takes her tongue and runs it from my balls all the way to the head, I forget all about any discomfort.

Her tongue circles the head a few times before her entire mouth descends on me.

Holy shit.

I lean my head back and let out a low moan, and my fingers run through her long hair as she starts to pump me in and out of her mouth.

Most women can't take my entire length when they suck me, but damnit, Tess sure does come close. I can feel the head of my dick run along the back of her throat, and I'm about to fucking lose it. Her big brown eyes look up at me as she pulls me out of her mouth. Her hand keeps stroking me while her mouth focuses its attention on my balls.

Good God, my heart is beating so fast I feel like it might come flying out of my chest. As her mouth moves back to tease me, her hands roam along my chest and abs, her fingernails lightly grazing my flesh sending shivers all over my body.

She takes one final deep suck, shoving me all the way down her throat before easing back and pulling me out of her mouth with a loud pop.

"Lay down." Her tone is seductive yet commanding. Usually, I never let women tell me what to do, but who am I kidding? Tess has me as putty in her hands after the way she just sucked my cock.

Before I do as she says, I lean down to my pants to retrieve the condom out of my wallet. Grabbing a few pillows to stack under my head, I lie down and wait for her to join me. I'm not waiting long before she is on all fours, crawling towards me.

Her hand reaches for the condom. When I give it to her, she rips the corner of the foil packaging with her teeth and slowly rolls it down my shaft.

One of her long legs swings over me so that she is straddling my hips, her pussy hovering just above my throbbing member. Her fingers wrap around me, and she slips the head inside. Her pussy is so fucking tight as she slowly lowers herself.

When I'm completely buried, she begins her movement. Although it's a ridiculously tight fit, she takes me in and out with ease. Up and down, she starts to moan a little louder with every pass.

I position my hands on her thin waist but am careful to still let her set the pace. Her hands reach up and massage her breasts and lightly tug on her nipples.

I want to be the one doing that.

Placing my hands over hers, I take note of how she wants to be touched. As she moves her hands, I take over where she left off...lightly pinching her nipples and grasping the perky mounds in my hands. A loud cry escapes her mouth as I increase pressure and pinch a little harder.

Her pace quickens, and I can see her getting close. Her eyes flutter underneath her hooded lashes, and I am absolutely entranced. She pushes her hair back from her face and braces her hands against my chest.

She glances down to look at me while her fingers trace along my abs. "Good lord, you're sexy," she whispers just barely loud enough for me to hear.

"Not half as sexy as you," I tell her before pulling her down to press my lips to hers. Her moan vibrates my mouth as I gently sweep my tongue in to dance with hers.

Pulling back, I whisper, "Ride me, sweetheart. Get yourself off for me."

Her teeth sink into her bottom lip as she sits back and begins to ride me harder and faster. This time, she grinds her pussy against me as she slides up and down to make perfect contact with her clit.

I can feel her begin to tighten and twitch around my dick, and I know she's close. I keep thumbing her nipples, rolling them between my fingers, as her cries grow louder.

"That's it baby, let me hear it. Let me see it," I command.

I pinch her nipples harder, and she begins to come around me. Her pussy tightens so much I can barely move in and out. She throws her head back and cries out my name as she rides out her release.

When she finally opens her eyes and looks down at me,

she smiles. "Damn, that was good."

She's right. It was fucking incredible, but I have news for her.

We aren't done yet.

And as sexy as it was watching her take the reins...it's my turn.

Chapter Nineteen

TESS

I'm still coming down off of the high of my mind-blowing orgasm when in one swift motion, Alexander switches our positions. This time, he gets on top.

My eyes gaze into his. Those deep pools hold so much...so much that I can't quite make out. So much that wants to make its way to the surface but stays buried deep within.

The one thing I can read in those eyes though is absolute carnal desire. He looks like he wants to do everything in the world to my body, and honestly, if he keeps looking at me like that, I might let him.

A moan escapes me as I feel him rubbing the thick head of his manhood up and down my slit. Just when I think he's about to plunge in all the way, he pulls back and continues his relentless teasing.

"Please," I whisper.

Who am I? I don't beg.

"Please what, sweetheart?" The way he whispers *sweetheart* always seems to have a strange effect on me. It turns me from an independent, competent woman to a bumbling teenager who is trying to score with the quarterback of the football team.

"Please fuck me," I say breathlessly as I writhe underneath his large frame.

Who cares if I'm begging? The way this man can fuck makes it totally worth it.

Without making me wait a moment more, he thrusts inside. The feeling of fullness makes me cry out as my nails dig into his muscular shoulders.

His head dips down as he lightly circles my nipple with his tongue before sucking it between his teeth. Every time he touches my sensitive buds, it sends a wave of electricity straight to my clit, and I pull him closer in an attempt to create more friction.

As if knowing what I crave, he sits back on his knees and places my legs on his shoulders as he continues to pump in and out of me. His thumb settles comfortably on my clit and begins rhythmically rubbing in slow circles.

My legs begin to tremble, and a sheen of sweat coats my skin as I feel myself getting closer. It was a slow, steady build, but I could tell the explosion was going to be huge.

"Right there. Don't stop," I moan as my chest heaves. The only sounds in the otherwise quiet room are the sounds of our passion…our moans, our slicked bodies coming together, our ragged breaths.

The moment I come is like fireworks. The heat begins in my sex and spreads through my entire body like wildfire as I buck underneath Alexander. He continues at the same pace and makes sure to wring every ounce of pleasure out of me.

As I'm coming down, he begins to increase his speed, and I can tell it's his turn to feel the fireworks. I look up at his face. That perfectly chiseled face begins to contort, and I can tell he's trying to hold on as long as he can.

I take a good look at him. He's got some stubble from the late hour, and his hair is tousled in just the right kind of messy way. I like Alexander like this…when he's not quite so perfect.

He takes my legs off his shoulders and leans down to kiss me. I pull his face closer to mine as our tongues swirl together.

My legs wrap around his back in an attempt to pull him deeper inside. Within moments, he is flying over the edge.

"Fuuuuuck," he says as he finds his release.

For a few brief moments, we lay there in silence, still wrapped in each other's arms and our bodies still heaving.

When he finally gets up to throw away the condom, I'm a little surprised when he comes back and joins me in bed.

"Look Ace, as much as I would love to go for Round 2, I'm afraid I have nothing left to give. You wore me the fuck out," I say with a sleepy smile.

Lying next to me, he props himself up on his elbow and laughs. "Nah, no more tonight. You wore me out too. I just figured I'd cool off a bit before I have to put that hot suit back on and head home."

I nod and give him a peck on the cheek.

His fingers graze up and down my side, so light I can barely feel them. As they wander further down, I mutter, "Ace, you're moving into dangerous territory if you don't want to get me all excited again."

He chuckles. "No, I'm just looking at your tattoo."

Oh, right.

"Do you like it?" I ask.

"I really do."

"Do you have any?" I ask the question even though I already know he doesn't. My eyes have traced over every inch of that sculpted body. No tattoos.

"Nope. Don't like needles."

That gets a cackle of out me. "You? Mr. Tough Guy doesn't like needles?" My laugh fills the room.

He smiles. "I don't know what's so funny, Miss. A lot of people don't like needles. It's a pretty common thing." Changing the subject from himself back to me, he asks, "When did you get this?"

"College. I actually had a smaller one that was supposed to be the same basic idea, but the tattoo artist did a shitty job. It looked awful. When I began getting a decent paycheck, I went and had it redone. Guess I might have gotten a little carried away with the size," I shrug.

"I think it's perfect. It suits you."

"How so?"

"It's a tattoo of wildflowers. Honestly, I can't think of a better description for you. You're wild, free, and untamed." His eyes continue to gaze at the ink.

I like how that is how he sees me…although I'm not sure how accurate it is these days. Back when I got this tattoo, I was far more wild and untamed. But I must say that being with Alexander gives me that same feeling I would get all those years ago.

And I love it.

He continues to trace the outline of flowers as he lays his head on my stomach. I run my fingers through his dark hair, and before I know it, we are both fast asleep.

Chapter Twenty
ALEXANDER

My eyes blink a few times as I struggle to open them. When I finally do, the room is still dark. I've always been an early riser, so I'm no stranger to getting out of bed before the sun comes up, but I'm definitely a stranger to the room I'm in.

Where am I?

Then, it hits me. The smell of flowers.

I'm still at Tess's. Shit, I stayed the night at Tess's.

It probably shouldn't be a big deal, yet somehow it is. I have rules that I never break. One of those is never spending a night in a woman's apartment. It puts out a signal that I'm not ready to give.

My gaze falls on the beauty that lay next to me. Her white sheets cover only the lower half of her body as she sleeps on her stomach. Her dark hair is fanned out all over the pillows, and I gently reach out to push a strand of it out of her eyes.

As much as I like Tess, I sure as hell don't think I'm ready for staying the night with her. Sex is one thing. Waking up in someone's arms is a whole other ballgame. We promised to keep this casual. Me sleeping in her bed seems the exact opposite of casual.

My head spins as I realize maybe this whole thing was a bad idea. I am not the man who sleeps with a woman and then wakes up with her the next morning. I'm the man who is out the door the minute after I fill the condom.

Our little arrangement we have going is more than I give any woman. I don't give anything more than sex. Ever. No dinners. No friendship.

I've already broken those rules with Tess, and I'm not sure I want to break any more.

I like my life just the way it is. I don't need a woman coming in trying to change everything. God knows I'm probably too fucked up for her to ever succeed.

A pit forms in my stomach, and I need to get the fuck out of here.

N*ow*.

Trying to be as quiet as possible, I get out of bed and walk over to my pile of clothes. I'm going to look like shit leaving this place with a wrinkled suit before it's even daylight. But, fuck it.

Less than five minutes later, I'm walking out the front door of Tess's building and taking a deep breath of fresh air… well, not fresh air…we live in New York. I call Barry and wait at the curb for what seems like an eternity. But what do I expect? It's the ass crack of dawn, and I gave him no indication of my plans last night.

When he finally pulls up, I slide in and tell him I'd like to go home. My head leans back on the soft leather seat, and I let out a sigh.

I just have to get home, take a shower, and try to get back to my routine. Change and I are not well acquainted, and I don't handle it well. The sooner I can get back to normal, the better I'll be.

****

The next couple days, I try to keep myself busy with work. It's the beginning of the month, which is when I sit down with the managers of each of my establishments. We go over all the numbers and see where there is potentially room for improvement.

I usually look forward to these meetings. It's nice to see how all the businesses are progressing. But this time, I just feel like I'm going through the motions.

Tess had texted me that morning after she'd woken up to make sure I was okay. When I told her I had broken one of my cardinal rules, she told me I was being ridiculous.

Maybe I was. Maybe I still am. But that's my choice.

I can't lie and say I don't miss her though. She keeps invading my thoughts at every turn.

When I'm at the club, I think about seeing her there for the first time. When I go to dinner, I reminisce about our conversations when we went out. And when I lie in bed alone at night, I think about that sexy body of hers underneath me.

With every passing thought, I tell myself that it's just the amazing sex that I miss. Nothing more.

Denial is a beautiful thing.

"Mr. Rockford, what do you think about that idea?"

I shake my head as if trying to shake the thoughts of her right out. "I'm sorry, what?"

Chet sighs. "Theodore here has just outlined an innovative new marketing plan he would like to use for the restaurant." He looks thoroughly annoyed with me. I always bring Chet with me to these meetings since he handles my books, but good lord, we drive each other insane.

"Oh right, that sounds perfect. I'll give you a little bit of leeway to run with this, and I will check back in a month to see how it's progressing."

Theodore's face lights up. It's a good thing one of us is happy because I have absolutely no idea what I've just agreed to.

Oh well. I trust Theodore, and I'm sure he will do whatever he can to get people in the door. Guess the whole thing will be a big surprise when I come back in a month.

"Are we done?" I ask, trying not to sound too impatient.

"Yeah, for now," Chet says with apparent hesitation.

"Great. I'll see you all later," I say, and I'm out the door before Chet can catch up with me. I'm not really in the mood for his inquisition or one of his new investment ideas. He's always trying to pitch me new ideas, but honestly, most of the time, they suck, and I don't have the patience to listen to them.

Besides, I still have to get to the gym before I make my way to Club Rock for the evening. My days are jam packed busy, and I like it that way. Leaves less time for distraction.

But as I'm lifting weights and running on the treadmill at the gym, distraction is all I have. Tess is firmly planted in my head, and she doesn't seem to be going anywhere. Hell, I'm not even ogling the girl ten feet away from me who is a knock-out. With a small frame and huge breasts, normally I would be asking for her number right about now...especially since she is clearly trying to put on a show for me.

I see you smiling at me and bending over.

But damnit if I'm not even the slightest bit interested. After fucking Tess twice, why isn't she out of my system? She seems to be a drug, and I need another hit just to be able to focus on anything else.

I keep pulling out my phone, tempted to call her and ask her to dinner, but I hesitate every time. An inner war rages within me as I struggle to figure out if we can keep out little arrangement intact while still following my rules.

Tess told me herself that she is a rule breaker. But I also wonder if she's worth *breaking* rules for.

Afterall, I would love to keep this whole 'friends with benefits' thing going. Tess and I are explosive in the bedroom. And I'm not quite sure I'm ready to let that go.

Chapter Twenty-one

TESS

After my morning run, I'm being lazy on my couch with some trashy reality TV. The episodes I'm on are close to six months old since I barely ever have time to watch them. My DVR is filled to capacity, and it keeps randomly deleting shit to remind me of that fact.

Guess I'm in for a fun-filled day of binge-watching. It sounds pathetic, but I don't care. What else have I got to do?

Ever since Alexander ran out of my apartment the other morning, he's been super weird.

Scratch that. He's been a dick.

His explanation that he has 'rules', and staying the night with me broke one of them is bullshit. I think he's just scared of even the slightest hint of intimacy. Hell, it's not like we made sweet, passionate love and fell asleep lovingly gazing into each other's eyes.

No. We had sex and passed out.

We haven't talked since.

Is it killing me? Yes.

But am I going to stand my ground and refuse to text him? Also, yes.

I've never been that woman to pine for someone. I've

never begged a man to be with me, and I am not about to start now...no matter how amazing he was in bed.

Just the thought of him inside me made the ache between my legs grow. I could go in my bedroom and take care of the issue with my vibrator, but as my head looks over toward the hallway, I come to the conclusion that it's just too far. I'll just lay here in a lazy heap on my couch...horny.

My phone vibrates on the coffee table, and my stomach flutters for a moment before I see that it's Tyler wanting to video chat.

I debate not answering, but I know he'll just keep calling.

When I hit the button to answer, two tiny little blondes show up on the screen. "Aunt Tess!!!"

"Hi, my beautiful babies!"

"Whatcha doing?" Lilah asks.

"Just got done going for a run. What are you doing?"

"A run?! You want to see how fast I can run?" Lilah shouts.

Before I can answer, she starts running laps around their living room.

"Well, what are you doing today, Miss Abby?"

She shrugs. "Probably hiding from Lilah."

I giggle and hear Tyler's voice. "Girls, did you use my phone to call Aunt Tess? What have I told you about stealing Daddy's phone?"

"Lilah did it!" Abby says.

"Nuh uh!"

Tyler takes the phone, and I see his face pop up on the screen. "Sorry about that. Little shits stole my phone."

"Daddy, don't say shit," Lilah exclaims.

"You're right. I'm sorry," he says while rolling his eyes at me.

"How's it going there, Papa Bear?"

"Oh, we are all okay. The girls are all amped up because Mom and Dad are supposed to be coming over today. I guess Mom is going to help Sam plan the birthday party for the girls. What's up with you? Why do you look like shit?"

"Gee thanks, baby brother."

"I mean I'm just saying you're looking a little rough. I heard you say you went for a run. Maybe go take a shower instead of laying in your own filth on your fancy couch."

Making sure the girls aren't in view, I shoot him my middle finger.

His hands shoot up in defeat. "Alright, alright, I'm sorry. I'm just busting your balls."

"I'll be sure to return the favor just as soon as I see you," I quip.

"Tess, when we were little you used to dress me up like a girl and have a tea party with you. Haven't you tortured me enough throughout our lives?"

I giggle. "No. Not even close. And I'm pretty sure you loved it. Still do. I've seen those tea parties you have with Lilah and Abby. You get way too into them."

"And with that, I'm going to hang up now," he chuckles.

"Tell the girls I love them!" I say loud enough for them to hear.

"Love you, Aunt Tess!" They echo each other.

As I hang up, I can't help but smile. Those girls are something else, and they always make me feel better. It also makes me smile that they're giving their dad hell.

Maybe Tyler is right. Maybe I should at least go shower. Then, I can be clean while I wallow on my couch all day.

But the shower is so far away.

Trying to find the will to get moving, I roll myself off the couch and begin to head down the hallway. Halfway down, I hear a knock on the door.

Damnit.

Sighing, I skulk back to the door. When I open it, there stands Alexander.

Trying to look as though I wasn't just being a lazy mess, I stand up straight and try to adjust myself.

"Hi." Although his voice is always sultry and sexy, today it's clouded with uncertainty.

"What do you want, Alexander?"

I can't decide if I'm happy he's here or pissed. Or both. Probably both.

"Can we talk?" He asks.

"About?"

I hear a door creak open, and one of my neighbors, Mrs. Monomar sticks her head out the door to see what the commotion is. She must have been spying because I know we aren't being that loud.

"Do you want an audience?" He asks, nodding toward the open door.

I don't respond but instead just move out of the way so he can step inside. Once I reach around his large frame and close the door, I start again. "Now, what do you want to talk about?"

"I want to talk about us."

"Oh, really? Now, you want to talk about us? The past few days you completely disappeared because you flipped out. And why? For breaking one of your precious rules?" I emphasize the word 'rules' with some air quotes.

"You're right."

I'm about to give him seven kinds of holy hell, but his words stop me as though I've run into a brick wall.

"What?" I exclaim.

"I said you're right. I woke up here, and I freaked out. Keep in mind that this is all very new to me." He leans his muscular body up against the wall and shoves his hands in the pockets of his dark jeans. "Tess, what you and I have going right now is more than I have ever done. Even friends with benefits is a lot for me. I'm not usually friends with women, and I usually only fuck them once. *Maybe* twice on rare occasions."

I scoff. "Well, there you have it. We have fucked. Twice. So, I guess that's it then, huh?" My voice grows in volume.

He matches his volume to mine. "Damnit, woman, will you listen to me?"

My arms cross over my chest, and I roll my eyes waiting for him to continue.

"What I'm trying to say is that you aren't like those other girls, and I shouldn't have treated you as such. I'm here to apologize, and I hope you can forgive me."

I pace around my living room for a moment trying to figure out exactly what to say. Have I missed him? Of course. I missed him like crazy, but I also am not going to be used as some pawn in whatever twisted game he is playing.

I try to keep my distance from him because he smells amazing, and every time I get close to his hard body, it seems to pull me in like a magnet. Fuck, I want to climb him like a tree, but I don't need his sex appeal making me lose my resolve.

I twirl my ponytail around my finger as I search for the right words. Finally, I face him again.

"Here's the deal, Alexander. You are either doing this or you're not. I'm not asking for some lifelong commitment from you, but I am looking for someone who isn't going to run off the next morning just because he fell asleep in my bed. If we are going to do this thing, I need you to say fuck the rules…at least some of them."

He nods, but I can see the hesitation written all over his face.

I continue. "Look, I am not the girl who is going to suffocate you with a relationship, but I'm also not the one to get walked all over. If we do this, you're at least trying to keep an open mind. So now, I ask you, Ace…are you in or are you out?"

Chapter Twenty-two
ALEXANDER

"Ace, are you in or are you out?" Tess asks me with her wide eyes and firm stance.

My head is screaming at me that I should walk away. Casual or not, I will hurt this woman. Eventually, the monster inside me will show itself, and she will never forgive me. I'll make her hate me as much as I hate myself.

But as selfish as it is, I just can't walk away. She's too damn addicting, and I need more.

"I'm in," I say, and a hint of a smile crosses her lips.

"Okay, Ace," she says, her face beginning to soften.

"So, what are you doing today?" I ask trying to lighten the mood.

Her shoulders shrug. "I didn't really have plans. Honestly, I was just going to lay around and do nothing."

I take her hand and pull her close to me, so our bodies are pressed against one another. "Do you mind if I stay and do nothing with you?"

She bites her bottom lip. "I don't think you'd have much fun watching trashy reality television with me."

"Whatever you want to do, we will do. You plan our day. If that includes reality TV, then I'll sit here with you all day."

I say the words but am secretly praying she changes her mind and wants to do something else.

She thinks for a moment before my prayers are answered. "No, I have a better idea of what we can do today."

"What's that?" I ask.

"It's a surprise."

I fucking hate surprises. No surprises is another one of my rules, but considering the tongue lashing she just gave me, I decide not to bring it up.

"Just let me take a shower, and we can get going."

Before she can get too far, I pull her close and plant my lips on hers. She melts into my kiss as my tongue gently dips into her mouth. My hand grips the back of her head, holding her in place while I take what I crave. But before we can go any further, she pulls away.

"Ace, if you keep doing that, we aren't going to make it out of this apartment today."

"What's wrong with that?" I whisper against her jawline.

A noticeable shiver runs over her whole body. "Patience, Ace. Tonight, you can have your dirty way with me. For now, I have other plans."

Before I can really turn on the charm and convince her to jump in bed with me, she leaves my arms headed for the shower. I start to follow her. Afterall, I don't know how much resolve she would have if I climbed under the water with her and started teasing her naked body.

But I stop myself. She wants to go do something today, and after the way I treated her, I can at least give her that. Even if that meant sporting a massive hard-on in my jeans.

****

"An amusement park?" I ask in disbelief.

After two hours of riding shotgun as Tess drove like a maniac in her Ferrari, where did we end up? A fucking amusement park.

"Uh huh," she says with an excited squeak.

"Why an amusement park? We could have just gone to

Coney Island which is much closer."

Without looking at me, she replies, "Rides aren't big enough."

"Exactly how big do you need them to be, Tess?"

Her eyes finally find mine, and she wiggles here eyebrows. "You know I like big things I can ride on. Come on, you don't like amusement parks?"

"Never been to one," I reply, looking out the window as she parks.

Once the car is firmly stopped, she turns to me, "Never? How is that even possible?"

I shrug. "Parents never took me when I was a kid, and when I became an adult, it was never really at the top of my to-do list."

"Well, Ace, it's at the top of your to-do list today!" She squeals while jumping out of the car.

"Has anyone ever told you that you are a reckless driver?" I ask, following close behind her.

"Yes. Plenty of times. I wouldn't be so reckless if people would just get the hell out of my way."

That gets a laugh out of me. "For a doctor, you sure do throw caution to the wind a lot."

She stops walking and looks at me for a moment. "As a doctor, I see how fast a life can be taken away. That's why I choose to live mine to the absolute fullest."

"Fair enough, sweetheart."

The smile finds its way back to her lips as we continue to make our way to the entrance. When we get to the gate, I pull out my wallet, but Tess insists on paying since the whole thing was her idea. Not wanting to argue in front of a crowd of people, I let her have her way...for now.

She grabs a park map, and we look at it together. She points out every single thing that she wants to ride, and my anxiety shoots through the roof. Isn't this woman scared of anything?

Grabbing my hand, she starts leading me through the

crowded park. As we approach some of the smaller thrill rides, I think maybe it all won't be so bad. Little kids are riding those, and they look like they're having a great time. But my heart picks up speed when I realize we are walking right past all of those small rides to a coaster that sits toward the back of the park.

Oh, fuck me.

This thing looks like it is straight out of a nightmare hellscape with all of its big drops and crazy loops.

"You ready, Ace?" She asks, practically bouncing up and down.

Before I really have time to answer, she is pulling me forward once more. Hell, if it makes her this happy, who am I to argue? Besides, how bad can it really be?

I'm Alexander fucking Rockford. I can do anything.

Five minutes later, I am about to hyperventilate as we are going up the first hill. My tensions were eased a little bit as we were getting strapped in. The girl checking my harness seemed a bit too eager with her hands, and Tess was staring daggers through the barely-legal girl. Pride surged through me as I watched her get a bit territorial.

But any pride or feelings of being an Alpha male went right out the window as the ride started to move.

I look over at Tess who is beaming from ear to ear.

"Tess, I don't know if now is the right time to tell you this, but I am terrified of heights," I say loud enough for her to hear over the chains on the track.

Her head snaps over to me, her eyes wide. "Why didn't you say something?"

"I thought it would be okay. But now that I am up here, and those people down there are starting to resemble ants, I'm kind of starting to freak out."

"Sorry to tell you, Ace, but it's a little late now. Don't worry, just close your eyes," she shoots me a wink. "Pretend you're flying."

"That doesn't make me feel any bett…"

Before I can utter another syllable, I realize we are at the top of the hill. My heart pounds against my chest, and I feel like it might fly out of my body and beat us to the ground. I squeeze my eyes shut as tightly as I can as we began soaring at crazy speeds.

"Holy shit!" I scream. Or at least I think I'm screaming. The sound might be blocked by my sheer terror.

On the other hand, Tess screams and laughs like she is having the time of her life. Her hands never leave the air as we fly through the loops and bank turns. Meanwhile, I'm white knuckling the shit out of my restraints. Pretty sure my fingerprints will be indented into them when it's all said and done.

When the ride finally slows, I manage to open my eyes and see the beautiful woman sitting next to me. I don't know that I have ever seen another person look so elated.

As we step off the ride, she gently punches my shoulder. "Why didn't you tell me you were afraid of heights?"

I shrug. "You were so excited. I wasn't about to ruin that for you."

She stops walking and looks at me. Without warning, she grabs my face and pulls my lips to hers. My hands hold her waist against me as she gently nips at my bottom lip.

"Thank you," she says, pulling back. "That was really sweet. But we don't have to ride anything else if you don't want to."

"Maybe something smaller. A lot smaller."

She giggles but agrees, and we go on some of the smaller rides. Eventually, she does talk me into another coaster, but this one isn't quite so intense. In fact, I even hold my eyes open for most of it. Although the on-ride photo makes me look like I am about to pass out. She insists on getting multiple physical copies of it.

"Blackmail for if you get out of line again," she says with a wink.

After the rides, we grab a couple of funnel cakes and just walk around looking at the scenery. It really is a beautiful park. Everyone seems so happy, and I can see why Tess loves it so much.

We find a few small tables alongside a garden, so we sit down to finish our food.

"Do you come here a lot?" I ask her.

"I used to. When my brother Tyler and I were teenagers, we would come down here damn near every weekend. He loves coasters as much as I do, so we would hit every ride in the park. Then, we would eat all kinds of junk and head home for the night. After he got married, sometimes I would still come up here by myself and ride a few things."

"You really like it, huh?"

She nods. "Don't get me wrong, it's always more fun to come here with another person," she shoots me a wink. "But I guess I never needed someone to come with me. When I'm on that coaster, it's like I am flying. Every worry or care I have disappears for three to four minutes, and I'm like a bird or something. It sounds stupid, I know."

My fingers graze the top of her hand. "No, it doesn't sound stupid. It's good to get out of your own head sometimes. Everyone has their own way of doing that."

"And what is your way of doing that, Mr. Rockford? Does it involve climbing between my legs?" Her smile turns into a seductive one.

"Well, as much as I love doing that to forget about all my problems, I have other ways."

"Like?"

I take another bite of funnel cake before answering. "I like to go camping."

"Camping?"

"Yeah. Alone in the woods. Just me and nature. Gives me that same sort of feeling of shutting out the world."

"Fair enough," she smiles. "Although I like my suggestion of you climbing in between my legs better."

"Oh, yes, I love that option too," I laugh.

"Thank you for coming today. And for being such a good sport even though it wasn't really your thing."

"You're welcome. But no thanks necessary. This funnel

cake is so good it makes up for it."

She leans across the table. "Well, I was thinking maybe there was something else I could do for you to make it up to you."

"What do you have in mind, sweetheart?" I ask, adjusting myself knowing that her answer is probably going to make the bulge in my pants quite apparent.

"Me. Naked. In bed. While you do whatever you want to me."

Good God.

"Let's go," I say.

A grin breaks out on her face as she stands up to throw our trash away. "And sweetheart?"

She turns to look at me.

"Let's see how fast you can get us home."

Chapter Twenty-three
TESS

"Lie down."

Alexander's voice is commanding. The rebel in me wants to tell him to fuck off. But an even bigger part of me is anxious to see what he has planned.

He has already stripped me down to my bra and panties, yet he is still fully clothed. Even through his jeans though, I can see the outline of his large cock. Just looking at it makes my knees go weak.

"Lie down," he says again, this time with more authority behind it. I guess I got busy staring at him I forgot what I was supposed to be doing.

My palms press down on the cool fabric of my sheets as I slowly make my way toward the headboard, making sure to shake my ass a little along the way.

"You love to drive me crazy, don't you, sweetheart?"

"I don't know what you're talking about," I say as I roll over onto my back, opening my legs just enough to give him a peek there too.

"Woman, you're going to pay for that," he grunts.

Call me crazy, but the caveman thing is seriously turning me on.

"Put your hands up," he says, pulling his shirt off over his head.

Damn, I will never get tired of looking at those abs.

Doing as he says, I lay my arms above my head on the pillow.

"Can I trust you to leave them there, or am I going to have to tie them up?"

"What do you think?" I work my bottom lip with my teeth.

"I think that you will end up being very bad and have to be tied up." He's now joining me on the bed.

"Probably," I don't even get the word out before his mouth devours mine. His tongue commands mine and takes all that I have to give.

His large body moves with ease on top of me, and I can feel the outline of every hard muscle. Not able to control myself, I wrap my arms around his neck and fist my fingers in his hair.

He breaks our connection and looks at me with those dark blue pools. "Didn't I tell you to keep your hands up?" His teeth nip at my lower lip.

"You knew I wouldn't listen," I moan.

He takes each one of my hands in his and holds them above my head while his mouth finds mine once more. I can feel his length through his jeans pressing against my sex, and I writhe beneath him, silently begging for more friction.

"Patience, sweetheart," he whispers into my ear sending shivers down my spine. "Now, can I trust you to hold your hands up here while I make you scream my name?"

Frantically, I nod my head even though I'm not sure I really can keep them still. I'll sure as hell try though if we can move onto the 'him making me scream his name' part.

My gaze follows him as he begins to work his way down my body. My fingers in his hair have messed up its usually perfect style, and a few strands hang in his face as he looks up at me.

His fingers lightly graze the skin right above my breasts, and my heartbeat quickens. His hands reach underneath me to undo the clasp of my bra. He pulls my arms down long enough to slip the straps off my shoulders. Once the lacy garment hits the floor though, he positions my hands above my head once more.

"Keep them there, sweetheart, or I stop," he says before swirling his tongue around my nipple. It immediately hardens as he exhales onto the wet flesh.

Moisture continues to gather between my legs, and I arch my back in an effort to get close to his mouth once again.

Taking the hint, he sucks my nipple into his mouth and grazes it with his teeth. I can barely sit still as his tongue flicks back and forth across one while his fingers mimic the motion with the other. Every touch to my nipples sends shock waves straight to my clit, and it aches to be touched.

Finally, his head lowers once more as he moves further down the bed to settle between my legs. Grabbing my thong with his thumbs, he pulls it down my legs and off my body.

He spreads my legs wide, and I'm completely on display for him. Instead of shying away from it though, I embrace the moment and angle myself closer to him.

His eyes dart hungrily from my pussy to my face. Alexander Rockford is usually a hard man to read, but the look on his face in this moment shows all he wants to do is devour me in every way possible. And I swear I'm going to let him.

His lips gently touch my thigh as he kisses a trail toward my sex but stopping just short of where I need him most. He teases me with kisses, and I can barely sit still. My hands ball into fists as I try to keep them in place.

"Good girl," he says, noticing my restraint.

And without warning, he sucks my clit into his mouth, and I buck my hips so hard I practically jump out of bed. All the teasing has made me so sensitive I can barely stand it. His tongue laps up my juices as he alternates between licks and sucks.

I'm getting close, and my whole body can tell. Every part of me responds to this man. Sweat beads on my skin. My heart races. My legs begin to shake.

When he pushes two fingers inside of me, I'm done. My hands fist in the sheets to keep from fisting in Alexander's hair as I ride out my release on his face.

Tremor after tremor of pleasure hits me as I have the most Earth-shattering orgasm of my life. It goes on for what feels like forever, and I'm still seeing stars as I start to come down.

Once my body stills, Alexander leans up to kiss me, and I can taste myself on him. Teasing him, I run my tongue across his bottom lip, licking it clean.

"You can use your hands now," he whispers, and I throw my arms around his neck and pull him back in to deepen our kiss.

It isn't long though before he is standing up and taking his pants off.

Finally.

"Turn over," he says.

I do as he commands and roll to my stomach. He pulls my hips towards him so my ass is up in the air. It's mere moments before I hear the foil of the condom wrapper ripping. He slides it on and pushes his head to my opening.

"Tell me if it's too much, sweetheart."

I don't know what he means, and I don't have time to ask because he's already working his way inside me. When he is fully buried, I begin to understand what he meant. I always feel full with him inside me, but this takes it to a whole new level. Every thrust makes direct contact with my g-spot, and after my orgasm from his mouth, every sensation is heightened ten-fold.

His moves are slow and deliberate at first, but when I push back against him, eager for more, he quickens his pace. Grabbing my hips, he plunges in and out of me hard and fast, and I'm crying out with every thrust.

Before I know it, I'm nearing release again, and he moves one hand between us for his thumb to focus attention on my clit. I begin coming just as hard, if not harder, than before. I beg him to give me everything he has, and it doesn't take long for him to follow through.

He lets out a low moan as he fills the condom. Before he pulls out of me, he leans down and gives me a tender kiss on my shoulder.

Once he has gotten up and disposed of the condom, he comes back to find me in a heap on the bed.

"You okay, sweetheart?"

"You fucked the life right out of me, Ace," I mumble.

"Back at you, beautiful," he chuckles while climbing in to lay behind me.

"Do you need to get going?" I ask.

"Nope," he replies, pulling me closer.

I can already feel his breathing starting to even out as he begins to doze.

"What about your rules?"

"Fuck the rules," he says, sleepily. "Why bother when you just keep making me break them?"

Chapter Twenty-four
TESS

Two weeks have gone by since Alexander showed up at my doorstep asking for another chance. He told me that he was going to try to look past all of his rules, so we could continue on with our...well, *whatever* this thing is that we are doing.

And you know what?

Things have been going pretty well. We see each other as often as we can, and usually our nights consist of dinner, talking, and then, some mind blowing sex. You'd think by now, I'd be used to him and his magic dick.

I'm not.

It's still just as good. Every. Single. Time. The man reads my body like an open book and has me experiencing things I didn't think were possible.

Aside from the fireworks in the bedroom, we have been following through on the 'friends' part of 'friends with benefits' too. We talk and laugh and joke with each other almost constantly. Of course, the other part of the time, we are arguing because he's trying to be Mr. Controlling by telling me how to live my life.

You'd think he would have learned by now that I am not

going to listen. I'm just going to get mad, and it's going to cause a fight.

Most of the time, both of us are too stubborn to admit when we are wrong, so we just drop it and move on. And maybe that would be super unhealthy if we were actually in a relationship. But we're not. This is still strictly casual.

There's just one problem.

Despite his dark and brooding nature, Alexander Rockford is beginning to make me swoon. When I know I'm going to see him, I get all excited and giddy like a damn teenager with her first boyfriend.

I keep telling myself that it's just the newness of the whole thing or that I am just excited about the upcoming orgasms, but deep down, I feel that it's more than that…although I won't say it out loud or even admit it to myself.

Instead, I hold onto the notion that there are absolutely no feelings involved and that it's all just harmless fun. And I assure myself that when the time is right to end it, I will know it.

Question is…will I be ABLE to end it when the time is right?

Earlier today, he texted asking if I was free for a late dinner when I got off work. The day dragged on in a blur as I impatiently waited for time to pass until I finally got off and came home to get ready.

Glancing in the mirror, I look over myself one more time to make sure I look okay. I touch up my bright red lipstick that perfectly matches the tight dress I'm wearing. And I run a brush through my straight hair one more time before there's a knock on the door.

Right on time. As usual.

When I open the door, I am surprised to not see Alexander's typical three-piece suit. Instead, he just wears jeans with a button-down shirt. He still looks fine as hell though. Honestly, the man could probably wear a burlap sack and still be the most attractive man I've ever laid eyes on.

"Hey, sweetheart," he says as I swing the door open all the way.

"What are you wearing?" I ask.

He looks down, clearly confused. "Clothes. Isn't that what I'm supposed to wear to dinner?"

"Yes, but you're usually much more dressed up, and now I look overdressed. See, this is what happens when you won't tell me where we are going to eat."

A sly grin crosses his lips as he pulls me close and rests his hands on my waist. "The place we are going isn't super fancy, so if you would like to change, feel free. But I must say that you look absolutely stunning in that dress."

"Thank you," I pout.

"So, do you want to go change?" He gestures toward the bedroom.

A loud sigh escapes me. "I guess not. I'm getting hungry, so I'll just wear this."

He laughs. "You're always hungry." Once he stops laughing, he leans down and whispers in my ear, "For what it's worth, I think that dress is going to look even better on the floor later as I peel it from your sexy body."

My breath hitches in my throat as I try to keep my libido in check. I look into his eyes as desire hangs in the air between us. My lips long to touch his, but I know the second they meet, there's no way we will make it to dinner. Hell, there's no way we will leave this apartment for the next twelve hours.

Deciding to give him a taste of his own medicine, I lean forward, almost close enough for our lips to touch while my hand gently grazes the front of his jeans.

I whisper, "As much fun as that sounds, Ace. I need food."

He exhales the breath he had been holding and finally breaks our gaze. "Let's go, gorgeous."

Half an hour later, we are walking into a quaint little bistro named Geraldine's. This place is so small and tucked away that I never would have even noticed it while walking down the street but surprisingly, inside the restaurant is fairly crowded.

An older woman with salt and pepper hair comes walking out of the kitchen holding a slew of plates. The moment she sees Alexander, she exclaims in a thick southern accent, "Well, hell's bells! Look who's here!"

After she sets the plates down at their appropriate table, she walks over to give him a hug. Mr. Cold and Distant embraces her with one of the warmest hugs I've ever seen.

"Nancy, good to see you."

She slaps him across the chest with the towel she was using to handle the hot plates. "Where the hell have you been?"

"Been busy working. You know how it is."

"I see," she says while picking up two menus and leading us across the inviting space. "You get some other big business ventures going and forget about this little old place."

He gives a sheepish grin. "Not at all. Clearly, this place is doing just fine on its own without me hovering around."

"Oh, hogwash. You know that you used to walk your butt through that door for a hell of a lot more than business reasons, but I can yell at you later." She stares daggers through him. "And believe me, I will, but first introduce me to your lady friend."

"Nancy, this is Tess. She and I have been seeing each other."

"No shit!"

I go to shake her hand, but she wraps me in a hug. "Welcome to the family, Tess. Do me a favor and make sure this one comes around more. We miss him around here."

"I'll do my best. You know how stubborn he can be," I joke, but the words ring true.

Her loud laugh fills the air. "No truer words have ever been spoken. I like this one Alexander. You should keep her around. Alright, I'll leave you two alone to eat. I have to get back in the kitchen. Boy, you better not leave without saying bye to me."

"Wouldn't dream of it," he says as we sit down in a booth.

Once we are seated, I look over the menu, trying not to look as confused as I feel. Everything listed is down home Southern cooking, and it all looks amazing. After a few minutes of perusing, I finally decide on fried chicken. You can never go wrong with fried chicken.

Once the waitress has taken our menus and delivered our drinks, I can't take it anymore. I blurt out, "Okay, I have approximately one thousand questions."

He chuckles. "I'd be surprised if you didn't. But how about this, let me tell you a story first. If you still have questions after that, you can ask me whatever you want."

"Deal," I say, hurriedly.

He took a long drink of his water before beginning. "After high school, I was eager to get out of the small town I was from and make something of myself, so I came here to New York. Everything I owned fit in a backpack, and I only had twenty dollars in my pocket.

"Once I got here, I walked around all day looking for work. When I was coming up empty, I stumbled across this place. The food smelled so good I decided it was worth spending my last cash on. I figured it would be good to have one last good meal before I was really, truly homeless.

"But once I came in, Nancy came over and talked to me. Told me I reminded her of her son who was killed in the war. I guess she took pity on me and offered me a place to stay in the upstairs apartment in exchange for working here in the kitchen in the evening."

"You worked in a kitchen?" I interrupt.

The look on his face says I'm supposed to be listening and not asking questions yet.

"Sorry. Go on," I prompt.

"Yes, I worked in the kitchen. I cooked, cleaned, and did whatever manual labor Nancy needed around here. She even gave me the numbers of some other business owners who would hire me for odd jobs during the day. So, I was actually pulling in a little bit of cash, and not having any real bills, I was able to invest some in the stock market.

"It didn't take a genius to look around this place and see that it needed a lot of work. Nancy was barely breaking even every month, and it was beginning to fall into disarray. Once I hit a lucky break in the market, I paid to have this place fixed up and started a couple marketing campaigns to really get the word out there. It worked. Nancy has been doing great with this place ever since. She insisted she make me part owner, so I do own some shares, but to me, this place isn't like the rest. I trust Nancy one hundred percent with every decision here, and I don't hover.

"So, there you go. That's why we are here. I wanted you to meet her because without her, I wouldn't be where I am today. I probably would have run back to my hometown with my tail between my legs. I know I don't always tell you much about my life, and I'm a bit of a closed book, so I just wanted you to see where it started for me…where it really started."

He takes another drink of water and sits quietly for a moment before saying, "Okay, beautiful, hit me with your questions."

Honestly, at this point, I don't know that I have any. His story was very…enlightening. I'm tempted to ask him what prompted him to move away from his hometown and why he was here with no real help from his family, but I decide against it, figuring there's probably a reason for his omission from the story.

"So, you know how to cook?" I ask instead.

He laughs. "Yes, I know how to cook. I invest in a lot of restaurants, so it's a good idea for me to have some inkling of how to advise them to tweak the menu. I'm no Gordon Ramsay, but I can fake it with the best of them." He shoots me a wink.

"Hm. I wouldn't know anything about faking it," I reply with a devilish grin.

"Sweetheart, you better behave. I'll spank that little ass of yours later."

Heat stings my cheeks at his words. Truth be told, it would turn me on like crazy to draped across his lap while he paddles my ass. But I don't put voice to that desire.

Instead, our food appears in front of us, and we dig in.

My eyes roll back in my head after the first bite. "This is seriously the best fried chicken I've ever had."

Alexander smiles at me. "Oh yeah, Nancy can cook like a motherfucker. I swear I had to stop myself from coming here all the time, or I would have gained 200 pounds."

"For this food, it would be worth it," I say between bites. "Besides, I'm sure you've always been sexy as hell."

There is a slight glint in his eye as I call him sexy, but he doesn't respond to that part. Instead, he says, "I used to be a bean pole as a teenager. I didn't actually put on any weight until my senior year, and then I started working out to try to turn everything into muscle. I still try to work out every day if I can."

"Me too," I reply

"Oh, I noticed," he says with a sly grin. "Which gym do you go to?"

I shake my head. "No gym. Usually, I just go running in the mornings, but if it's too cold, I do have a treadmill. I turned the spare bedroom in my apartment into a little at-home gym."

"I'm impressed."

"Don't be. A personal trainer would probably be appalled by my workout routine. There's no rhyme or reason to it. Like I said, usually, I run, and I just keep running until my body feels like it's damn near about to give out. So, I stop and do it all again the next day."

He shrugs. "Whatever works."

"I might have to run extra hard tomorrow to work off this fried chicken though," I giggle.

"Same. But as you said, definitely worth it."

We spend the rest of our meal talking and laughing. It seems strange to me that just a few weeks ago, this man was so closed off, and now, he's beginning to let me into the more intimate parts of his life.

Maybe the big bad wolf isn't the monster he wants me to think he is.

As we were about to leave, he insisted we walk back to the kitchen to say goodbye to Nancy.

"Boy, are you out of here already?" She asks while stirring something on the stove. "Benjamin, come over here and finish this for me."

A scrawny kid jumps at his chance to take over leading the kitchen.

Alexander leans down to hug her, and she wraps her arms around his large shoulders.

"It was good to see you, Nancy. The food was amazing as always."

She lightly punches him in the chest. "Boy, don't try to suck up to me. It's been too damn long since you've shown your face around here, and you know it. I miss you. You need to promise me you'll come back soon."

"I promise. In fact, here," he pulls out his wallet and grabs a business card. "My new cell is on the back. If I don't come back soon, feel free to call and read me the riot act."

"You know I will," she replies while grabbing the card.

He chuckles. "I have no doubt."

Next, she gives me a warm hug. "It was good meeting you, Tess. Keep him in line for me, okay?"

I smile. "I'll try. But as I'm sure you know, he can be a huge pain in the ass."

Her loud laugh fills the kitchen. "Oh honey, believe me, I know all too well."

After saying our goodbyes to Nancy, we are seated back in Alexander's car with Barry driving us home.

We ride in a comfortable silence, and as I look down, I notice Alexander's fingers are locked with mine. His thumb gently rubs the back of my hand. To most, the gesture would seem small, but to me, it seems enormous. Sure, we have shared a bed together more times than I can count, but this seems much more intimate. It's a gesture that he actually cares about more than what's in my pants.

Noticing where we are, I turn to him. "Hey, you passed the turn to head back to my apartment. Oh my gosh, is this where you kill me?" I joke.

"No, not tonight," he says before pausing a moment. "I thought tonight, we could...stay at my apartment."

My eyes go so wide I feel like they're going to pop out of my head. "Really?"

"Only if you want to. If you'd feel more comfortable at your place, we can go there instead."

"No!" I interject a little too excitedly. "Let's go to your place."

Okay, now we really must be in the Twilight Zone. First, he introduces me to a woman who acts as his surrogate mother. Then, he holds my hand. Now, he's taking me to his apartment? What is happening?

My eyes drift over to him, and I take him all in. The way his large body commands everything it does. The way his dark eyes are fixed out the window. The way his jaw slightly twitches as if he's mulling over something in his head.

Tonight, something is shifting between us, and I wonder if he is feeling it too. We are slowly moving from 'fuck buddies' into something else, although I'm not entirely sure what that something is.

Fifteen minutes later, we pull into an underground garage of a high-rise building. Once we are inside, Alexander hits the button for the Penthouse, and it asks for a key code. I turn my head as to not invade his privacy.

Next thing I know the elevator doors are opening to an absolutely stunning penthouse. He takes my coat and offers me a drink. I tell him anything with vodka is fine.

As he is busying himself at the minibar, I walk around the large open floor plan. "Ace, this place is gorgeous."

"Thanks," he says. "I'm good at designing restaurants, but my own space is a whole other matter, so I hired someone to come in and make it look presentable."

"They did a good job," I reply. And they did. The space perfectly reflects Alexander. It is decorated mostly in hues of black and white, and it's very minimalistic. Although there are a few pieces of art on the walls, they don't step into the realm of pretentious.

The floors and kitchen cabinets are a dark wood that perfectly accent the white of most of his furniture.

In one corner of the room stands a beautiful grand piano. It's also white but is outlined in a bright gold.

"Do you play?" I ask, walking over to it.

"I do. Helps me to clear my head," he says, now handing my drink to me.

Setting his down on an end table, he takes a seat at the piano and begins to play. Despite his large hands, his fingers move as if they are as light as air as he taps the keys in perfect harmony. I never would have guessed Alexander Rockford to be an avid piano player. But here we are. I guess I never would have thought a lot of things about him, but he keeps proving me wrong.

With his fingers leaving the keys, he stands up and gives me a gentle peck on my lips. "Be right back beautiful," he says in a low voice.

I watch his tight ass as he walks away, and I smile, eager to see what else the night will bring.

Chapter Twenty-five
ALEXANDER

Walking into my bedroom, I light a couple candles that I am pretty sure have never been lit. The designer put them in here. I'm sure she was thinking it would be a nice touch when entertaining the ladies. Trouble is, I never bring women to my actual apartment...only to my fuck pad on the other side of town.

Except Tess.

What makes Tess so undeniably different?

Every fucking thing.

For starters, she's beautiful. Absolutely stunning...most of the time without even trying. It makes me one proud son of a bitch to have her on my arm when we go out.

It's not all about her looks though. She's smart. I guess you have to be smart to get through medical school and become a doctor.

Most of all though, she is independent. I've always held women at arm's length enough to never even get close enough to become clingy. But Tess and I have been doing this thing a few weeks now, and she hasn't crossed that line.

Hell, maybe I'm the one who's clingy considering I am usually the one asking when we can see each other next.

I could tell myself that the sex is fantastic, and that's why I keep coming back for another taste, but I know it's more than that.

So much more.

As I'm finishing up in the bedroom, I hear music from the living room. As I walk back in, Tess is sitting at the piano playing what might just be the most beautiful song I've ever heard. Her eyes are closed as she sways to the music her hands are producing.

I stand a few feet away just watching, careful not to disturb her. She's in her element, and I love it.

Of course, I play the piano in hopes of impressing this woman I am so fond of, and then, she goes and does it better. If that doesn't perfectly describe Tess, I don't know what does.

In every room she's in, she shines the absolute brightest.

When the melody comes to an end, she opens her eyes to look at me. "Sorry," she says, embarrassed.

"For what?"

"I should have asked before just touching your stuff."

"Sweetheart, if you play like that, you feel free to do it any time you want," I say, taking a few strides until I am behind her.

She smiles as I begin to rub her shoulders. "Where did you learn to play?" I ask.

"While I was growing up, my mom put me in piano. All their rich, snobby friends said that I should have some sort of 'creative outlet', so I guess piano was the first thing she thought of. My dad promised I could quit if I didn't like it, but turns out, I was pretty good. So, I just kept playing all through high school."

"It sounded beautiful," I leaned down to whisper in her ear. "Just like you."

"Has anyone ever told you that you're a real smooth talker, Ace?" Her hand reaches to tangle in my hair as I lightly kiss her neck.

I chuckle against her skin. "I think you're the only one with enough balls to say that to me."

And it's the truth. Most woman let me call every shot and

let me make the rules. Tess challenges me all the time and isn't scared to tell me if she doesn't like something. As much as I love being in control, I have to admit hearing her put me in my place turns me on a little.

She turns around on the piano bench and pulls me down for a kiss. I brace my hands on the keys, and they make a low noise as our tongues begin to dance. My dick is already hard as stone just from our kiss.

I pull away and stand up, reaching for her hand. When she takes it, I lift her and set her on top of the cool surface of the piano.

"Lie back", I tell her, and she does without hesitation.

I grab the bench and scoot it over, so I am right between those long, perfect legs of hers. Spreading her thighs, I see her tiny red thong that matches her dress. Slipping my thumbs under the strings, I pull it down until it's free of her body.

Tess never shies away from my gaze, and it's sexy as hell watching her spread herself open for me to look at. God, she is fucking gorgeous. Her pretty, pink center is so wet and ready for me, but I intend to drive her a little crazy first.

Pulling her hips closer to me, I lean in and slide my tongue along her slit which makes her quiver under me. I delve my tongue deeper and find her clit and begin to circle it, and she begins to come alive.

My hands reach up to pull her dress down far enough to begin thumbing her perfect nipples.

"God, yes!" She moans. "Alexander!"

I swear my name has never sounded sexier. When her fingers begin fisting my hair, I know she's close. Her legs start to shake, and I angle them on my shoulders to help steady her. When I slip two fingers inside and crook them at just the right spot, she begins to get louder.

She screams my name as she releases on my tongue. I keep lapping up her juices until her body stills. When I look up at her, her cheeks are flushed, and she's biting the side of her lip.

"Take me to bed, Ace," she says, gazing at me with those

bedroom eyes.

She doesn't have to ask me twice.

I reach for her hand to help her off the piano. Once her feet are firmly on the floor, she shimmies out of her dress and leaves behind. She heads for the hallway wearing nothing but her high heels, and I swear I'm about to come right there in my pants.

Without turning back, she says, "You coming, Alexander?"

Just about.

When I hit the bedroom, she is laying in the center of my large bed with her legs spread, ready and waiting.

"How do you want me?" She asks.

"Just like that, sweetheart," I growl as I lose my clothes as fast as I can. I grab a condom out of my drawer and roll it on before climbing in between her legs yet again.

I get on my knees and toss one of her long legs on my shoulder as I begin to sink into her. Her pussy tightens around me like a glove as I push further and further. Once I'm in, I begin to take long, hard thrusts in and out of her.

She seems to enjoy every movement just as much as I do as we both get lost in the passion. I could sink my cock into this woman all night long and never get tired. Her eyes stare into mine, and we are locked in our own perfect moment that I never want to end.

Tess is the first woman I've had in this bed, and I can't think of a better woman to break it in with. Her dark hair is fanned all around her on the black sheets. She moans with every thrust I make. Her hands grab the sheets as she edges closer to her release.

She's fucking beautiful.

And as much as I hate to admit it, I want her to be all mine.

Chapter Twenty-six
TESS

My eyes flicker open as I try to take in my surroundings. It doesn't take me long to realize I am in Alexander's room. The room is still fairly dark, but the clock on the nightstand says it's almost 9 AM.

My arm reaches over to find the large man occupying the space next to me, but he's not there. All I feel are cold sheets beneath my fingers.

Rolling out of bed, I head for the bathroom connected to the master bedroom. When I walk in, my mouth drops. Now, don't get me wrong, my apartment is nice. Being a doctor as well as a trust fund kid has always kept me pretty flush.

But this place is on a whole other level. Everything in this bathroom is a gorgeous marble. I poke my head in the shower which has different sprayers along every surface. The top of it appears to be a rain shower. If I get in this thing, I might never get out.

I think it's my favorite part of the room...until I see the oversized bathtub that could probably easily fit three or four people. And it looked pristine. I'm guessing that Alexander isn't a relaxing bubble bath kind of guy.

My bladder starts reminding me of the original reason I

entered the room, so I hurry and do my business. Before I walk out, I run my fingers through my hair, trying to make it look somewhat presentable.

When I walk back into the bedroom, one of Alexander's white t-shirts sits on the bed. Now, I know that wasn't there a few minutes ago.

Was it?

I toss it on over my head, and I'm swimming in the soft material. I can smell his scent all over it, and I can't help but smile.

Making my way out of the bedroom, I hear him in the kitchen. Once I catch sight of him, my breath hitches in my throat. He has that effect on me every time. Will I ever get tired of looking at this man? He stands at the counter, cracking eggs into a bowl...shirtless.

Every one of his muscles ripples underneath the skin as he moves around. As he backs away from the counter to move to the stove, I can see he was wearing a pair of pajama pants that hang low on his hips.

Geez, even him in his pajamas is turning me on. I have the sudden urge to lick every one of his abs and that cute little V shape etched below them, but it looks like he's putting a lot of effort into cooking.

"Morning, Ace," I say, strolling in from the hallway and trying to act like I wasn't just staring and drooling

When his eyes find mine, he smiles. "Good morning, beautiful. How'd you sleep?"

"Like a rock apparently. I never sleep this late. Did you just wake up?" I ask, while taking a seat on one of the barstools along the counter.

"No, I've been up since five."

"Well shit, I don't get up that early."

He laughs. "I usually don't either on a weekend, but one of the restaurants called and said they had a water pipe bust, so I called and got a crew out there to work on it."

"Oh no, is everything okay?"

"It will be. Probably just going to have to replace a few pieces of equipment and maybe the floors. I don't know. We will see what they say once it's all said and done. Anyway, enough about business. How are you doing this morning?"

"I'm pretty good. I would be better if my sexy man was in bed beside me when I woke up." I poke out my bottom lip to feign pouting.

"Oh, trust me, that would have made my morning better too, but I didn't want to wake you. And when I heard you up and moving, I decided to make breakfast. I know how cranky you get when you're hungry," he gives me a wink.

"I would argue with you if it wasn't true," I said, while reaching for a strawberry out of a bowl he had sitting on the counter. "What are you making anyway?"

"Breakfast burritos."

"Mmm, sounds heavenly," I say with a mouthful of another strawberry.

"Yeah, and we are going to have some fruit with it if you will stop eating all the strawberries."

"Okay, okay," I say before shoving a final one into my mouth.

Ten minutes later, we are chowing down on breakfast burritos, and they are absolutely phenomenal.

"So, you really can cook, huh, Ace?" I ask between bites.

"I told you," he smiles. "Nancy was one hell of a teacher."

"Well, remind me to thank her next time we see her." I wait for a response to see if he is going to shoot down the idea that I might see her again.

He doesn't. He just says, "Oh, she will love taking all the credit for that, I'm sure."

"I'm glad you can cook because I am seriously awful at it. Growing up, our housekeeper, Jacinda, always tried to teach us kids but it was a waste of time. I think since Tyler found Sam, he has at least learned a few things from her. Me? I'm just a hopeless cause."

"Oh, I'm sure you're not that bad. I could show you a

couple things if you want."

"I wouldn't bother. One time, Jacinda told me to boil water. That was it…boil water. I don't even remember what we were making. But I got so distracted that I let all the water boil out of the pot and actually destroyed the pot and the stove in the process."

"How…"

I interrupt. "No idea. Since then, everyone thinks it's best that I just stay out of a kitchen. That's why in my kitchen, you will find mostly microwavable items or things I don't have to heat up at all. I also have a very personal relationship with the food delivery man. His name is Frank. Good guy."

Jokingly, he says, "Do I need to worry about this Frank guy?"

"Hmm. Let's see. Frank is about nineteen years old with braces, acne, and only weighs about 90 pounds soaking wet…so yes, I'd say you should definitely be worried."

His laugh fills the space between us. "Well, then sweetheart, I guess I'll just have to keep cooking for you, so you can avoid Frank all together."

"I just don't know if you can live up to Frank's impeccable skills in the bedroom," I quip.

He launches a strawberry from across the table, and it hits me square in the chest. I look down at the red spot now speckling the white shirt.

"You ruined your shirt," I say.

"Worth it," he smiles.

Once we are finished with our breakfast, I get up to begin clearing the table.

"You don't have to do that, sweetheart. I'll get it later."

I hold up my hand. "Look, I may be a shitty cook, but I at least know how to clean up after myself. Despite the fact that Jacinda was our housekeeper, she still taught us how to take care of the things we had and the space around us."

"Sounds like she was more than just your housekeeper," he says while pouring himself another cup of coffee.

"She was. I guess some would have considered her our nanny, but my parents always hated that word. And Jacinda was always family. She practically raised Ty and me."

"What about your other two siblings?"

I shrug while I fill up the sink with hot water. "My parents had Tristan and Tawna when they were younger, and their business was still pretty small. They were able to really focus on the whole parenting thing. I was born so much later, and then Ty, that they were so wrapped up in work that they just didn't have a ton of time. We would go to our house in the Berkshires sometimes and be the whole perfect family, but it wasn't all that often, so Jacinda picked up the slack. Made sure we turned out to be halfway decent human beings."

"I think she did a great job," he gives me a peck on the cheek. "So, what are your plans on this lovely Saturday?"

"Oh, shit, it's Saturday," I mumble to myself. "I have to go to my nieces' birthday party. They are turning three."

For a split second, I wonder if that is disappointment that I see in his eyes, but it's gone so fast, it's hard to tell.

"Hey Ace, do you want to come with me?" The moment the question is out of my mouth, terror washes over me as I wait for his response.

"To a kids' birthday party?" He asks, looking at me over the rim of the steaming mug.

"Yeah. But I mean it won't just be kids. It'll be my family. You kind of showed me a part of your life last night. Now, maybe you can see a part of mine."

The look on his face isn't convinced, so I continue. "Look, don't read too much into this. We are going just as friends. That's it. Friends can meet each other's families."

Hesitation is still etched into his face, so I try to take back the words. "I mean if you don't want to, no big deal. I have to go, but we can get together afterwards if you want."

"No."

"No?" A pit slowly forms in my stomach.

"I mean no, I don't want to just see you after. Of course,

I'll go with you. You just have to save me if your family gets too crazy." He smiles, but I can tell he is serious.

"I can do that."

"Do you want to go for a run before we start the day?" He asks.

I dry my hands on a dish towel and walk over to him. "I was thinking there are much more fun ways I would like to burn off some calories with you this morning."

"And what way is that, Dr. Wendell?"

"Well, Mr. Rockford," I say while sliding my hand underneath the waistband of his pants and fisting his already hard cock. "I think you know."

"Bedroom. Now." He commands.

I begin to walk toward the hallway, but apparently, I'm not moving fast enough. Suddenly, I'm whisked up and over Alexander's shoulder.

"Going a little caveman, aren't we, Ace?" I ask, my head at just the right height to gawk at his perfect ass.

"Oh, sweetheart, you haven't seen anything yet."

Chapter Twenty-seven
ALEXANDER

After taking Tess hard and fast in my bed, I seduced her again in the shower. Our second round was more slow and sensual than the first, and I think it was my way of trying to prolong the inevitable. It didn't work though because now, we are in the car on the way to the birthday party.

The closer Tess drives to her brother's house, the larger the pit of lava in my stomach seems to get.

When Tess asked me to come, I honestly didn't know what to say.

She assured me that we were just going as friends, but it feels like more. This feels like a thing that couples do. Then again, I introduced her to Nancy and showed her my apartment last night. Both of which seem like 'couple' things to do, but I didn't want her to read into those either.

I'm beginning to wonder how long we can keep up the 'friends with benefits' routine without turning it into something more. Tess already means more to me than any woman ever has, and I know keeping her around is probably a horrible idea. But I just can't seem to let her go.

So, for now, I guess I'll play the part and pretend I'm not a monster. Pretend that maybe for just a moment, I could make this woman happy in the long run.

A few minutes later, we are pulling up to a beautiful house that sits on what appears to be a pretty large piece of land.

"Nice house," I say while parking off to the side, giving us a quick getaway whenever we decide to leave.

"It is. They actually got it for a super good price because it needed a ton of work done, but they fixed it up and seem to be pretty happy with it," Tess replies as she gets out of the car.

We go to knock on the front door, but there's a sign taped to it reading:

IT'S LOUD. THERE'S NO WAY WE WILL HEAR YOU. JUST COME IN.

I chuckle, "You could never leave a note like that on your door in New York."

"You got that right."

We walk inside, and the sign was right. It's loud as hell. Tess takes my hand and leads me into the kitchen where everyone is standing around talking and snacking on appetizers.

At the sight of us, everyone stops talking and stares.

This is it. I'm going to throw up in front of all these people.

When Tess squeezes my hand in hers though, a strange sense of calm washes over me.

Tess clears her throat before she begins to speak. "Hi everyone, let's get this out of the way. This is Alexander. We are friends. No, we are not dating. No, you don't get to interrogate him. And no, you don't get to whisper behind our backs. Everyone just back the hell off. Got it?"

Everyone nods and goes back to the conversations they were having.

"Impressive," I say softly.

"They know when I get mad, there isn't a safe place in the world for them. They'll behave."

After that speech, I don't doubt it.

A petite blonde woman comes over and wraps Tess in a hug. "Oh, I've missed you! You have to come to Boston more often. Your brother is driving me insane."

"What's he doing?" Tess asks.

"He is hell bent on getting the girls a trampoline for out back…which wouldn't be so bad if Lilah wasn't already trying to jump off everything in the damn house. I can see a shit ton of medical bills in our future." The woman sighs and turns her attention toward me. "Hi, I'm Sam, and I'm married to her brother, Tyler."

"Nice to meet you," I say, holding out my hand for her to shake.

She leans in to whisper, "If you ever need to get away from the crazy show, come find me. I know what it's like to be the newcomer in this family."

I nod and look over to see if Tess heard what she said. Apparently, she didn't. "So, where is my hardheaded brother?"

"Outside with your…free spirited…nieces."

Tess laughs. "Free spirited?"

Sam shrugs. "Better than calling them tiny assholes. They have shorter hair now because the other day, they decided to give each other haircuts."

Tess's eyes grow wide. "You're kidding?"

"Not even a little bit. And this time Abby was the one who started it. She saw someone getting a haircut in a TV show, and thought 'hey, I can do that'. Spoiler alert…she *couldn't* do that. Luckily, I stopped them before it got too far."

"I have to see this," Tess says, grabbing my hand and leading me toward the back door.

Once we walk through the French doors leading onto the deck, I spot a man who I assume is Tess's brother. He has the same dark hair and pointed features.

He's throwing a frisbee to two little girls both of whom have dark hair but big green eyes. They look like the perfect combination of their two parents.

One of the little girls sticks the frisbee in her mouth and runs to her dad. The other little girl exclaims, "Lilah, stop! You're not a dog!"

"What if I want to be a dog?"

"You CAN'T be a dog!"

They are staring daggers through each other, and I swear they're about to throw down right there in the yard, but when they spot Tess, any animosity they had toward each other, fades away.

"Aunt Tess!" They both scream.

Tess kneels on the ground, and when they both run over, she wraps them in a hug.

"My angels!" Tess cries.

Her brother says, "Angels might be a little lofty for them."

But she just waves him off. "Have you girls been good for Daddy?"

They both nod.

"Are you telling Aunt Tess the truth?" She asks. "Remember, I told you that when you lie, your ears turn red. Now, have you been good for Daddy?"

They both cover their ears with their hands and continue to nod. I can't help but chuckle. I have had absolutely zero experience with children, but these two are seriously adorable.

Tess's brother walks over to me and holds out his hand. "Hey man, I'm Tyler."

"Alexander," I say, gripping his hand to shake.

Before we can get any more niceties out of the way, the back door opens again, and two older people walk out. I can tell right away that they are Tess and Tyler's parents. We all exchange pleasantries as the girls give hugs to everyone.

Their mother is named Maria. When she talks, I can detect a Hispanic accent although I'm not quite sure where from. Trying to make pleasant conversation, I ask, and she explains she is from Columbia.

Their father is named Theo, and he is a tall, blonde man. The only way in which his children favor his looks is in their sharp cut jaws. After speaking with him for a little while, I learn he's from New York originally and now he and his wife live there too when they aren't traveling for work.

They all seem like nice people. Great people, even. But do I really fit in here?

Throughout the day, I don't have much time to contemplate that answer. We move from lunch to cake to presents all in what seems like the blink of an eye. I didn't realize how much went into children's birthday parties. Hell, I don't even remember having a party for my birthday when I was growing up, and I don't remember ever being invited to one.

Tess makes the rounds, talking to everyone, while still trying to make sure I don't feel left out. Everyone asks questions but tries to not step over any boundaries.

At one point, she excuses herself to go to the restroom, and I seem to be left all alone. Trying to avoid the large crowd, I opt to head out into the backyard hoping for a little bit of quiet. When I see the twins out there playing though, I know quiet isn't in the cards.

I take a seat on the steps of the deck that lead down into the grass. The girls are actually giggling and seem to be getting along. I wonder if that whole twin connection thing that people always talk about is true.

Once they spot me, they whisper something between themselves and casually walk over, each of them taking a seat beside me.

"What's your name?" Abby asks.

"Alexander," I respond.

"Do you have a shorter name?" Lilah chimes in.

I can't help but laugh. "Well, your aunt Tess calls me Ace."

"Ace," they both say the word in unison.

"You're really big," Lilah says. "Are you a giant?"

"Nope. Not a giant. Just big I guess."

"Like a tree!" Abby says. "Do you want to see something cool?"

I'm not sure if the answer to that question is really yes, but the excitement in her eyes makes it impossible for me to tell her no.

"Sure," I say, and each of the girls grab my hand and begin

to lead me away from the deck.

We walk for a couple of minutes until we come upon a garden. It's hard to tell what's growing in it because it looks like most of the plants are just starting to poke through the soil.

"Did you guys plant this garden?" I ask kneeling down to get on their level.

They both nod, and Lilah says, "Daddy helped us with it. He says pretty soon all sorts of flowers will grow, and we can pick them and give them to Mommy."

"I think that's a great idea, and I think your mom is really going to love that."

Abbey points over to another small mound of dirt. "And over there, we planted an apple tree!"

I rub my stomach and say, "I love apples. I might have to come over and get some of those."

They both smile, showing off their cute little dimples.

I hear footsteps behind me, and I figure it's Tess, but when I turn around, Sam stands before me.

"Girls, are you being nice to Mr. Alexander?"

Lilah says, "Tess calls him Ace, and he said we could call him Ace too!"

She looks at me questioningly. "Ace?"

I shrug. "You'll have to ask Tess."

She smiles and nods. "Girls, why don't you run up there and see what your dad is doing?"

Once they take off running to see who can get to him first, she looks at me again. "I'm sorry if they annoyed you. They just get excited around new people."

I hold up my hand. "Really, they were fine. They just wanted to show me their garden. They seem like great kids."

"They are...when they're not pushing every button I have. They can absolutely annoy me to the point where I'm practically ready to sell them, and then, they hug and kiss me and somehow all is forgiven."

We both chuckle and begin to walk back towards the house. "So, Alexander, how are you honestly holding up? I know the Wendell's can be a lot to take it all at once. Hell, I met them one by one, and it didn't always go smoothly."

"I'm doing okay. Yes, it's a lot especially because I don't come from a big family, but it's alright," I reply, walking with my hands in my pockets.

"I'll tell you something. I was night and day with everyone in this family when I came in. I'm the little farm girl from Kansas, and needless to say, I didn't fit in."

"How'd you deal with it?"

She glances at Tyler who is now walking towards us. "At the end of the day, it didn't matter what any of them thought. Only him. I fit with him, and that was the only thing that counted. He became my person, and everyone else just kind of eventually fell in line."

"That's nice," I say. "But Tess and I are just friends. We are doing the whole 'casual' thing. I don't think we will ever be more than that."

She gives me a warm smile. "You're both idiots."

Before I can ask her what that means, Tyler reaches us and pulls his wife in for a kiss. When he pulls away, he says, "Have I told you how much I love you lately?"

"Every day," she smiles.

"Well, have I told you thank you for putting on this amazing party?"

Since they are caught in their own little bliss, I quietly walk away and head back to the house. Taking a seat on one of the deck chairs, I try to envision what it would be like to have a life like this.

Could I ever be the man who gets married and settles down? Moves to the suburbs? Has babies?

No.

As great as all of this is, it's not me. Monsters don't get to have happily ever after's.

And as crazy as I am about Tess if she wants all of these things, I don't think I can be the one to give them to her. I'm never going to be her knight in shining armor. Never going to be her Prince Charming.

Truth is, I'm never going to be anywhere close to what she deserves.

She deserves a man who isn't broken on the inside. She deserves the world handed to her on a silver platter. She deserves someone who can give her every single thing she wants...especially if that means marriage and babies.

I need to clear out any delusions that we will ever have the idyllic life that Tyler and Sam have. Maybe it would be better to just end this whole thing before it goes any further...before Tess gets hurt.

Because once she finds out my past, I will hurt her. It's inevitable.

In the middle of my pondering, I feel two arms wrap around my neck and a soft kiss on my cheek.

Tess.

"Hey handsome, you okay?"

"Yeah, I'm good. It's just a little crowded in there, so I've been sitting out here. Are you having fun?"

She shrugs. "It's been alright, but I think I'm ready to get out of here with you. You ready to go?"

"Whatever you want, beautiful."

And I wish to God that I could truly give Tess whatever she wanted.

Chapter Twenty-eight
TESS

The ride back to my apartment is quiet. Too quiet. Alexander will barely look at me, and certainly doesn't seem in the mood for conversation. He has the radio cranked up to really ensure the silence between us.

I knew bringing him today was a huge risk, but he seemed to be doing fine. Everyone loved him, and he held his own really well. Even the twins seemed to be crazy about him.

But then, it was like a switch flipped, and suddenly, we are back to him being cold and distant.

He walks me up to my apartment once we get back, and the second we are inside, I can't take anymore.

"You want to tell me what's bothering you?" I ask.

"Nothing. I'm fine…"

"Bullshit!" I snap. "You've been weird ever since we left, and I want to know why."

He rakes his fingers through his hair and starts to pace. "I just don't know," he mutters.

"You don't know what?" My arms cross over my chest showing my defensiveness.

"I don't know that I can ever be that guy who can give you that perfect life. I'm never going to be that guy who lives in the suburbs with his big family and white picket fence. I can't give that to you."

"I'm sorry, but who the hell asked you to? Have I said to you 'Alexander, I would like to move to suburbs and play Mrs. Mom'?"

"No, but..."

"But what, Alexander? You and I have never even discussed the future, yet you presume to know what it is that I want. Not only that, but you proceed to run the other direction from your assumptions." My volume is starting to rise as my anger boils.

He walks over to me, so we are face to face. "Isn't it though? Don't you want the whole package?"

I take a step back because when he gets close, it's as if he invades all my senses, and I'm not able to think straight.

Taking a deep breath, I try to find the best way to put this so that he gets it through his thick skull. "Alexander, of course, I want the whole package, but who are you to tell me what *my* package is? Who's to say that my 'whole package' looks the same as Sam's. Because let me tell you, it doesn't. You're acting like I took you there and introduced you as my boyfriend and told everyone how we are going to ride off into the sunset. News flash...I didn't. You're acting like something has changed between us."

"It has," he says the words in barely more than a whisper.

"What? What has changed?"

He runs his fingers through his hair as he begins to pace. "Everything."

"I'm going to need you to be more specific because I don't get how so much changed in just a few hours."

Finally, he stops to look at me. "It's not just today. It's been ever since I met you. I don't chase after women, yet I showed up at your door. I don't go out on dates, yet you and I go out damn near every night. I don't show women my apartment, yet having you in my bed felt so damn right. And I sure as hell don't go meet families, but I did today. For you."

I interrupt. "So, is this just about you breaking more of your precious rules?"

"No. Fuck the rules. This is about us denying that we are in a relationship, yet doing everything that people do when they're in a relationship. We can keep up the 'friends with benefits' thing all we want, but we both know it's gone further than that."

"And?" I question. "What does that mean?"

"Tess, I've told you I'm not a good man. Deep down, I'm a fucking monster."

"You keep saying that, but you have yet to show me that or explain what the fuck it means."

"It means that I will hurt you. And I don't want to do that."

Tears begin to sting behind my eyes as I can feel which direction this is heading. "Isn't that my decision to make? Isn't it my choice if I want to stick around and take the risk?"

He doesn't answer. Instead, we stay locked in a silent battle of wills. Staring into each other's eyes as one of us tries to break the other down.

Finally, he says, "No, because this isn't a risk you should take."

I realize pretty soon I am going to lose the battle with my tears which are threatening to fall any minute now.

"Alexander, you need to figure your shit out. I'm not asking you for forever. Maybe we are past casual, but no one is talking about a life-long commitment. So, you need to go home and really think about what it is that you want. If you can't do this, fine. But if you decide you want to try, then fucking try and stop trying to push me away. I'll talk to you later."

I say the words and walk into the bedroom unsure as to whether I want him to follow me or show himself out. When I hear the door shut behind him, my tears fall, and I realize that I wanted nothing more than for him to stay.

****

Two hours later, I'm sitting on my couch feeling sorry for myself when my phone vibrates on the table next to me. I told myself I wouldn't pick it up when Alexander texted me, but I can't help myself. When I look at the screen though, it isn't him at all.

Chris's name pops up on the screen.

Chris: Baby girl, when are you going to leave that man candy of yours alone long enough to have dinner with me?

Me: That man candy of mine is being an ass.

Chris: Oh, no! What happened?

Me: Long story.

Chris: Dinner?

Me: I don't much feel like going out. Plus, I look like shit.

Chris: First of all, I doubt it. You're fucking fabulous. Second, I don't care about going out. I'll be over in 30.

I'm not entirely sure I want company but being alone doesn't sound super appealing either.

True to his word, thirty minutes later, Chris is knocking on my door. When I open it, he has a bag of Chinese food in one hand and a large bottle of Vodka in the other.

"My hero," I say with a small smile.

Once he's inside, we eat until we are stuffed and talk about Alexander.

Chris says, "So, what are you going to do, sweet cheeks?"

I shrug and sigh. "Well, honestly, I don't know what I can do. I left the ball kind of in his court. He needs to figure out if he wants to keep doing the casual thing or not without being all wishy-washy."

"Can I tell you something without you getting mad?"

Just the fact that he asked makes me assume I *will* get mad, but I assure him he can go on.

"I think he's right. You two are past the casual thing. If it was just 'casual', you wouldn't stay the night with each other. You wouldn't go to dinner all the time. You wouldn't have met each other's families. You both are crazy about each other and too stubborn to admit it."

I scoff. "He's not crazy about me. I'm beginning to think I'm just another piece of ass to him."

"Bullshit. Since you two have started this whole thing,

that man comes into work *in a good mood!* Do you know I have never seen that man smile until you came into his life? He is joking with the staff. People aren't running around scared of him!"

"That's just because he's getting his dick wet."

"Honey, I have watched a lot of women fawn over that man, and I'm sure he's taken a fair share of them home. He's had an endless supply of pussy, yet he's never been happy like he is lately. Maybe it's the woman the pussy is attached to that matters."

That puts a little smile on my face, but it slowly fades.

"And what if he can't get over all this bullshit baggage he's got going on?" I ask.

"Then, he's an idiot."

"Chris, he thinks he knows what I want. He thinks that I want the whole perfect wife and mom in the suburbs life."

"Do you?"

"Fuck no." I laugh.

"Did you tell him that?"

I nod.

"When you weren't in a fight? Tess, before today, have you two sat down and talked about what it is that you want?"

"No because it was always just supposed to be casual. It didn't seem like that talk was necessary."

"Baby girl, we just decided it's gone past casual. Time to have that talk. If you want different things, then you both can call it quits and move on. But at least you'll know."

I sigh. "I hate when you're right."

I'm going to give Alexander the night to think it over, and tomorrow after work, we are going to discuss what it is we both want.

Chapter Twenty-nine
ALEXANDER

After I leave Tess's, I decide to go to the gym to see if I can work off any of my stress. Although it doesn't exactly clear my mind, I keep going until my muscles burn and my chest heaves.

That evening, I must pick up my phone a thousand times to text Tess, but honestly, I have no idea what to say.

Because although I feel bad about what I said, it doesn't mean every word isn't true. Maybe I am jumping ahead trying to figure out where this all was going, but isn't that the end goal of most relationships? Marriage? Kids? A house with a fucking white picket fence?

Was I wrong to assume that is where we are heading? I never had any of that shit as a kid, and I sure as hell am not equipped to give it to someone now that I am an adult either. I'm too fucked up for all that.

I want to keep going. I want her in my bed underneath me every fucking night. But I can't promise her more, and I don't know that I ever will be able to.

That's why I said what I did. I needed to draw my line in the sand and let her know exactly where I stood. And if that's not okay with her, I don't want to waste any more time.

But what does she do? She throws the damn ball back in my court and leaves it up to me. She tells me that she is okay with keeping it casual, but is she really? It's not like she's very good at telling me what she wants…unless it's in the bedroom, and then she is an expert.

I lay in my bed at the end of this never-ending day and wish she was beside me, my arms wrapped around her while her hair gets in my face. I want to text her and tell her I miss her. Tell her to come over and crawl in bed with me. Tell her I'm crazy about her, and I am fine with keeping things casual as long as we can.

But I don't do any of those things. Maybe it's best if she just thinks I'm the cold-hearted asshole. If she sees the real me…the monster…will she still want to keep going?

Or will she just give up on me like everyone else?

****

The next day, I wake up early and head into Club Rock. I have a meeting with Chet to go over all the finances from the different business holdings. As much as I usually despise meetings with Chet, I'm hopeful it will help me keep my mind off Tess.

She flooded my thoughts all night, and I don't think I slept more than a few minutes at a time. I know I will have to talk to her eventually, but I have no idea what to say. Until I do, I figure maybe it's best that I don't pick up the phone.

As I enter my office, Chet is already waiting inside.

Bastard. He knows he's not supposed to come in here without me. I hold my tongue though. I'll bust his balls about it when I have more energy.

"Morning, boss," he says.

"Good morning," I reply, taking a seat across from him. "I assume you have all the numbers and figures all printed up."

"I do," he says, pulling a large binder out of his bag.

We spend the next two hours going over spreadsheets. I take notes on which businesses need the most work and pencil them into my schedule to visit them in the next week.

Once we have finished the last one, Chet starts to put his binder away. "It's good to see you finally interested in all of this again."

"Excuse me?" I ask.

"It's just lately you haven't seemed too invested in all of this. It seems like ever since you got a girlfriend, business comes second."

I interrupt him. "First of all, she's not my girlfriend, and second off, if she was, I don't think it's any of your business. How do you even know about her?"

"Alexander, you have taken her to multiple restaurants you either own or invest in. I also frequent these businesses for work purposes. You had to know that people would find out. You're taking her out in public for God's sake. You're lucky there haven't been pictures plastered on the internet yet."

No, I'm not lucky. I'm smart. That's why I try to take to Tess to places I own or I have a personal connection with. I know they won't fuck me over by letting any photographers snap any shots.

"Chet, you're walking a really fine line. I'd watch it if I were you," I lean back in my chair and study the weird little guy. He's busying himself with the zipper on his bag to avoid direct eye contact with me.

"I'm sorry. I just don't want some woman gumming up the works and washing years of hard work down the drain."

"Why the hell do you care?" My voice is getting louder now. "You get paid either way, right? Unless, of course, you piss me off, and I fire you."

His eyes finally meet mine. "You're right. I shouldn't overstep."

"No, you shouldn't. Who I am or am not seeing is none of your fucking business. And this is the last time you will bring her up again. Are we clear?"

"Crystal, sir." He walks out of my office without another word.

Maybe it's time to start looking for a new financial advisor…one who isn't so worried about my love life.

The rest of the day passes in a blur. I go to the gym, pick up my clothes from the dry cleaner, and take a walk around the city, but the entire time, it feels like I'm on Auto Pilot.

My mind can't escape Tess. It's beginning to become more and more clear to me that she's more than just a good fuck. I genuinely miss her. I don't think I've ever felt this way about anybody in my entire life. When she isn't around, it's like a part of me is missing.

I might be a son of a bitch who will absolutely be awful in a relationship, but damnit, if I'm not willing to throw in the towel and try.

For her.

She's worth it.

After thinking about it all night, I decide to call her and ask to see her so we can talk. Maybe we can try to come to some sort of solution to move forward.

But when I dial her number, all I get is voicemail. Not really knowing what to say, I hang up without leaving a message. I begin to get ready for bed, figuring I can try again tomorrow… after what I know will be another sleepless night.

Just as I am beginning to shut off lights, my phone dings. There is a message from Tess.

Tess: I'm downstairs. Can I use the elevator to come up?

Thank fucking God.

I quickly type in the code for her to ride the elevator all the way to the penthouse. I stand at the sliding doors for what seems like an eternity waiting for her.

When the elevator finally comes to a slow stop and the doors open, it's not the typical confident, fiery Tess that greets me.

No. This Tess is wearing scrubs. Her hair is piled in a messy bun on top of her head. And she has smeared eye makeup from tears streaking her cheeks.

"Sweetheart, what's wrong?"

She drops her purse on the ground and walks to me. I open

my arms, and she lets me wrap her in a hug as she quietly sobs against me. I can't help but feel responsible for this.

But before I can apologize, she looks up at me. "I lost a kid today."

"What?" I'm so overwhelmed I don't quite understand what she is saying.

Taking her by the hand, I lead her to the couch and sit her down next to me, holding her close.

She wipes away another tear. "Today, at work…I lost a kid. A four-year-old kid."

Shit.

"Tell me what happened," I say softly.

"He came in with a gunshot wound. Apparently, it was a drive-by, and they were aiming for his stepdad. But while we were working on him, I noticed all kinds of bruises…like this kid hadn't lived a very good life. I worked on him for hours. Every time we would get him stabilized to go into surgery, he would flat line again. His poor little heart just couldn't take it."

Her tears were falling harder now, and every word she said became more difficult for her to get out. "Alexander, he wasn't much older than the twins. The whole time I was thinking about how I would feel if it was them lying on the table." The lasts words came out as a choked sob.

I pulled her head and rested it on my chest. "But it wasn't them."

"No, it wasn't. But it was someone's baby. Being a doctor, I see a lot of death, but this one just seems different. When I was in the Congo, I had a few teenagers die on me but never a small kid like this."

I know no words that I can say will take away the pain she's feeling. Nothing I can say will make this day any less tragic for her.

Instead, I hold her close and let her tears fall. I will sit here as long as she needs me to.

When her sobs finally quiet and her body settles, I quietly ask, "What do you need? What can I do?"

For a few moments, she doesn't say a word. I wonder if she's fallen asleep. But her head slowly rises up to look at me. When her eyes meet mine, I stroke her cheek with my thumb.

"Just tell me what you need, sweetheart."

Her lips lean forward and press against mine for a tender moment. "I need you to help me to forget. Just take away the awfulness of his night and replace it with something better."

I might not be good at a lot of things, and I might not be some knight in shining armor, but I can make damn sure this night ends better than it began.

Chapter Thirty
TESS

My tears may have stopped, but my heart still aches as Alexander leads me into his large bathroom. He turns on the water to begin filling the larger than life bathtub, and surprisingly, he pours in what appears to be bubble bath.

Who knew Mr. Dark and Brooding would have bubble bath?

He pulls me close to him and places a gentle kiss on my forehead before wrapping his muscular arms around me for a hug. The tears threaten to fall again, but I will them to stay in my eyes. I'm trying to forget the awfulness of this day, not keep reliving it.

When I worked with Doctors without Borders, I saw awful things. Things that a person should never have to see in their lives. Despite that, I had never lost a little kid before today. That sounds crazy, right? Bad things happen to good kids a lot in the part of town where I work. But I'd never lost one before.

Usually, I can compartmentalize my job and my personal life. I know once I leave those hospital doors, my time there is done for the day. I did all I could, and there was no point dwelling on it. But I think anyone would be crazy not to dwell on losing a kid. Anyone would wonder what more they could have done to save him.

Interrupting my thoughts, Alexander takes my hand and leads me into the tub. I sink into the hot water and let it soothe my tired muscles. It's just now hitting me how exhausted my body really is.

I look up and see Alexander's hard body becoming visible as he removes his clothes. I scoot forward as he climbs in the tub and situates himself behind me. Leaning back, I lay my head against his chest as he begins running his fingers through my hair.

Between the sound of his heartbeat, the hot water, and the amazing work his fingers are doing, I feel like I could fall asleep for days right here and now.

"I'm sorry," he whispers in my ear.

"For what? It's not your fault I had a bad day at work," I respond without opening my eyes.

"Not for that. Well, I am sorry for that too, but I'm sorry for yesterday."

I don't say anything but instead look up at him waiting for him to continue.

"Maybe I shouldn't have freaked out like I did and assumed you wanted something without talking to you first. It's just that I'm not good at this whole relationship thing, Tess, and I don't know that I ever will be. But I'm willing to try…for you."

I sit quietly for a moment trying to comprehend what he's saying. Is this man telling me he wants a relationship? Is this the same man who told me he would never do more than fuck a woman a couple of times before sending her on her merry way?

Maybe Chris was right. Maybe Alexander does care about me more than I realized.

I turn my body around, so I am facing him. I pull him close and press my lips to his. "I don't need you to be great at this. I'm not exactly skilled in the fine art of relationships either. Let's just have fun and see what happens."

"Okay, sweetheart," he says, pulling me closer.

"Now, enough talking," I whisper, kissing him once more.

This time, pulling his bottom lip with my teeth.

I can feel him growing hard beneath me as I straddle his waist. I position myself right above him, and my eyes meet his.

"I'm on the pill, but if you want to get a condom, tell me now," I say.

Without a word, he takes my hips and lowers me down onto his thick shaft. I moan as he begins to fill up every inch of me, my body perfectly molding to him.

Our tongues dance together while I move up and down at a steady pace. His hands alternate between grabbing my hips to help him thrust up into me and teasing my nipples.

"Alexander," I moan out as he twists the tiny bud between his fingers.

"God, I love hearing you say my name," he growls before replacing his fingers with his mouth. His teeth would slightly nip the tender flesh before his tongue would flick over it.

The man knows how to ignite every pleasure receptor my body has and makes them all come alive at once. When he feels me getting close, he slides a hand between our bodies to give my clit the attention it craves.

A couple circles of his fingers, and I am tensing around him, every muscle in my body being set on fire. My arms wrap around his neck as the quakes of pleasure hit me one after another. Grabbing my hips, he pumps into me harder and faster until he is coming too.

Once both of us have stilled, we give each other one more tender, sensual kiss before deciding to get out of the lukewarm water.

Alexander gets out first and quickly dries himself before wrapping the towel around his waist. He reaches for my hand and dries me with what feels like the softest bath towel I've ever felt.

"Do you give all the girls this treatment?" I ask, only half-jokingly.

"No, I must say that I have never taken a bubble bath with a woman."

Something about that small statement makes me feel insanely special. "I'm glad I'm the first."

"Me too, beautiful," he smiles. "Are you hungry? I can fix you something if you haven't eaten."

The man is always insistent that I eat, but honestly after the day I had, I don't know if my stomach can handle anything right now. So, despite the fact that I haven't eaten, I tell him I have.

"No, I ate a salad earlier. I'm just tired."

"Well, then, let's go lay down, sweetheart. Do I need to set an alarm or anything for you?"

I shake my head. "had a bit of a break down at work, and they decided I should use some of my vacation time. So, I have no plans for the whole week."

Most people would be thrilled at a week-long vacation, but I'm dreading it. That means a whole week of being trapped in my head along with my own thoughts. I don't know why my employers thought that would be a good idea.

I walk over and yank off my towel before crawling into his enormous comfortable bed. I watch Alexander do the same.

"You should probably put some form of clothing on," I say to him while wrapping myself in the blankets.

"Why's that?"

"Because you expect me to just lay next to your perfect, naked body all night and keep my hands to myself?"

His laugh fills the air. "You ever think that is maybe my intention? Maybe I don't want you to keep your hands to yourself? And maybe I won't keep mine off you either." The last words are whispered into my ear which makes goosebumps erupt over every inch of my skin.

Good lord, the man hasn't even touched me again, and my body is craving round two.

"What are you waiting for? Touch me," I say, pulling the blankets back, revealing my naked body.

"Woman, you drive me fucking insane," he growls against my kiss.

And he does touch me…every inch of me…all night long.

****

The next morning, I wake up once again to an empty bed. *Does the man never sleep in?*

I get up and see he has set out another one of his t-shirts at the foot of the bed. I quickly throw it on and head to use the restroom before going to find Alexander.

He's on the phone when I walk out of the bedroom. The conversation doesn't sound like it's going well, but when he sees me, his face lights up.

"I don't care. I'm sure you can handle things for a few days. You're my financial advisor not my fucking mother. Deal with it, or I'll find someone else to handle my finances," he spits and hangs up the phone.

"Whoa, rough morning?"

He rubs his forehead. "Just dealing with ignorant people. You're a doctor. I'm sure you see a ton of them."

"Yep. When I was interning in the ER, I saw all kinds of people doing dumb stuff. One time, a guy stuck a light bulb up his ass."

His forehead creased. "Why?"

"No clue. And when I asked him that same question, he had no clue either. Just said he wanted to know what it felt like," I giggle. "Anyway, what are you up to today? Do you have to go deal with said ignorant person?"

"Nope. Actually, I had some other plans, and I thought maybe my beautiful, dark-haired woman would like to join me."

I walk over and take a seat on his lap, wrapping my arms around his neck. "And where exactly are you asking her to go with you?"

"It's a surprise. But let's just say I thought we could get out of the city for a couple of days."

"Really?"

"You said you had the whole week off work, and I know you're just going to sit at home overthinking everything. And I've been so busy with work lately, I could probably use a break too," he says, rubbing his fingers up and down my thigh.

"That sounds nice," I say. "Do I need to go back home and pack a bag?"

"No, I think I have everything covered."

"But what about my clothes? What am I going to wear?" I ask.

He grins. "Well, if it were up to me, you'd wear absolutely nothing. But I'm sure I can handle getting a couple things for you to wear."

"You don't have to do that, you know?"

He looks confused. "Do what?"

"Spoil me with your money. It's not like I'm hurting for cash or anything."

"I know. I'm not doing it because I think that you can't buy stuff yourself. I was doing it so you had absolutely nothing to worry about on this trip. But if you really want to run by your place, we can."

I can see that his face has fallen a little bit. Although I have no idea what he's going to pick out, at the end of the day, I really don't care. It's nice to have someone who wants to look out for me.

"No. I think you can handle it."

The smile on his face is infectious. "Great. I have to run a couple of errands and drop off some paperwork at Club Rock, but I shouldn't be gone long. Do you want to stay here, or do you want me to drop you back off at your place for a bit?"

I shrug. "I can stay here. I might go back to bed for a little while."

"You lazy bum," he jokes.

"Well, *somebody* kept me up all night doing naughty things to me. I didn't get much rest."

"I can't help it. Beautiful woman in my bed…I have to touch her."

I lean in, "Maybe you should hurry up and get back so you can touch me some more."

"Woman, you are insatiable," he says with a quick swat to

my ass.

"Hurry back, Mr. Rockford," I say while pulling his shirt over my head, leaving me standing stark naked before him.

I hear him growl and curse under his breath as I walk my ass back to his bedroom.

A few minutes later, I hear him gather his things and head out the door. I roll over in bed onto his pillow and pull it in close, inhaling the scent of him.

The events of yesterday plague my thoughts. Visions of me still working on that kid even after they called time of death run through my head. I can still hear my sobs echoing through the empty hospital room.

When I refused to leave him, I was told my boss wanted to see me. It was his suggestion that I take some time off. Said he thought I was working too hard, and it was making me too emotional.

Bullshit.

He just thought I was being a hysterical woman.

Despite that, I held my tongue as I grabbed my stuff and walked out. Without even thinking about it, I told the cab driver to take me to Alexander's. For whatever reason, my home had become wherever he was…not my empty apartment. He was the only face I wanted to see…the only presence that would make me feel better.

Just being in his arms seemed to make all the bad stuff melt away. Sure, we still have a lot to talk about, and I have no idea where this is heading, but I'm glad I'm by his side.

As I begin to drift off to sleep, I try to quiet that inner voice that is telling me what I already know but am desperate to deny.

I am falling in love with Alexander Rockford.

Chapter Thirty-one
ALEXANDER

Later that day, I'm sitting across from Tess on the private jet that I chartered. I don't think she expected that we would be going far enough to need a plane ride, but she went along with it nonetheless.

I can't take my eyes off of her. Since I have absolutely no eye for fashion, I had my personal stylist, Suzie, pick out a few things for Tess on this trip. I'd glanced at the size on her clothes from the day before and given Suzie a roundabout guess of her measurements. At first she insisted, she needed more than a couple of hours to shop, but when I informed her I would pay triple her normal salary, she suddenly found the time.

Money talks. Go figure.

Tess had put on one of the sundresses Suzie had picked out, and I can't stop staring at her gorgeous, long legs.

Apparently, she notices because she looked up from her phone. "Ace, will you stop staring at me?"

"Can't help it. You're just so much fun to look at."

She smiles and looks at me. "Back at you, Ace. Now, are you going to tell me where we are going?"

"Does it matter?" I ask.

"I guess not. I'm just antsy…and bored."

"We could go in the back, and you could wrap those legs around my neck for a while if you want," I wink.

"Mr. Rockford, you dirty, dirty boy." Her teeth sink into her bottom lip. "When are you going to get sick of me?"

"Not any time soon, beautiful." I get on my knees in front of her and part her legs. I can already smell her desire.

"Alexander, what are you doing? What if someone sees?"

"I paid the flight attendants very well to leave us alone until we land," I mutter while moving the thin fabric away from her pussy.

"You are so fucking sexy," she says, looking down at me.

I push her legs further apart, resting one on my shoulder as I run my tongue up and down, tasting her. She has the sweetest pussy I've ever tasted, and I don't know that I will ever get enough.

I bury my face between her legs, going to work until she has had three orgasms beneath my tongue. When her legs are shaking and she's begging me to stop, I pull her on top of me and watch her ride me as she loses her mind over and over again.

We drive each other crazy for so long that when I am finally unloading inside of her, it's almost time to land.

****

"Okay, I've done a lot of traveling in my day, but this place is seriously amazing," Tess says, walking around our large condo I rented. "And you're telling me you rented out this whole island for us? Just us?"

I walk toward her and pull her close, "Yes, sweetheart. Just you and me. Our own island and a chance to escape the world for a few days."

A gentleman I had met a while ago through mutual business dealings owned this place, which is nestled in the Bahamas. I now owe him one hell of a favor, but the look on Tess's face makes it completely worth it.

"So, what do you want to do today, beautiful?" I ask, placing a soft kiss on her neck.

"Well, if you don't stop that, we are going to head straight into that bedroom and not come out until it's time to fly home."

I shrug. "I'm okay with that."

Playfully, she swats my shoulder. "I'm not! We are on a tropical fucking island! We need to go exploring! We can fuck like animals later!"

I can't help but laugh at her excitement. "Okay, well, go get dressed, and we can go explore whatever you want."

She skips off into the bedroom to change out of her sundress, and I walk outside. Our little bungalow sits right on the beach, and the waves of the ocean are enough to take away every care I have.

When I told Tess, this trip wasn't just about getting her away from her shitty day, I meant it. I'd been working so hard for the past ten years, I had barely stepped foot outside the city. In fact, I don't even think I've had a vacation since I was maybe five years old. And even then, I don't really remember it.

The past ten years had been full of nothing but working, eating, sleeping, and getting my dick wet when I wanted to. Fun was never in the cards nor was relaxation. And for ten years, I'd been perfectly fine with that. Perfectly fine with nothing but chasing the almighty dollar.

But now, things seem so different. Despite me trying to try on the whole 'relationship' thing, I feel like Tess and I have an expiration date, and I am not going to squander all of our time together working. Why not make the most of the time we have?

"Now, I know you are not wearing jeans to walk around this island, Mr. Rockford," Tess says from behind me. "Get that tight ass of yours inside and change into something more comfortable."

I am beginning to kind of like her ordering me around. Her independence has definitely grown on me.

So, I obeyed and went and changed clothes, throwing on a sleeveless shirt and some basketball shorts.

Half an hour later, we were in the heart of the island... or what I assume was the heart of the island. This place didn't exactly come with a map. The guy who owns it though said that it was a couple hour walk from one side of the island to the other, so I figure we are probably close to the center.

Tess is a few steps ahead of me following a trail that leads who knows where. But I am staring at her perfect ass, so I really don't care where we are headed. She traded the sundress for a pair of cotton shorts and a tank top.

Something seems to catch her eye, and she jogs ahead of me a bit. I lose sight of her for a moment, but she yells, "Ace, come here, you have to see this!"

Picking up my pace, I quickly join her. Beyond a thicket of trees, she's standing on a large ledge overlooking a beautiful lake with a waterfall flowing into it.

"Holy shit," I gasp, taking in the surreal scene around us.

"That's what I said," she says, her eyes as wide as saucers. "You want to go for a swim?"

"Sure, but how do we get down there?" I look around for another trail of some sort.

"We jump, silly," she replies, already taking off her shoes.

"What? We can't jump that."

"Why not?" She asks, still removing articles of clothing.

"You could get hurt. You don't know how deep the water is. No, we aren't jumping."

She gives me a half-cocked smile. "Good thing I'm not asking for your permission." Without another word, she gets a running start and leaps over the edge.

I look down to see her cannonball into the water with a splash. The few seconds it takes her to make her way to the surface might be the longest of my life.

"Come on, chicken shit! The water is great!" She screams up at me as her head bobs out of the water.

This woman has absolutely no fear. She's constantly chasing her next rush of adrenaline, and here she is pulling me right along with her. I'm a man who enjoys living in my own comfort zone. And Tess is the woman who came in and said fuck your comfort zone.

"I'm waiting!" She calls.

Cursing under my breath the entire time, I begin to remove my clothes. I walk to the edge of the rocks, and I think I might have a heart attack. This is even scarier than those damn roller coasters she dragged me on.

I close my eyes and take a couple of deep breaths, trying to work up any nerve that I may have. Apparently, I have none because my body is firmly planted exactly where I'm at.

I look down at Tess again who is now removing her bra. "Come on, Ace. I'm naked and all alone down here. Come and get me."

The woman is a fucking she-devil, but when my dick starts to tent my boxers, I know she's onto something. Apparently, my will to get laid outweighs my survival instincts.

No wonder women live longer.

Taking another deep breath, I leap off the edge. And the only thought that crosses my mind is how I am going to make her pay for this later.

Chapter Thirty-two
TESS

"You jumped! You actually jumped!" I squeal as Alexander's head pokes up from the water.

He shakes out his hair and looks at me. "Yeah, I guess I did. You're a little crazy. Do you know that?"

I shrug. "Maybe a little bit. But you seem to enjoy it. Besides, look at you! You did something you probably never thought that you would, and you're fine!"

He pulls me close to him. "Sweetheart, you have me doing a lot of things I never thought I'd do."

I smile and can't help but hope that maybe one of those things is changing his outlook on our future. But I don't put voice to those words. This moment is too perfect.

He kisses me, and I wrap my legs around his waist as we bob up and down in the water. One of his hands holds my face as his tongue begins to swirl with mine. The man's kiss is exhilarating, making every cell in my body surge to life.

There we are...making out like a couple of teenagers underneath the most beautiful waterfall I'd ever seen. Flowers bloom on the shores around the crystal clear water, and the whole thing is so perfect it looks like a screensaver on a computer rather than real life. I could stay here with him forever...

getting lost in his kiss and forgetting about the rest of the world. Every problem we face and every worry we might face back in New York. Maybe we could just stay here forever and outrun all of the bad. Maybe we could grow old together here. Maybe we could start over.

Damn, I wish it was that easy.

****

After a sexy night with Alexander, we spend most of the next day swimming in the ocean and lounging on the beach…or at least I do.

Despite this being our trip to get away from everything, Alexander's financial advisor won't stop calling his phone every five minutes, so I finally tell him to just go handle his business. He's been inside for who knows how long.

I feel bad for the man on the other end of that phone because every time that phone rang, I could see every muscle in Alexander's face tense a bit more. Every phone call got him more pissed off, and the guy is going to be lucky to have a job when it's all said and done…especially if it's for anything other than a true emergency.

I decide to give him something nice to come back to, so I strip off the tiny bikini I'm wearing and lie back on the lounge chair completely naked.

My phone chimes next to me, and although I have mostly been ignoring it, I'm a little bored, so I see who it is. It's a text from Chris.

Chris: Hey gorgeous! Lunch?

Me: Well, I'm not exactly home.

Chris: Where are you? I can meet you somewhere.

I turn around and snap a selfie with the ocean in the background, careful to not show my exposed boobs. Not that Chris would get any sort of arousal out of them anyway.

Chris: You bitch! Where are you?!

Me: Bahamas. Something happened at work, so they insisted I take a week off to deal with things. Alexander brought me here to get away for a few days.

Chris: Number one, I hate you, and I'm so jealous. Number two, when you get back, I want to hear how you two went from at each other's throats to vacationing in paradise.

I promise to tell him all about it when I get home, and we say our goodbyes.

A few minutes later, my phone chimes again, and I roll my eyes wondering what Chris wants now. But when I look down, it's not from Chris. It's from a private number.

Private: Leave Rockford alone. You've been warned.

My skin prickles with goosebumps as I look around me. We are supposed to be here alone, but that doesn't mean I don't suddenly feel like I'm being watched.

Who the fuck knows Alexander and I are seeing each other? That has to be a pretty short list because both of us have been fairly quiet on the subject. At least I have.

I'm so consumed with worry over the text that I about jump out of my skin when Alexander walks back over to the empty chair next to me.

"Everything okay?" I ask, trying not to get him as frazzled as I am.

He takes a seat on the edge of the lounger and links his hands together. "I need to tell you something."

My heart thumps so loudly in my chest that I worry it's going to fly right out my body and into the ocean.

He continues. "Apparently, some paparazzi took some photos of us and has sold them to some different websites and magazines. So, if people didn't know we were dating before, they do now."

"We're dating?" Out of all of the things to say in the entire world, that's what I come up with? I sound like a damn teenage girl whose crush just admitted he liked her.

He laughs. "Isn't that what we are doing?"

"I guess," I smile. "So, how do you think they got the photos?"

"I have no idea because usually, I make sure we hit places that I have a stake in. They won't do anything to jeopardize my business relationship with them. And the photos are in more than one restaurant which tells me they are actively seeking us out. But I just wanted you to have a heads up. Once the photos are out, the rumors start flying. You're from a wealthy family, I'm sure you've seen your fair share of crazy stories."

He's right. The Wendell's have always had trash posted about them. My parents have been set to get divorced about sixteen times now according to the media. Thankfully, they always tried to keep us kids out of the limelight as much as possible.

My eyes glance towards my phone as I consider telling Alexander about my mysterious text, but when he starts telling me about Chet fucking up some more finance stuff, I decide that he has enough on his plate right now.

Besides, it's probably just a woman obsessed with him or something that's freaking out after seeing the photos. I'm not going to be scared off by one little mysterious text.

Instead, I completely shut my phone off and try to be present in the moment. Alexander walks back in the house to grab us some drinks but assures me that he's done with work for the rest of the trip.

I gaze out at the endless waves hoping they will provide me some answers to the sea of questions I have swimming around in my head.

But as much as I long for some clarity, they give none.

I wish we could stay in this paradise forever. As much as I love the hustle and bustle of the city, this beach seems like a nice place to park my ass for the next fifty years. Besides, it's not the city itself I am dreading, but the demons lying in wait within it.

Every time I think about stepping foot back in that hospital, my anxiety shoots through the roof. I've always loved being a doctor. The thrill of being on the front lines and saving lives has always kept me going. I know one life shouldn't derail all of that, but somehow, it is. I saw the look in everyone's eyes as I sobbed over that poor boy the other day. They all looked at me like I had finally lost my marbles.

I've seen a lot of doctors hit their breaking point over the years, and I wondered if I had found mine. For a while now, I have been heading down that road. I have seen it coming for months now. Every time the hospital denies care due to lack of insurance. Every time we are under-funded due to the financial status of most of our clientele. Every time I wanted to work harder to save someone that everyone else deemed beyond saving.

The thrill of it all seemed to be slowly replaced by a yearning for more. Although I have no idea what that 'more' is. Becoming a doctor has been my entire life. What else would I do?

"What are you thinking about?" Alexander's voice pulls me from my thoughts.

"Lots of stuff," I smile up at him.

"Care to share?" He leans back in the lounger next to me and takes my hand in his.

"Thinking about work I guess. About how I am questioning whether it's what I want to do anymore." I go on to explain some of my concerns to him, telling him all about how I loved Doctors Without Borders, but all of the travel got exhausting. And now, the hospital just doesn't do much for me anymore in the way of self-fulfillment.

"Sweetheart, I don't think that it's that you don't want to be a doctor. I think you love being a doctor and helping people. I think it's that you don't like doing it according to someone else's rules."

"What do you mean?"

"I mean when you were working in the Congo, you weren't necessarily working in a hierarchy like you are a hospital. You were saving lives based on YOUR instincts. No one else's. Maybe it's time to use your skills in a way where you don't have to listen to someone else tell you how to do it."

I grin at him. "You're pretty smart, Ace. You know that?"

"Back at you, gorgeous. Now, let's talk about how you're laying out here with no top on." The tone in his voice says we are done with any serious talk for the moment.

"I don't want tan lines," I say, rubbing my fingers over my

bare chest. "Besides, we are all alone. Who's going to see me?"

He leans over and kisses me hard and fiercely, gripping my hair at the base of my neck with one hand. He pulls back and says, "You're lucky we are alone because I'll never let *anyone* see that beautiful body except for me."

"Fair enough. But no one else gets to see yours either," I demand.

"Wouldn't dream of it, sweetheart. You know what? I can't look at you like this and not touch you," he says, picking me up from my chair and carrying me in the house.

"What are you doing, Ace?" I giggle.

"Having my filthy way with you. You can't expect to show me that sexy little body of yours and not get fucked."

He's right. I would expect nothing less.

Chapter Thirty-three
TESS

Two days later, we are back home, and I'm already missing the beach. In fact, I was already missing it the minute we stepped foot onto the jet to come home.

Alexander has to get back to work, so I decide it is time to come back to my apartment...at least for the day. Heaven knows, I need to catch up on some laundry and clean up the place. It's funny how it's such a mess, and I haven't even really been staying here.

My day is spent running loads through the washing machine, doing dishes, running the vacuum, and blaring music to dance around to while I do all the other things.

By mid-afternoon, I'm wiped, so I sit down and turn on some mindless television while I piddle around on my laptop. I check my work email and respond to couple fellow doctors checking in to make sure I'm okay.

I'm fine. I don't need your pity.

I know they're trying to be nice, but I also know that my meltdown the other day is probably still the talk of the hospital which makes going back in a few days increasingly more difficult.

Pulling up the search engine, I type in Alexander's name.

Maybe I shouldn't be doing it, but I'm a little curious to see what pops up about us.

Most of the articles that pop up are about his newest business ventures that have been printed in various business journals.

There are a few plastered with titles like:
Rockford and Renown Doc Snuggled Up
Who is Alexander Rockford's Mystery Lady?
Rockford Slumming it With Doctor!
Slumming it? Really?

And then, when I click images, there are a few photos of us shot at a few restaurants around town but nothing too scandalous. Honestly, I'm surprised photos of us haven't leaked before now.

Most of the other photos are the ones accompanying his business articles which just consist of him with his arms crossed standing in front of a giant window or something else that seems super pretentious.

Then, there are a few that look like they've been snapped with a cell phone camera of him with a few various women.

I zoom in trying to get a better look at the low-quality images. Each woman is different, yet they all have similar qualities.

Petite.

Light hair.

Huge boobs.

Which ones of those columns do I fit into? None of the above.

Don't get me wrong, I think I'm a fairly attractive person, and I'm proud of my body from all of my running and workouts. But I can see in the beginning why Alexander said I wasn't really his type.

I look down and grab my barely-there chest.

Yeah, pretty sure those aren't going to get any bigger.

A knock on the door about makes me jump out of my skin.

I leave my laptop open on the table and walk over to answer it.

"Hey Ace!" I smile as I see my sexy man standing in the

doorway. "You're early."

"I know. Figured I would come whisk you away a little earlier than we planned."

"Okay, well, come in. I probably need to take a shower real quick. I've been cleaning all day," I say.

"Not necessary. We are going to be getting dirty tonight," he winks.

"What kind of dirty? Because if it's *that* kind of dirty, then, yes, I really should take a shower."

"Not that kind of dirty. At least not yet," he replies with a smile.

I shrug. "Okay, let me just go change. Jeans and a tank top okay for this little adventure?"

"Perfect."

After I finish changing, I come out to find him looking at the open laptop on the table.

Shit.

"Little light reading?" He smiles.

"I was bored," I say like it's no big deal.

"Don't feel bad. I Googled you too…before our first date."

"Believe it or not, this is the first time I've looked. And let me say, Ace, you really have a type," I say pointing to the busty women on the screen.

"I guess it must seem like that looking at these photos. But keep in mind, I have been with more women than what's on that screen," he says while standing up.

"You know, that really doesn't make me feel better. Is that why you were so against us going out at first? Because I don't look like a pinup model?" My words come out far more hostile than I mean them to, but really, I just want an answer.

He walks toward me and lays a hand on each of my cheeks. "No, I said that because I knew you were very independent, and you'd be a huge pain in my ass. And I was right. You still are."

I scoff but can't help but laugh. "Really?"

"Really. You are a *huge* pain in my ass."

I playfully hit his chest. "You know what I meant."

"I know. And I had my reasons, and clearly, you proved them all wrong. And for the record, I don't have a type of woman based on looks. I like beautiful woman, and you certainly fall under that category." He follows his words with a gentle kiss.

"Okay, Ace. Let's get out of here," I say, closing my laptop and vowing not to look into the past again.

Half an hour later, we pull up outside a restaurant which appears to be empty. In fact, it doesn't look like it's been open for a while.

I turn toward Alexander to ask him a question, but he's already stepping out of the car.

"Okay, then. I guess we are going inside the creepy looking building," I mumble to myself.

We reach the door, and Alexander pulls out a set of keys to unlock it.

Once we enter, he flips on the lights, and I see a restaurant that looks like it's in the middle of a massive overhaul.

"Welcome to Gino's," Alexander says, taking my hand in his.

"Gino's?" I ask.

"It's my newest business investment. Well, it's more than an investment. I actually bought it outright."

Still holding his hand, I walk around a little bit taking the place in. It's small and quaint, but I can see that with some hard work and elbow grease, this place could spruce up pretty nicely.

"I like it," I said while giving him a quick peck on the lips. "I'm glad you brought me here to show me."

His face softens. "Well, actually, I brought you here for a little more than that."

My eyebrows raise waiting for him to continue.

He walks behind the counter and picks up a gallon of paint a couple brushes. "Maybe you'd want to help me out for a bit?"

"Oh, now I see why you told me we might be getting dirty!" I laugh. "You just brought me here to use for manual labor!"

"Maybe," he smiles. "But I'll make it worth your while."

I hold out my hand. "Hand me the brush, Ace."

A few minutes later, we are getting busy painting the doors throughout the building.

"So, tell me about this place, Ace. Why Gino's? You must have a ton of options in deciding where to invest or what properties to buy."

"This place was owned and run by a man named Charles. Charles loved two things in his life, his wife and Gino's. His wife has fallen ill recently, so he decided he wanted to spend every moment he could with her. I offered to be just an investor, but he said he was ready to say goodbye. I probably paid more than this place was worth, but I wanted he and his wife to be comfortable in whatever time they had left together."

My heart swells so big I feel as though it might bust out of my chest. "That was really sweet of you."

"Don't go thinking I'm a nice guy now, sweetheart," he smiles.

I hold up my hands. "Wouldn't dream of it."

We sit in a comfortable silence for a few minutes before I have another question. "So, why do so much of the work yourself? I know you could easily pay someone to come in here and do all this."

"I feel like when I pour my own blood, sweat, and tears into a place, I care about it more. I put my own stamp on it, and it gives me more of a personal connection with the business. In the end, the more I care about it, the more time and effort I put in, the more money I make."

He can pretend it's all about the money, but I see through him, and I know it's about so much more than that. Despite what the man thinks, he has a heart. A big one.

"When does this place open?" I ask.

"It was supposed to be in about two months, but my financial advisor who happened to be doing some marketing for me, fucked up and made it a month early. So, now, I am busting ass to get it done. That's what the big emergency was when he called me in the Bahamas."

"Gotcha. Well, let me know when opening day is for sure,

and I'll be here."

"Really?"

I smile. "Wouldn't miss it for the world."

He orders us some pizza while we continue to work into the night. We talk and laugh, having so much fun it doesn't even feel like work.

When we decide to call it a night, Barry drives us back to my apartment. When he pulls up out front, I ask Alexander if he's coming up, but he shakes his head.

"Not tonight. Can I take a raincheck?"

"Sure. How about tomorrow?" I ask.

"I can't tomorrow. I'm actually going to be out of town for a couple of days. There's something I have to take care of. I don't know if you'll be able to reach me either." His voice is suddenly stern and cold.

"What's going on, Alexander? We've spent practically every second together for a week, and now, you're telling me you're going to ghost on me for a couple of days?"

"It's personal," he says.

"Personal? So personal you can't tell me?"

"I don't have to tell you everything!" He raises his voice at me.

That's it.

I open my door. "You're right. You don't have to tell me. I just thought you'd want to. Forget it. Call me when you get back. Better yet, don't bother!"

Walking inside the building, I half expect him to come after me and apologize, but anger boils inside me as I hear the car door shut and Barry drive away.

What the fuck is going on? Why is it that he can be perfect one minute and an absolute asshole the next?

I have no idea, but I know that the back and forth is really starting to take its toll on me.

Chapter Thirty-four
ALEXANDER

I'm an asshole. I'm the biggest asshole in the entire world.

My plan was to get away for a couple of days…just like I do every year…so that I don't show anyone the darkness in me. I know I'm insufferable to be around on these days, so I disappear, so I don't take it out on anyone.

Too late. My plan backfired because now Tess probably hates me. She should. I was awful to her.

She holds such a special place in my heart (or where my heart *should* be), yet I pushed her away like she was nothing more than a call girl.

Damnit.

I tell her I want to try and do the whole relationship thing, yet I treated like whatever she and I have meant absolutely nothing. She must have a million questions, and I just drove away after yelling at her.

If I would have told her why, would she have understood?

I have no idea because I didn't give her a chance to even try to understand.

It has been twelve years since the fateful day that changed my life forever. It turned me into the man I am today. It made me grow up fast. It forced me to get my shit together and make a good living. But it also brought out the cold-hearted son of a bitch that I have become.

My head thumps against the headrest of my sports car as I am driving out of the city ready to yet again confront my dark past. I never let Barry drive me on these trips. It's something I have to do alone. Usually, this experience is a cathartic one. It helps me remember why I am the way that I am. Why I don't let people into my world.

But the guilt that I am feeling now makes me think I won't get shit out of this trip unless I attempt to make things right with Tess.

Who am I?

Maybe it's best to let her be mad at me. If she hates me, maybe she will realize how bad I am for her.

I'll just let her hate me.

Even as I think the words though, I am pulling my car off an exit ramp heading straight in the one direction I know I shouldn't.

Chapter Thirty-five
TESS

After getting zero sleep last night, I decide to go for a run this morning hoping it would help me release some of my pent-up anger. It doesn't really help, but maybe I'll be exhausted enough to fall asleep later.

When Alexander had first dropped me off, every time my thoughts would go to him, my eyes would well up with tears. Now, when his stupid attractive face pops into my head, all I feel is rage.

Rage at how he could just be an asshole and walk out on me without so much as a single word of explanation. Rage at how he could treat me like I don't even matter to him. Rage like all of our time together has meant absolutely nothing.

I keep running until every muscle in my body feels like it's on fire, and I slow down to a brisk walk back to my apartment. I glance at my phone wondering if I should call Chris and see if he wants to do lunch. I decide to wait a little while until I know he's awake. Being a bartender makes him keep late hours.

I stick my phone back in my pocket and round the corner of the hallway to my front door when I see a very large figure standing at my door knocking.

Alexander.

He must see me out of the corner of his eye because he turns to look at me. "There you are...I've been knocking."

"I wasn't home," I respond sarcastically.

Pushing past him, I unlock the door and head inside. He follows behind me.

"I know you're upset with me," he begins. "But if you want to take a drive with me, I think I can explain everything."

My head snaps around. "Why would I want to get in a car with you right now? You treated me like shit, and now you want to come here like suddenly everything is going to be okay?"

"I didn't say that. I said I came here to see if you wanted to get some answers to those questions you have." His voice was beginning to grow in volume. "You want to know why I disappear for a couple days, but it's not something I am going to tell you. It's something I'd like to *show* you. Please."

The last word came out more as a command rather than a plea, but I can see he's trying to be at least somewhat genuine. Despite my anger toward him, my curiosity is certainly peaked. What could he possibly have to show me that he couldn't just explain?

"Fine," I snap. "But let me take a quick shower. I'm gross from my run."

He doesn't respond. Only nods.

Trying to hurry, I take a fast shower and toss my hair in a messy bun. I don't bother with any makeup because I certainly don't want to look like I am getting all dolled up for him. I'm still pissed at him after all.

When I walk back to the living room, he's standing in the same spot as if he hasn't moved at all. When I announce I'm ready, his head jerks to me as if I pulled him out of his own thoughts.

The ride to wherever we are going is a fairly quiet one. And by fairly quiet, I mean the only sound was the music on the radio. I sit with my arms crossed, trying to still portray my annoyance. I think about asking where exactly we are going or how long it's going to take because it seems as though we have been driving forever, but I continue to keep my mouth shut. If nothing else, I'm stubborn as hell.

This is my first time in his fancy Porsche, and I have say that she's gorgeous. Once again, I'm not going to open my mouth to tell him that. I'll just admire it inside my own head.

Between the dull sound on the radio and the comfort of Alexander's car, I finally find myself beginning to drift off. I guess not getting any sleep is beginning to catch up with me.

My eyes only open back up when I feel us start to drive on what feels like a gravel road. Suddenly, the ride isn't smooth enough to nap through anymore.

When I sit up and look out the window, I see we are pulling up to a small house in the middle of nowhere. And by house, I mean it looks more like a shack because it has fallen into disarray over the years.

I know I've said it before, but this is probably where he is going to kill me. Maybe that's his deep dark secret...that he brings women here and kills them.

"Come on," he mumbles, opening the door and stepping out.

Here we go.

We reach the front door, and he pulls out a set of keys to unlock it. Why does the man have keys to everything? Exactly how many properties does he own?

We walk inside, and there is some old, tattered furniture that looks like it's from the 80's. Most of the room is covered in dust, and it has a very musty smell to it as though it needs to be aired out.

I walk over to the tiny kitchen table that has a chair on either side and have a seat. "Okay, Ace. I'm listening."

He sits opposite me at the table and runs his hand through his hair. "This used to be my home when I was growing up."

I don't say a word but instead wait for him to continue at his own pace.

"My parents bought this house before I was born. It was a bit of a fixer upper even back then, but they made it nice enough to call home. They talked about adding onto it and having more kids, but that never happened. My dad died in a car crash when I was five."

"I'm so sorry, Alexander," I say, unable to keep quiet when he makes that admission.

"It was a long time ago. Anyway, my mom was a hopeless romantic. She thought my dad was her soulmate, but when he died, she thought maybe she was wrong. So, she went on a never-ending quest to find the person she thought was 'the one'. Our house was a revolving door of men coming and going…each one a little worse than the last.

"When I was about fifteen, she met Paul. Paul was a drunk son of a bitch who liked to keep her all drugged out on pills and beat her up when no one was around. I'd see the bruises all over her, and I'd beg her to call the cops, but she never would. One day, I got fed up, and I went to the cops myself. They came to the house and questioned her, but she denied it saying she was anemic and bruised easily. Without her statement, there wasn't much they could do. After that, Paul made it very clear that he would make it worse for her if I called the cops again."

He stopped for a moment to take a breath and collect his thoughts.

"The next few years were hell. I tried getting out of the house as much as I could so I wouldn't have to be around either of them. I hated Paul with every fiber of my being, but I felt like there was nothing I could do. I was a scrawny teenager who barely weighed 100 pounds. How was I going to take care of my mom?

"My senior year though, that all changed. I finally started to put on some weight and began working out to build some muscle. Problem was that Paul suddenly seemed to calm down a bit. They started to somewhat resemble a happy couple…until they didn't show up to my high school graduation."

I can tell this story isn't going to have a happy ending, so I lay my hand on top of his letting him know I am there for him, no matter what comes next.

He continues, "I came home to find him smacking her around. Apparently, he wanted her to give it up to him, but she was too high to probably even understand what was going on. I had known for years that he was beating her and slipping her drugs, but it was the first time I'd seen it with my own eyes. I don't even really remember details of it all. I just remember pulling him off of her, and we began wailing on each other. He got in a few punches, but I wasn't that small scared kid anymore. I was ready for a fight, and I started beating him like crazy...until he reached for his gun..."

I audibly gasp and put my hand over my mouth.

"He pointed it at me, but I wasn't going down without a fight. We struggled over the gun, and then, it went off between us. He fell to the ground and blood began pooling beneath him. My mom screamed as if the sound of the gun pulled her out of her stupor. She crawled across the floor to him, trying to get him to wake up. But it was no use. He was already gone.

"I called the cops. When they came, I told them what happened. Seeing the bruises on my mom and the marks all over me, it wasn't hard for them to believe. I still had to go down to the station though to give my formal statement. An officer said he would stay with my mom and try to convince her to go to the hospital to get looked at, but shortly after I left, she kicked him out. By the time I got home, she had swallowed a whole bottle of pills and was dead on the couch. Left a note saying that she'd lost two of her soulmates and she didn't want to be stuck on this Earth looking for another."

Tears are now silently sliding down my cheeks. Truly, I have no idea what to say. "Alexander," I begin. "Why do you come back here to this place that has so much grief attached to it?"

"Tess, that day might have been awful. It was one of the worst things a person can go through. But it helped mold me into the man I am today. Every year, I take a few days to go camping and completely disconnect, and I always stop here along the way."

"I don't understand," I whisper.

"Every year, I come here on the anniversary of that awful day. When I come here, it reminds me of why I never let anyone into my world. People just get hurt. When I come here, I remind myself of what I did…the monster that lives inside me, and I don't want anyone else to have to experience that."

"Alexander, you aren't a monster. You were trying to save your mom. And you said it yourself, the gun accidentally went off," I try to argue.

"Yes, it did. But Tess, if he hadn't have pulled out that gun, I probably would have beaten him to death. In that moment, all I wanted was his blood on my hands no matter what the cost. I know that anger is deep inside me, and no matter how far it is buried, it's there. No one should have to experience that."

I shake my head. "I'm sorry, but I don't see it that way. I see a man who was trying to save his mom from getting beat up and probably raped. That's a *good* thing."

He slams his hand on the table. "God damnit, Tess! I am not ever going to be some knight in shining armor! I'm the beast in this story!"

He can say whatever the fuck he wants. He doesn't scare me. I walk over to him and sit down on his lap, wrapping my arms around his neck. Leaning in, I whisper, "I don't care if you're a beast…as long as you're *my* beast."

His arms pull me close to him as he looks at me. "You're infuriating. Do you know that?"

I nod. "Maybe you should teach me a lesson."

"Don't tempt me, sweetheart."

"Why don't we make a good memory in this house that you can remember when you come here?" I say, standing up to remove my shirt and bra followed by my jeans and panties.

I stand before him completely naked, and he looks me up and down. "Fucking beautiful."

My hands reach down and undo the button and zipper of his pants, pulling them down just enough to let his cock spring free.

Some might say that this is as wildly inappropriate time

to have sex. The man just poured his heart out to me in a deeply moving, yet disturbing, story from his youth. But honestly, I just want to be close to him. I want us to find a connection in the midst of our anger. I want us to add a happy memory to all the dreadful ones.

I pull his shirt off over his head and run my hands along every sculpted curve of his chest and abs before straddling him. Positioning my pussy above him, I grab his shaft and hold it in place while I slowly lower myself onto him.

"Fuuuuck, Tess," he moans when he fills me all the way.

My eyes meet his as I slowly begin to move up and down. Those dark pools suddenly don't seem to be quite so mysterious. Now, I can see all of the hurt and fear that lies within them. I see the man who had something heinous happen to him and now believes he isn't worthy of love.

God, I wish he knew how wrong he is.

He pulls my hair down out of its bun and runs his fingers through it while pulling me close to kiss him. His tongue expertly explores my mouth, and I fist my hands in his hair. The man's kiss is absolutely everything.

Alexander and I have fucked countless times, but this feels different. This feels like making love. Two souls trying desperately to cling to one another despite all the forces trying to keep us apart.

We get lost in that moment, keeping our slow and steady tempo, our bodies slicked with sweat, the only sound being our labored breathing.

Every stroke up and down I can feel him stretching my walls and hitting every nerve ending in my tight channel. I angle my hips so that I am getting more friction on my clit and begin to speed up. I can feel his cock start to twitch inside me, and I know he's getting close too. I'm going to pull him over the edge with me.

When my orgasm hits, it makes my entire body clench and pulse around him. I hold him as close as possible, and I cry out his name while I ride out the waves of ecstasy.

Just as mine takes hold, he's right behind me, letting out a primal growl as he spills into me.

When we have both stilled, he continues to hold me close, his arms wrapped around my waist and his head laying on my chest.

It seems like an eternity that we stay locked in that moment before I hear him whisper, "I'm sorry I was a jerk to you last night. Although I had my reasons, it is no excuse for me to act that way."

"It's okay," I say.

He finally looks up at me. "No, it's not. Treating you that way will never be okay."

"Then, just don't do it," I smile, trying to lighten the mood.

The smile he gives in return is a forced one, but I appreciate the effort. Climbing off of him, I begin to put my clothes back on.

When I'm fully dressed, I turn to him. "Look, Ace, I might not completely understand why you come here. Hell, I think it's even a little unhealthy for you to keep reliving that day, but if this is what helps you, then okay. You can have your dark days, and I'll leave you alone. You stay here or go camping or whatever it is you need to do, and I'll take a ride share back to the city."

"Come on, don't be silly. I'll give you a ride home, Tess," he says, pulling up his pants.

"No, you won't. This is your time, and you have already wasted enough of it driving back and forth. I will call a car. No big deal."

"Tess..."

I hold my hand up. "This isn't up for discussion."

"You're a pain in the ass," he spits.

"Yeah, you said that. But you're my beast, and I'm your pain in the ass," I wink. Pulling out my phone, I open the ride share app and ask him what the address is.

He gives it to me, and we wait for the car. I walk over to him, wrapping my arms around him in a hug. Despite him thinking he's dangerous, he makes me feel so safe.

In my mind, I go over the story he's just told me. Looking up at him, I say, "I do have one question though."

"Yes, sweetheart?"

"Why didn't any of this show up when I Googled you? I mean there should be some of record of it, right?"

He pauses for a moment. "I changed my name when I got to New York. My birth name is Alexander Harrison. I didn't want this incident to follow me when I tried to make something of myself.."

Leaning up on my toes, I kiss him. "I like Alexander Rockford much better."

Twenty minutes later, I am heading back to the city in the back of a grey sedan. Definitely a step down from Alexander's sports car...or my sports car for that matter...but after hearing his story, I know he needs some time to himself.

So, I will give him his space and let him come to me when he's ready...even though it might be a very long couple of days.

Chapter Thirty-six
ALEXANDER

Two days later, I am on my way back to the city.

And I can't fucking wait.

Although I usually use my days away to reflect on the past, I use it as some quiet time to think about the future. Being in the house that saw me at my lowest point reminds me of how I never want to go back to that stage and encourages me to move forward. Then, I go camping to completely clear my head.

I've had some of my best business ideas sitting in those woods all alone.

This time though, all I could think about was Tess. Even after she left, I could still smell her all over that room. Her hair that smelled like flowers. The fruity smell of her soap. The sweet scent of her arousal.

I fly down the highway, trying to get back to her as soon as I can. I have missed her like crazy. Despite my 'no talking to anyone' rule, I sent her a text asking if she was okay. It was her first night back after her week off, and I couldn't help but worry about how she was handling it.

She assured me she was fine and said she was just tired and would see me soon.

Soon couldn't come fast enough for me, so I ended up cutting my trip short. Besides, sitting around worrying about her wasn't letting me focus on anything else.

Geez, what the hell is this woman doing to me?

When I finally get to her apartment, I hear yelling on the other side of her door.

"I'm fine!" I hear Tess scream.

"You're clearly not fine! Look at you, damnit!" A man's voice shouts back.

Not waiting to hear any more of the conversation, I try the doorknob, and it's unlocked, so I proceed to let myself in.

She's got her back to me, and I see that her brother, Tyler, is the one she is yelling at.

"Oh Look, Alexander is here. Maybe *he* can talk some sense into you."

Her head whips around to look at me, clearly not aware that I had just walked in. As quickly as she turned toward me though, she looks away again.

"What's going on?" I question.

"Nothing. I'm fine," Tess reiterates.

"She's not fine! If you're fine, why don't you show him?" Tyler crosses his arms waiting for her to respond.

She finally turns completely around, and I see she has a huge black eye and another bruise along her jaw.

My blood boils in record time. "What the fuck happened?!" I roar.

"I..." she begins, but Tyler interrupts her.

"She was attacked coming out of work last night. Guy really did a number on her."

"You were what? Who the fuck was it?" I ask.

"I have no idea," she says, clearly annoyed. "But I was able to fend him off. I've gone through enough self-defense training, I know how to take care of myself. Trust me, he will be hurting today."

"Was it a robbery?"

She shrugs. "I don't know. I mean he didn't take anything,

but I also fought back, and he ran off. So, maybe he just didn't get the chance."

"Motherfucker," I mutter.

"Both of you need to settle down. I am clearly fine," she tries to say in a calming voice, but neither of us are having it.

"No. You need a new job," Tyler argues. "I've been telling you that for years. That place isn't safe, and you aren't careful enough. Look!" He points to the door. "You didn't even lock it after I came in. Alexander just walked right in! Damnit Tess, you live in New York; you have to be more careful!"

"I agree," I say. "That job is clearly too dangerous. It's in the worst part of town. Maybe it's time to start looking elsewhere."

"Like where? Like the Congo or a war zone? Oh yeah, I've already done that! This is nothing for me. I've had worse, and I was able to take care of myself then, too. I don't need you two over-protective brutes telling me how to live my life!" She cries while waving her arms in the air.

Tyler shakes his head. "We are just worried about you. Sorry if I don't want anything to happen to my sister. Do you know how hard it would be lose you? How hard it would be to tell your nieces something happened to you? You're too fucking careless. Stop living your life as if you don't care if it ends! Alexander, maybe you can talk some sense into her, but I'm done."

Without another word, he walks out and slams the door.

She holds up her hand. "Don't start."

"Too late, sweetheart. We have to talk about this."

I can't deny that maybe Tyler is right. Tess can be careless at times, and it's finally catching up to her.

She walks away from me toward the bedroom where she has a laundry basket full of clean clothes sitting on her bed. She picks up a shirt and starts to fold it, but I grab it from her hands and toss it back in the basket. Taking her hand, I sit her down on the bed next to me.

"Tell me exactly what happened," I try to keep my voice as calm as possible even though on the inside I feel like I might explode.

She takes a deep breath. "I was coming out of work, and it wasn't even completely dark yet. I figured I'd be fine to take the subway to get home, but in the parking lot, someone grabbed me from behind. I managed to get him off me, and he swung on me a couple times. I swung back and kicked him in the balls. He ran away after that."

"Did he say anything?"

"Called me a bitch."

"When you kicked him in the balls?"

She shakes her head. "No, before that. When he first grabbed me."

"Did you see his face? Recognize his voice?"

"I caught a glimpse of his face despite the fact that he had an oversized hoodie on. When he ran away, I did call the cops and file a report, but I mean how they are going to find one skinny, blonde guy in a city of 18 million?"

I rub my face with my hand trying to make sense of everything she's telling me. The fact that he was lying in wait and called her a bitch right off the bat makes me think that maybe he knows her. I'm not going to say that to her though and scare her.

"Alexander, I told you I'm fine. A few bruises which will heal in a couple of days."

"It could have been worse," I retort.

"But it wasn't," she argues.

"Tess, I am allowed to be worried about you. Damnit, I care about you, and it comes with the territory. I'm sorry if I'm acting like a caveman here, but I don't want anything to happen to you. And why the fuck didn't you tell me last night when I texted you?"

She shrugs. "I was busy talking to the police, and I knew you were doing your own thing."

I stop her. "I don't care what the fuck I am doing. I don't care if I am in the most important meeting of my fucking life. If something happens to you, you call me. Period. If you are going to keep your job, you at least have to make me that promise."

She nods. "Okay, I promise. While you're already mad, I

have something else to tell you."

My blood boils as she shows me her phone with a text from an unknown number telling her to stay away from me.

"Why wouldn't you tell me?!" I shout.

"We were on vacation, and it didn't seem like the right time. You would have gotten mad, just like you're doing now, and it would have ruined our trip."

I try to lower my voice a little. "Sweetheart, you still should have told me. I could have had someone looking into this. I just want you safe."

"I know. I'm sorry. I just didn't think it was a huge deal. If more texts would have came, I would have showed you, but they stopped."

I rub my hand along my stubbled jaw. "I need you to be more careful. Please. I can't have anything happen to you."

She agrees, and I wrap my arms around her. My mind keeps racing as to who would want to hurt her. I know I've made a few enemies over the years, but honestly, I try to fly under the radar most of the time. Guilt washes over me as I feel responsible for her attack, but something else replaces it as I realize now I will be personally responsible for her safety.

We sit quietly for a moment before she says, "You're home early."

My shoulders shrug. "Eh, I guess I kind of missed you."

"How much?" She smiles.

I hold my finger and thumb about an inch apart. "About this much."

She adjusts my hands to make the space between them bigger. "I only get naked for this much."

My eyebrows raise at her. "Take off my pants, and I think it's about that much."

She giggles, and I kiss her as we fall into bed together.

Chapter Thirty-seven
TESS

The next morning, I open my eyes to find Alexander still lying in bed next to me. Usually, I wake up, and he's already been up for hours. It's nice to feel his warm body still against mine.

He's on his back with one arm wrapped around me as I lay my head on his chest. I can hear his heart beating…strong and steady…just like him.

My eyes glance up and down his chiseled body before landing on his handsome face. His stubble is thick from not shaving for a few days, and I have to say that I like the scruff.

"Why are you staring at me, sweetheart?" He mumbles.

Busted.

My fingers trace along his jaw line. "Just thinking how I like this look on you. Goes very nicely with your caveman attitude."

"Maybe I'll just stop shaving altogether and grow a mountain man beard," he smiles.

"Eh, let's not go that far. But I do like a little bit of hair."

"Even when I do this?" He flips on top of me and starts rubbing his chin all over my neck, tickling me like crazy.

"Stop!" I laugh. "Get off me, you brute!"

"Oh, sweetheart, I'll show you a brute," he says while his hands join in on the tickling.

When I can't take anymore and admit defeat, he pulls me into his arms and holds me close.

"What are you doing today?" He asks.

"Not much. I have the day off which is insane because I just had a whole fucking week off. I guess I'll do some more laundry since *someone* distracted me from it last night. And I suppose I should call Tyler and try to smooth things over. I don't think he's too happy with me."

"Don't be too hard on him. He is just worried about you," he says, placing a kiss on my forehead.

"I know. I'll apologize. I never feel right when we argue. It's like something is off until we are okay again. Anyways, what about you? What are you doing today?" I ask.

"I was supposed to have a meeting with Chet, but he said he had a family thing and asked if we could do a conference call instead. Fine by me. Over the phone, he can't see me tuning him out."

We both laugh and continue to make some small talk before finally getting out of bed.

Alexander stands in my kitchen looking into my fridge. "You know, I can't make you breakfast if you have an empty refrigerator."

I shrug. "Yeah, I need to go shopping."

He laughs. "Understatement of the year, sweetheart." He pulls a bottle from the back. "Tess, this expired four years ago."

I just shrug.

"You're something else, woman."

There's a knock on the door as he is about to kiss me, and I wonder if it's Tyler. If it is, I'm going to kill him for having the worst timing.

But when I open the door, Tyler isn't the one standing there.

It's Mark…as in…my ex.

Holy shit, I haven't seen this man in years, yet he looks

exactly the same. Well, now he looks a bit more clean cut than he did when we were living in Africa together.

"Mark?" I ask.

"Hey T," he smiles. "Been awhile."

"No shit!" I laugh and pull him in for a hug.

Alexander clears his throat behind me, and I had almost forgotten he was there. Seeing a ghost from the past will do that to a person.

"Mark, this is Alexander," I say. I'm about to introduce him as my boyfriend, but Alexander greets him and holds out his hand.

The two shake, and he turns to me. "Hey, I have to go get on that call with Chet. Stop by later if you want." He holds my hands while he says the words but then is out the door.

No kiss?

Once he's gone, my attention focuses back on Mark. "What are you doing here?" I ask with a warm smile.

He returns the sentiment and says. "I just moved back to the city. Decided to look you up. Can we talk?"

I step out of the doorway and let him into the apartment. We walk to the couch, and I offer him something to drink. Thank goodness he says no because I'm sure all I have is vodka and tap water.

"What's going on, Mark? Why are you here?"

"T, I've been doing Doctors Without Borders for years, and as much as I love it, I think I'm finally ready to put down some roots. So, I came back to my hometown and got a job at a hospital where I'm pretty sure a very sexy trauma doc works," he winks.

God, Mark is charming. He always has been. He has shaggy blonde hair that always looks messy, but in a perfectly styled way. His skin is kissed by the sun from spending so much time outside. His eyes are baby blue, and his smile was wide and white.

To look at him, you'd never know he is from New York because everything about him screams West Coast.

Back in the day, he and I had something good going. We

would spend all day in the trenches saving lives, and it would leave us on such a high that we would fuck all night. We were best friends in the middle of a hopeless landscape.

But when I was ready to leave the program to resume a normal life, he wasn't.

Until now apparently.

"T, I missed you. I have missed you so damn bad. I was hoping we could start something up again."

"Mark," I begin, but he interrupts.

"And I didn't come here thinking that you were going to be single. You're far too brilliant for that. I didn't come here because I thought it would be easy. I came here fully prepared to fight for you. Even against Mr. Tall, Dark, and Handsome who just blew out of here."

I literally have no clue what to say. I never thought of Mark and I more than just a good time, but here he is telling me he has missed me?

And now, there is Alexander. And I can't picture my life without him.

Before I can inform Mark of this fact, he starts talking again. "Look, I'm not asking for you to make any type of decision right now. I'm just telling you I'm tossing my hat in the race." He gets up and heads toward the door. "I'll see you at work," he says with a wink and walks out.

What in the literal hell just happened?

Chapter Thirty-eight
ALEXANDER

"Alexander, are you even listening to me?" Chet barks over the phone.

"Yes."

No.

"Are you sure because you sound like you haven't heard a word that I've said."

"I've heard everything."

Not a single word.

As much as I am trying to listen to Chet about this new 'awesome' business investment he wants me to look into, I can't concentrate on anything he is saying.

Tess fills my mind in a hazy fog, clouding all other thoughts that try to emerge.

She'd mentioned Mark before. I guess they worked together in Doctors Without Borders. But she'd never given me specifics on how serious they were or what exactly happened.

She got excited and hugged the guy when she saw him, so clearly, there weren't feelings of animosity there. Were there feelings of something else?

Why the hell am I getting jealous over this guy? I'm the one who took her to bed last night. It was *my* name she was screaming out as she came.

Besides, why the hell do I care if this whole thing is supposed to be casual? If it has an expiration date, why am I so worked up?

Honestly, I've probably let the whole thing go on longer than I should have. But I can't help it. There's something so intoxicating about her that just keeps drawing me back in.

She's my forbidden fruit that I have to have a taste of every single time…my soul be damned.

I finally end the call with Chet, explaining to him for the hundredth time that I am not interested in any business dealings at the moment until I have Gino's up and running. He's none too happy with my answer, but I don't care. I am just ready to stop talking to him.

Tossing on my jacket, I head to Gino's for a bit to do some more painting. I figure maybe keeping my hands busy will help to also keep my mind busy, but as I swipe the roller up and down the wall, I still think of Tess.

I wonder what she is doing. I wonder if *he* is still there. I wonder what he wanted, and what she told him.

Most of all, I regret not kissing her before I left. I should have kissed her like she's never been kissed before just to show him that she's mine, and he should keep his fucking hands off.

But I didn't. And I think I know why.

I work at Gino's all day and into the evening. There's a slight tap on the front door, and when I look up, I see Tess staring back at me.

I jog to unlock it for her.

"You told me to come over, but I went to your apartment, and you weren't there. And apparently, you don't answer your phone, so I figured I'd try here," she says walking in.

Walking over to my phone, I see I have four missed calls.

"I'm sorry. I took it out of my pocket earlier and forgot it was still on silent I guess."

"It's alright. I found you," she smiles, but when she notices I don't smile back, hers quickly fades.

Quietly, she says, "So, I guess we should talk about earlier."

"What about?" I ask trying to sound like I wasn't chomping at the bit to ask her for every single detail.

"About Mark."

I keep painting and avoid looking at her.

"Okay, say what you want to say, Tess."

"I know I have mentioned Mark to you before, but I don't think I really ever told you much. Mark and I met in Doctors Without Borders. The last trip we were on, it was just him and me and one other doctor on site. When you're in high-stress situations like that, you get to know each other pretty damn fast. We became best friends, and one drunken night, it became something more.

"It was fun...our little light in a dark situation. But when I was ready to come home, he wasn't. He thought he wasn't done saving the world yet, so we called it quits. Back then, it seemed so important...so wonderful, but now, I look back on it, and it feels almost like nothing more than a fling."

"So, what did he want today?" I interrupt.

"Apparently, he's giving up that life and has moved back here. He grew up here, so he's always used New York as his home base. And I guess he got a job at the hospital I work at."

"So, he's back here for you?"

She shakes her head, but I can see it all over her face. "No, I never said that."

"Tess, he moved to New York, where *you* live. He got a job at the hospital *you* work at. He came to see *you* today. Guess what the common denominator is here, sweetheart?"

"It doesn't matter. He knows I'm seeing someone."

"Doesn't mean he will stop trying," I retort.

"I guess. But it doesn't mean that I want him."

"Does he want the whole package?" I ask.

"What do you mean, Alexander?"

"Does he want the marriage...the kids...the house in the suburbs with the white picket fence?"

"What the fuck is up with you and white picket fences?

And, I don't know. We never really talked about the future like that. Besides, I told you that's not the whole package that I want."

The words that begin to spill out of my mouth feel like they are ripping a hole clean out of my chest. "Maybe you should be with someone like Mark."

"Excuse me?"

"Let me ask you this. Is he a good man, Tess? I mean deep down, is he a good man?"

She thinks for a moment. "I guess so. Alexander, what the fuck are you saying?" Her voice goes up an octave.

Taking a deep breath, I know I am about to say words that will rip me apart.

"I'm saying it's over."

Chapter Thirty-nine
TESS

"It's over? The hell, it's over!" I scream.

"You said it yourself, Mark is a good man," Alexander replies.

"So?"

He gets in my face. "So, maybe he is the prince coming to save you from the monster. Did you ever think of that?"

"No, I didn't think of that because you're not a monster!" Tears are stinging my eyes, threatening to spill over.

"I am! And the sooner you realize that, the better. Tess, I'm crazy about you, but this will never work. You deserve someone so much better than me. You deserve someone who is going to be able to make every one of your hopes and dreams come true. I am not that man. God, I wish I could be, but I'm not. It's time to call a spade and a spade and stop pretending this is going anywhere."

"But..." I say even though I'm not sure how to finish that sentence.

"No buts. No excuses. We need to stop making excuses for why this is a good idea. I wish that it could be, but it isn't. Let's stop lying to ourselves. This thing has always had an expiration date. That date is today."

I can't contain the tears anymore. I came here tonight to tell him that I was going to tell Mark that I was in love with someone else, and I couldn't be with him. Instead, I come here, and he breaks up with me.

Anger boils inside me. "Alexander, you may claim that you're a monster, but I've seen the good in you. I've seen the relationship you have with Nancy. I've heard you talk about the owners of the businesses you invest in and how you genuinely care about them. I've seen how you care about me. No matter what you say to me…breakup or not…you'll never be a monster to me."

"Think whatever you want to, sweetheart. It doesn't change my mind on wanting to settle down." There is a finality in his words that breaks my heart.

I wipe the tears from my cheeks, but his hand replaces mine.

"Tess, you deserve so much in your life. You deserve someone who is going to love you every single day. Someone who is going to be able to always put you first. Someone who is going to be your true partner. I need you to go find that…whoever it might be with." His voice cracks at the last words, and I know this is hard for him too.

"I'll really miss you, Ace," I choke out.

"Sweetheart, you have no idea."

I long to kiss him. If we kiss, I know it will lead to more. I yearn for that time together…even if it's the last time. I want to tell him to kiss me. To fuck me hard right here on one of these tables. To tell him I don't care what the future holds as long as it has him in it.

But I don't do any of those things. Because I know in the end, it will make it harder to say goodbye. And clearly, that's what he wants. I'm not going to beg him to be with me.

When we first met, he told me I wasn't his type because I was fierce and independent, and I'd be damned if I didn't live up to that.

I am Tess Fucking Wendell. I told him I was the fire. And I

meant it.

Quickly, I wipe my remaining tears and hold my head up high.

"Goodbye, Alexander," I say quietly and walk toward the door.

My head stays held high as I exit Gino's and walk out into the evening. I keep my eyes forward and my jaw locked tight as I walk home.

It isn't until I hit my front door that my façade finally shatters, the dam breaks, and my tears begin to fall once more.

Chapter Forty
ALEXANDER

Two days later, I sit in my office at Club Rock. I'm trying to bury myself in work, so I don't think about Tess. Though it's not really working, I still try.

I try because I know what I did was for the best. Everything that is fucked up about me would eventually destroy her. She doesn't deserve a ticking time bomb. She deserves the best.

She deserves everything.

As much as I wish I could be the man to give that to her, I can't. Bad people don't get to have things go their way. Maybe being forever alone was my penance.

Maybe I'm just an arrogant asshole who fucks up everything.

Yeah…that too.

As I watched her walk out of Gino's that night, every cell in my body was screaming at me to go after her. My heart ached to hold her in my arms, but my head reminded me how bad of an idea that was.

We should have never gotten as far as we did. I should have let her go a long time ago. Maybe even after that first night.

But damn it if the woman didn't call me in like a sexy siren leading me back to her every time. And I was just too weak to resist those big brown eyes. That long silky hair. Those gorgeous full lips.

Stop it.

I shake my head a few times trying to get the images of Tess out of my head before I get a raging hard-on in my office. I may be in here alone, but that doesn't mean I want to be sitting here with a boner all day.

I let the numbers scattered on the spreadsheets on my screen carry me away for the next couple of hours. After all, I still have my empire to run.

The wheels of business don't stop turning...even for a broken heart.

I'm taken out of my concentration by a knock on my door. "Come in," I order.

Chris peeks his head in, and I already know this might be awkward. Chris is a damn good bartender...but I also know he is Tess's best friend. He's the reason she stepped foot inside this place to start with.

"Chris, how can I help you?" I ask.

"I'm sorry if I'm stepping over some personal line here, but have you heard from Tess? I've been trying to call her for two days with no answer. I was thinking she was with you, but you're here..." The worry in his voice is apparent, so I resist the urge to tell him his question is wildly inappropriate. I know he is just looking out for his friend.

"No, she's not with me. Last time I saw or talked to her was two nights ago." As I say the words, suddenly, I become a bit worried.

Is she okay?

It's very unusual for her not to answer the phone for Chris.

He asks another question. "Again, forgive me...but did something happen between the two of you."

He was coming dangerously close to stepping over the line, but I need to give him some scrap of information so that he will go check on Tess and make sure she's okay. Heaven knows she would probably rather see him than me right now.

"I ended things with Tess." I say in as calm of a voice as I can muster.

"You did what?" He said. "Why?"

"Now, that really is stepping over the line, Chris. Watch it," I bark.

As if I hadn't just scolded him, he walks over and sits in the chair across from me. Leaning forward, resting his elbows on his knees, he looks me dead in the eye.

"Rockford, you may scare a lot of people in this place, but I'm not one of them. If you want to fire me, go ahead. I'm a bartender...in New York...I'll be fine. But I think you've lost your damn mind. You're never going to find a woman as good as Tess."

I consider taking him up on his offer to fire him, but I don't want that little piece of news getting back to Tess.

So, leaning forward and closing the space between us, I respond with, "I know. Problem is that she *can* and *should* find a man way better than me."

As if a light clicks on in his head, he nods. "For the record, Tess is a big girl who is completely capable of making her own decisions. If she saw something in you, it must mean you're special."

"Or it means she has terrible taste."

He laughs. "Maybe. But in the end, I think you'll regret it because women like Tess Wendell don't wait around for men who don't want them."

I know. That's what I'm hoping for.

He continues, "But I guess after I pissed you off, now I'm going to make you even more mad by asking for the night off. I need to go check on her. It isn't like her not to answer the phone."

"Who is your number two tonight?" I ask.

"Sheila. She's already here and prepping the bar."

I nod. "That's fine. Tell me if you end up needing tomorrow too."

"Thank you," he says sincerely but follows it up with, "Now, time to go get baby girl out of her funk. The funk that *you* caused."

As he is about to leave, I say, "Hey Chris…she really likes amusement parks. *Really* likes them. I don't know if you knew that or not."

He smiles. "I didn't. But I'll make sure to keep it in mind. And Rockford?"

"Hmm?"

"You're kind of an idiot."

Before I can respond, he was out the door. He probably thought that I was going to reprimand him for talking to his boss like that and calling him an idiot.

On the contrary.

I was going to tell him he was absolutely fucking right.

Chapter Forty-one
TESS

"Get off me, you bitch!"

Two blonde women fighting on some reality show scream through my television. At this point, I couldn't even tell you what they are fighting about.

Men? Money? Whose boobs are bigger? All of the above?

My TV plays episode after episode as I lie on my couch. My racing mind keeps me from sleeping more than a couple hours at a time, so I keep nodding off randomly. I have my blanket curled up around me covering everything but my face, and my arm only pokes out long enough to grab another cheese puff.

Since I really didn't want to leave yesterday, I ordered groceries online and had them delivered. Well, if you can even consider them *groceries*. Mainly, it's just liquor and junk food. Last night, I drank my weight in vodka hoping that it would help me to get to sleep.

It didn't. It just made me throw up.

So, I was sad and sick. What a fucking combination.

There's a knock on the front door, but I don't answer. My body stays perfectly still in hopes that whoever it is will just go away. The knocking finally ceases, but my phone buzzes next to me with a text from Chris.

Chris: Tess, open this door right now, or I'm going to assume your dead and go get the super to break it down.

Knowing he will absolutely be that dramatic, I quickly get up and shuffle over to the door. When I open it, Chris is there holding a grocery sack.

"Hi, beautiful," he says with a sympathetic smile.

Damnit, he knows.

"How'd you find out?"

"When I couldn't get ahold of you, I walked into Mr. Brooding's office and asked him where you were. At first, he was vague, but I pried it out of him."

"Glad to know he's bragging about dumping me," I mutter, walking back to the couch.

"Honey, it wasn't like that. I wouldn't leave him alone, and he gave me the speech about how you deserve better than him."

"Yeah, I got that speech too. What a load of bullshit, right?"

He follows me and sits down taking my hand in his. "Maybe not. Hell, I think you're too good for the smug asshole."

"Deep down, he's a good man," I say no louder than a whisper, but he still hears it.

"I'm sure you have seen a side to him that I haven't. Even so, any guy to let you go has to be a moron."

I can't help but laugh and give him a hug.

He pulls back and looks at me, "But in the future, when something like this happens, you call me. Period. I don't want you laying around in this apartment all day sulking. It's not good for you. I mean baby girl, look at you. You have a cheese puff stuck in your hair."

Jokingly, I ask. "Does it look old, or do you think I can still eat it?"

He laughs and grabs it out of my hair "Not a chance in hell you are eating this."

I pull my stash from next to the couch. "That's alright. I have a whole bag," I say reaching my hand in the giant sack.

"No! Put those down! I stopped and got us sushi."

"Mmmmm...you know me so well."

He pulls all of the containers out of the bag, and my mouth begins to water. When I go to reach for one of them, he bats my hand away.

"Get in the bathroom and wash your hands. You are not touching this delicious sushi with those orange stained fingers of yours."

My eyes look down at my hands, and I realize my fingers really are a bright hue of orange. I go to just lick them, but Chris stops me and points to the bathroom. "Soap and water."

"Okay, *Mom*," I groan sarcastically.

While washing my hands, I avoid even the smallest glance in the mirror. I don't need to see that mess of a human being staring back at me.

After I dry my hands and let Chris examine them to make sure they were no remaining bits of cheese puffs, we dig in.

"God, this is good," I say while my eyes roll back in my head.

"Thanks, I hear that a lot," he quips.

Playfully, I smack him in the shoulder. "Oh, stop it. But for real, are you *sure* you're gay? Because I mean if you tell me you're straight right now, we can just run straight to the alter. You bring me sushi, check up on me, you're damn fun to look at..."

"Honey, if I were straight, you wouldn't know what hit you! But unfortunately, you and I are in the same boat dealing with the dumber sex. I wish I had some pearls of wisdom for you, but I'm up the same creek you are, sweetheart."

The mention of the name 'sweetheart' causes an ache in my chest. Part of that ache is caused by wishing I could hear Alexander call me that again. Part of it wiswondering how long it would take for him to give that name to someone else.

Trying to expel that thought from my head, I say, "Well, I guess we can just watch reality TV and trash talk men all night... unless you have to work." My heart sinks thinking about Club Rock.

"Nope, I'm all yours for as long as you need me."

As much as I would like to keep Chris here with me forever, I figure tomorrow, I will pretend that I am feeling better and send him on his way. After all, I'm going to have to pick myself back up eventually...might as well start sooner rather than later.

But not tonight.

Tonight, we will lay on my couch with our bellies full of sushi watching trashy TV. Chris will let me lay my head in his lap, and he will twist my hair around his fingers until I finally drift off to sleep.

****

The next morning, I awake to Chris making pancakes in the kitchen, and they smell heavenly.

Getting up off the couch, which apparently is now my bed, I walk in the kitchen, my nose leading the way.

"Morning, gorgeous," he smiles at me.

"Morning. You know you don't have to do this. I'm sure you're tired. I know mornings aren't really your thing."

"Right now, *you're* my thing. Besides, I can sleep when I'm dead." He gives me a wink.

"Well, thank you. It smells delicious."

"Good. Eat up. I have a big day planned for you."

A sense of dread fills me because I really don't want to go anywhere or do anything. "Does your big day involve me lying on the couch some more?"

"No, baby girl, it does not. You sulking on that couch is not helping to make you feel the least bit better. So, we are going to go have some fun!"

Fun? I doubt it.

But I don't express my hesitation because he seems so excited. I guess it's time for me to put on my happy face and try to act like I am feeling far better than I actually am.

He hands me a plate of warm pancakes, and I cover them in butter and syrup and dig in. "Damn, these are good. Where'd you learn to cook?"

He shrugs. "Honey, I have five sisters. You wouldn't believe the things I learned to do over the years. I can cook, sew, clean, and if you sweet talk me really nicely, I'll even French braid your hair for you."

I laugh. "A jack of all trades."

He smiles. "Something like that. I figure you should never stop learning because if you aren't moving forward, you are standing still. And what fun is that?" He asks while scooping his own breakfast out of the pan.

Maybe he's right. I've always thought of myself as a person who is chasing that next goal or dream, but the past few years, I've just been *living.* Nothing more. I stopped fighting to be better. I stopped moving forward.

Pulling myself out of my own thoughts, I say, "Speaking of fun, what fun things do you have planned for today?"

"You really want to know?"

I nod.

"Figured we could hit up an amusement park."

A smile hits my face. "How'd you know I love those?" Realization hits me that Alexander probably told him. "Did *he* tell you that?"

He shrugs. "He might have mentioned something about it. But today isn't about him. It's all about having fun and living our best lives!"

"Okay!" I say, trying to muster up as much enthusiasm as I can.

"But first, for the love of God, you have to take a shower. For real. You're gross."

I laugh, but I know he's right. I'm a mess, and maybe if I make myself look better on the outside, it will help me to feel a bit better on the inside.

While I shower, I blare music on my phone to try to drown out any thoughts going on in my head. If I'm singing along, I don't have time to wallow.

After I get out and dry off, I'm actually starting to feel a little bit better. There's actually even a hint of a smile on my face as I walk back out to the living room.

"Ready when you are, chief," I say to Chris.

"You look gorgeous, baby girl! There's just one problem."

My face drops. "What?"

"See, I'm not going to be the one going with you today."

"Chris, I'm really not in the mood for games. What the fuck is going on?" I snap.

"Well, roller coasters aren't exactly my thing, but I know someone who loves them just as much as you do. And I think you are due for a day with him anyway."

A knock on the door sends Chris skipping over to answer it. When he opens it, Tyler is standing there with his hands in his pockets.

"Heard you needed a ride buddy for the day," he says with a smile.

Even after getting mad at me the other day, my brother still stands at my front door. I walk over to him, and he holds out his arms for a hug.

The second I reach him, my demeanor, which was just so put together, completely falls apart as I begin to cry once more.

Chapter Forty-two
TESS

Tyler let me cry on his shoulder for a few minutes before I pull myself together so we could get on the road.

"Do you want to tell me what happened?" He asks once we were on the highway.

"I fell in love with a man who isn't ready to love me back."

"Do you think maybe he does love you, and he just can't say it?

I look over at Tyler who has his eyes fixed on the road. "I don't think it really matters…whether he can't *say* it or can't *show* it, I think he's ready to move on. Part of it is my fault. He told me from the beginning he wasn't going to want to settle down. I told him I was fine with keeping things casual, but deep down, I thought I could change him."

"Can't change someone who doesn't want to be changed, sis."

"Sam changed for you," I said, referring to how guarded his wife was when they first met. She spent months denying her feelings for him.

"Sam was pretty emotionally messed up because of her past."

So is Alexander.

"Ty, when did you know Sam was the one?"

He thinks for a moment before answering. "Although I was drawn to Sam from the first moment I met her, I don't think I really knew until we finally kissed. She had been pushing me away for months, and we were nearing our breaking point. But when I kissed her, it was like all the bullshit just faded away. And there was just us in that moment. It's like my soul had been missing something until that very second. To this day, I could still just kiss her for hours on end."

The way my brother smiles when he talks about his wife makes me so happy for him, albeit a little jealous. They had been through so much in their relationship...more than any couple should have to go through...yet they came out stronger than ever.

I guess some couples are just made to weather the storm, and some just drown in a little bit of rain.

But I knew what he meant when he talked about their kiss. There was so much heat between Alexander and I when we kissed, I thought we might explode. But maybe that was all just brought on by our physical attraction to one another.

We talk a little bit more about our love lives, but I change the subject to something a bit lighter on our way to the park.

"How are the girls?" I ask.

"They're good. The past few days they've actually been getting along, and it's fucking weird. They never get along this well. Sam and I are convinced they're plotting to kill us and take over the house."

"Wouldn't surprise me. Which one do you think is going to take you out? Lilah or Abby?"

He rubs his chin. "You know, if it were something physical, Lilah for sure. She'd stab us or something crazy. Abby, on the other hand, is much more sinister. I think she would poison us. Pretty sure she'd be the mastermind behind the whole thing."

I slap him on the shoulder. "You know they love you. Besides, if they killed you, who would they have to annoy?"

"Oh for sure, I'd make sure they came to live with Aunt

Tess," he chuckles.

"Haha. Very funny."

"They love you too. I didn't even tell them where I was going today because they would have wanted to come, and when I said no, they would have given Sam hell all day for it," he says.

"Thank you for coming, Ty. It means a lot."

"You're welcome. But you know I'd do anything for you. Besides, you and I have not been here together in years, and we are due for some adrenaline!"

I laugh at his enthusiasm, and he turns on some music for us to sing and dance to all the way there. It feels just like we are teenagers again. Driving to the park early in the morning to get in right when the gates open…ready to ride everything and eat all the junk we can.

Although I miss those days, nothing beats seeing my baby brother as a dad. He's by far one of the most caring, compassionate people I have ever met, and now, he gets to give all that love to two beautiful little girls.

And yet still finds time to take care of his big sister when she needs it.

We get to the park and immediately head for our favorite coaster. Last time I was here, I was riding this ride with Alexander. I can still see the scared look on his face as we go over the first hill. It's a long cry from the excited face of my brother who is laughing and holding his hands in the air the whole time.

As we soar over the large hills, every thought I have completely falls out of my head. I throw my hands up, close my eyes, and pretend I'm flying. If I was a bird, I could fly far away from here and start over.

After hitting every coaster in the park once, we decide to take a break and get some lunch. While we are eating a delicious meal of pizza and breadsticks, Tyler breaks the silence between us.

"Tess, can I ask you something?"

I simply nod.

"I know this Alexander thing is hard for you, but I can't

help but see it's not the only thing bothering you. It seems like you've been in a funk for a while now. Before him, you were out partying all the time, and..."

"How'd you know about that?" I ask, knowing I was always super careful not to let my family into that part of my life.

"One of my friends saw you one day and asked me about it. Doesn't take a genius to figure out that's why you were being so secretive."

Leaning back in my chair, I pause to think for a moment. "Ty, you know I've always been chasing that next rush of adrenaline, that next high. For years, my life moved at the speed of sound, and I loved it. When I did Doctors Without Borders, every single day held that excitement for me. There was never time to catch my breath.

"Then, I came back and started work at the hospital, and while I love being a doctor, I just don't think it's the same. I deal with so much political bullshit. I've got people telling me not to give as much care to patients who don't have insurance, and it's not right. I don't know that I want to be just some cog in the hospital money making machine. I'm just not sure the hospital is the right place for me anymore."

Knowing I don't need to relive it, I don't mention the part about the kid I lost. Instead, I say, "Plus, Mark just started at the hospital. Not sure how that's going to go."

His eyes widen. "Mark? Like guy you dated while working..."

I cut him off. "Yeah, that's the one. He showed up at my apartment while Alexander was there. And later on, he tells me that he came back for me and is ready to settle down."

"And you said?"

"I said I was seeing someone. At the time, it was true."

"What are you going to say if he puts the same offer on the table again?" He asks while sipping his drink.

"No fucking clue. Mark and I had something great, but it was forever ago. And I am not sure when I will be ready to jump into anything again. And I mean if it's not right, it's not right.

Look at what happened with you and Marisol."

Marisol was his long-time girlfriend who came back into the picture before he and Sam got serious. They tried dating, but he just couldn't get over Sam, so they ended things.

"Touché," he laughs. "I just want you to be happy."

"Me too. But I think maybe I need to make a few changes to make myself happy before I go trying to make someone else happy."

As I utter those words, I realize that I have been avoiding saying them for quite some time. I'd been looking for things to make me happy for years instead of trying to get to root of the problem as to why I was *unhappy.*

Maybe it is time to start figuring that out...after more roller coasters, of course.

Chapter Forty-three
ALEXANDER

Three weeks have gone by since I ended things with Tess, and I wish I could say it was getting easier.

It's not.

But I bury myself in my work so much that I just try avoiding my feelings altogether.

I miss her. I miss her so damn bad that it hurts to breathe sometimes. Every single night, I reach for my phone and consider calling her, but every time, I put it right back down.

I even go to the hospital every evening when she's getting off and watch her walk out and catch a cab. Call me a stalker if you want, but I have to make sure she's safe. I'll never forgive myself if she gets attacked again.

Every time I see her, I yearn to take her in my arms, kiss her, and tell her that I miss her. But I don't.

You broke her heart. Why the fuck would she want you back?

A few times, I have considered asking Chris how she's doing, but I don't. I'm not sure I would want to know the answer. What if she is still in a bad place? What if she has moved on?

Which one of those answers would hurt me the most?

My time has been split between working out of my office at Club Rock, keeping tabs on all of the businesses, and remodeling

Gino's. Because of all my free time, I haven't had to hire hardly any contractors at all.

Although it's nice to save the money, I mainly do it so I have something to do in the evenings. Lord knows I will go crazy sitting in my apartment…which still has Tess's smell all over it. No matter how many times I wash my sheets, I can still smell the scent of her shampoo all around me.

Sleeping at first was hard because I would dream about her every night. But now, I relish those dreams. In those dreams, we still get to be together. In those dreams, I'm able to be exactly what she needs.

I glance at the calendar on my phone and am reminded that I am supposed to go have lunch with Nancy today. Although I know she's going to bombard me with questions of Tess, she'd be heartbroken if I cancelled.

So, I am walking into her restaurant at noon on the dot. When she sees me, she immediately tells one of the other workers to take over her spot on the grill.

She walks over and gives me a hug and pulls me down so she can kiss my cheek. "My boy! You look tired. Let's go sit down, and you can tell me all about it."

Leading me to a booth in the back, she instructs our waitress to keep the tables around us clear so we can have a little privacy. She then tells the young girl what we would like to eat. After all these years, she still knows my order by heart.

"Now, are you going to tell me what's on that big ol' mind of yours?" She asks, adding some sugar to her iced tea.

"Just busy getting ready for my new restaurant opening. I'd love for you to come if you can make it," I say, trying to deflect her from the one topic I know she is itching to discuss.

It doesn't work.

"You know I wouldn't miss it. But why don't you tell me about why you look like someone just kicked your puppy. Does it have anything to do with that girl you brought in here a few weeks back?"

"Yeah, that's over," I say solemnly.

"Oh honey, I'm sorry. Any woman not smart enough to see your worth doesn't deserve you."

"I actually broke up with her, Nance," I say.

She takes the lemon out of her drink and throws it at me.

"Hey!" I exclaim. "Why'd you do that?"

"I could be asking you the same thing, Alexander! You actually care enough to bring a woman in here, and you break up with her. You better have a damn good reason for that one."

I sigh. "I just thought we were getting too serious. She told me we could keep it casual, but I could see that we were flying full-speed *away* from casual. And if she is going to settle down with someone, it sure as shit should be someone better than me."

"Why do you say that?"

"Nancy, I'm no good. Some shit that happened in my past made it so that I just don't think I can be as good as person as she needs me to be."

"You mean when you shot your mama's boyfriend?"

Nancy asks the question, and I choke on my water. After coughing for a minute, I look at her.

"How the fuck do you know that? I never told anyone."

Aside from Tess.

"Alexander, you came here when you were still a little puppy. You don't think I saw right past your fake documents labeled Alexander Rockford? I knew that wasn't your given name. And you were going to be working in my restaurant and living in my extra apartment...I had to do my research to find out who you were."

My mind tries to wrap around the information she just gave me. She's known for all these years and never said a word. Neve treated me any differently.

"Why'd you still let me move in? I killed a man. Didn't that scare you?"

She shakes her head. "Why would it? You were trying to protect your mama. The gun went off. Accidents happen. Alexander, I'll tell you right now that if I had been in that desert when my son was killed, I would have shot the bastard that did it right between the eyes. Hell, I still might if I meet the son of a bitch. Human instinct is to protect the ones we love. Let me ask you this…would you do it all over again if you were in that same situation?"

"In a heartbeat. That's the problem. I have that anger inside me that makes me capable of those things."

She leans forward. "No, that's the love you have inside you. Do you know what makes a woman feel safe? Knowing a man would go to the ends of the Earth to protect her and hoping to God he doesn't have to."

A sudden wave of emotion hits me, and I feel tears sting my eyes. Tears that I haven't felt in years.

"Nance, I don't know that I can ever be that perfect partner to anyone. I'm just not wired like that."

Her laugh fills the air between us. "Son, I'm here to tell you there is no such thing as the perfect partner. I was married to my Stan for 30 years when he passed and let me tell you that I loved that man with every breath in my lungs. But there were days I wanted to hit him over the head with a frying pan. Love isn't all flowers and chocolates, hon. It's being there for each other when it gets hard. It's loving the other person and accepting all their faults no matter how much they might drive you insane. Did you tell her about your past?"

I nod, unable to speak, worrying the tears will finally spill over.

"Did she run away? Did she act like it scared her?"

This time, my head shakes no.

"So, she was willing to accept you just as you were? It doesn't matter what's behind you. Stop looking in the rearview mirror and keep your eyes on the damn road in front of you. Know in your heart that you are not that same kid you were back then, and you *are* worthy of love. Stop running from it, you big oof."

A single tear falls down my cheek, and I wipe it away as quickly as I can. "I think I really fucked up, Nance. I gave up a woman who I'm miserable without."

"What did I just tell you? Stop looking in the rearview mirror. It's in the past. The question is how are you going to move forward and try to fix it?"

When I leave Nancy's, I know exactly what I have to do. I have to talk to Tess. I have to tell her I was wrong. I have to ask her to forgive me one last time.

I know her schedule pretty well, so I know she's at work, and I drive straight there.

Parking my car across the street from the hospital, I wait for her to get off. I spend the next hour trying to figure out what I am going to say to her when I see her.

I figure it's best to just lay it all out on the table and hope to God she feels the same way. I feel like an idiot for wasting the last few weeks not being with her.

But what's done is done. Now, I can tell her that I don't want to ever be without her again.

The minutes tick by slowly as the pit in my stomach grows. I'm no good with emotions.

Finally, I see her make her way out the hospital doors. God, she is beautiful.

But this time, she's not alone.

Mark is with her, and she's laughing. Her head leans back as she giggles.

Pain erupts in my chest at the realization that I'm too late. She listened to me and ran right into his arms.

Despite me wanting to go over there and still make my confessions to her, I don't. Instead, I tell Barry to take me home. This will be my last time coming here. She's got someone else looking after her, and clearly, I have caused her enough heartache, and I don't think she needs anymore sadness brought on from me.

Now or ever.

Chapter Forty-four
TESS

"Mark, that is seriously the corniest joke I have ever heard," I say as he walks out to catch a cab.

"Maybe, but it got you to laugh!" Mark said with a grin.

"True," I reply.

Working with Mark the past few weeks hasn't been as bad as I thought it would. We seem to fall back into the same rhythm we had when we were working in the Congo…apart from the sex. We definitely weren't doing that.

"So, T, when are you going to let me take you to dinner?" He asks for probably about the tenth time in a week.

"I told you that…"

"I know. I know. You're not ready for a relationship. I'm just asking for dinner. Let's get to know each other again. I will act like a perfect gentleman. Scout's honor," he says while holding up his hand.

"Fine," I sigh hoping it will get him off my back.

"Tonight?"

"Bold," I say. "But I'm having dinner with my mom tonight. We can do tomorrow if you want."

"Perfect. I'll pick you up at seven," he says, opening the cab door for me.

I can't help but shake my head at him. The man is persistent. I'll give him that.

But I'm still not sure that I am ready to start dating again. Yes, I'm still trying to get over Alexander (who still plagues my thoughts constantly), but I'm also trying to make a few other moves in my life. Trying to find what would really make me happy...that isn't something tall, dark, and handsome.

I head home to quickly change before meeting my mom at the restaurant. She and I used to have dinner every week, and I feel bad that lately, I just haven't had the time.

Or I just haven't MADE the time.

"There she is!" My mom screams out when she sees me, frightening the couple sitting at the next table.

I mouth the word 'sorry' to the couple as I hug her. Maria Wendell was always a bit over the top and could be a bit much for people who don't know her.

"Well, come on, sit down!" She says.

I take a seat across from her, and we begin to catch up. She tells me that she and my father are thinking of selling their real-estate company that has made them millionaires.

"Mom, what? You love that company! You've poured everything you have into it."

"I know, honey, but your father and I have been working so hard for years that it seems like we have missed giant chunks of our lives. Look at you and Tyler...look how much of your childhood we missed. And now, we have grandbabies that we want to see grow up. Besides, selling the company would give us more time to travel without having the burden of work attached. Your dad and I can actually spend time together and *relax* for once!"

I smile listening to her talk about my dad. They met when my mom came from Columbia to New York to go to college. Starting out in a tiny crappy apartment, they got a loan to flip their first property. They spent years working their way up until they eventually had their empire. Through it all, no matter how busy they got, I never questioned their love for one another.

'Whatever makes you happy, Mom," I smile.

And I mean it. Despite her not always being present when I was a kid, she and my dad always made sure we were taken care of. They blessed us with a wonderful life. You won't hear me being a whiny, rich kid.

"Can I ask you something, Mom?"

"Anything," she said while sipping her wine.

"How did you know Dad was the one?"

Yes, it is the same question I asked Tyler. Call it my research.

She smiled and without hesitation, she said, "The butterflies."

"Huh?"

"Every time your father would do something sweet or show up at my door, I would get butterflies in my stomach. And when he kissed me, they went crazy. I still get them when he kisses me."

Good lord, my parents and my brother make me sick with how in love they are.

But maybe they were onto something. Afterall, Tyler and Sam were solid as a rock, and my parents have been together almost forty years now.

Maybe it really *is* all about the kiss.

I can tell my mom is dying to ask me questions about Alexander, but she doesn't. I figure Tyler must have called her and given her a heads-up that maybe I didn't want to dwell on the subject too much.

Thank goodness. My mind was already racing with thoughts of my Ace. He was on a constant loop that played in my brain. I didn't need yet another reason to think about him.

And how his skin felt against mine.

How his lips tasted.

How his eyes locked with mine as he thrust in and out of me.

Good lord, knock it off.

I try to force the thoughts out of my head as my mom and I catch up. But as she talks about every aspect of her life, my mind slowly daydreams back to Mr. Tall, Dark, and Handsome.

Chapter Forty-five
ALEXANDER

When I first saw Tess with Mark, all I felt was sorrow. I just wanted her in my arms again. I wanted to touch her, feel her against me.

But that sorrow quickly turned to rage at the thought of Mark getting to do those things with her. He would get to see her beautiful hair fanned around her as she lay beneath him. He would get to feel her moan against his kiss. He would get to hear her scream as she came.

If she came.

I'm sorry, but I refuse to believe that another man could read Tess's body the way that I could.

I force my cock to calm down in my pants because I'm heading to Club Rock. I need alcohol, and it's far closer than my apartment.

When I arrive, the club is busier than usual for this time of evening, but I'm not complaining. More money in my pocket.

Immediately, I walk to the bar and notice Chris isn't working. Sheila is the one pouring drinks tonight.

"Hey, boss!" She smiles.

"Hi Sheila. No Chris tonight?"

"No, he's off. You're stuck with me," she winks. Most would

assume she's hitting on me, but I know for a fact that Sheila is dating the bouncer, Vince. They try to keep it under wraps, but both of them came to tell me about it when it first started to make sure they weren't breaking any type of rules.

Some bosses might care, but I don't. Both of them are the height of professionalism while they're on the clock, and that's all that matters to me.

"What are you drinking, Boss Man?" Sheila asks.

"Vodka on the rocks," I reply.

"Coming right up!"

A few seconds later, she places the glass in front of me, and I chug it down before she can even put the bottle away.

She refills the glass without being asked. "Bad day?"

"You have no idea. Keep them coming."

She sets the bottle on the bar in front of me, so I don't have to keep asking.

Four drinks in, and I'm still not feeling any better. I feel like such a dumbass. Tess was mine, and I let her go just for her fall into someone else's arms. The someone that I told her she should be with! How fucking stupid is that?

Turning my body around on the barstool, I look at all the people occupying the club. Everyone seems to be having a good time. Or maybe I just think that because I'm having such a shitty time.

A petite blonde appears on the stool next to mine. She orders a dry martini and makes a bit of small talk with Sheila... although I have no idea what they are talking about, nor do I really care.

The blonde slips off the jacket she is wearing, revealing a low-cut halter top that shows off her enormous tits. I guess they are probably fake with how small the rest of her is, but who cares? Tits are tits.

As to not seem like I'm leering at them, I turn my attention back to the people on the dance floor.

"Tracy." I think it's the woman next to me who has spoken, but when I look over at her, her eyes are staring down into her drink.

"I beg your pardon?"

"I got tired of waiting on you to ask me for my name, so I figured I'd just give it to you." She finally looks at me and smiles.

I can't help but crack a smile in return. "Alexander."

"It's nice to meet you, Alexander."

We make small talk for a few minutes, and I'm careful not to give away too many details. This woman doesn't need to know anything personal about me. My name is more than enough.

Finally, she looks at me and says, "Look Alexander, I've had a pretty shitty day, and I'm guessing from the bottle sitting in front of you, you have too. So, why don't we go somewhere quiet and forget about it?"

My heart is screaming at me to say no. The only woman I want wrapped around my cock is Tess. But the thought of her wrapped around Mark's cock is enough to have me grabbing Tracy's hand and leading her off the barstool.

Without a word, I lead her upstairs to my office, shutting and locking the door behind us. She notices me flick the lock and a twinge of uncertainty settles over her.

"The lock is to keep people out. You're free to go any time you wish," I say.

Seeming to relax, she pulls her shirt over her head and begins to walk toward me.

"Let's just have fun for the night," she says. "I'll do *anything* you want."

I can't help but remember the first time Tess was up here and how badly I wanted her yet still somehow refused. I wish so badly it was Tess standing in front of me now.

But it's not.

And at this point, I'll do anything to forget her.

"Get on your knees."

Chapter Forty-six
TESS

I sit across the table from Mark trying to figure out what I'm going to order. I finally decide on the salmon figuring it would be good to eat something somewhat healthy since the past few weeks, I've been on a non-stop junk food binge.

"So, how's life been the past few years, T?" He asks with a smile.

Mark's smile used to make me weak the knees. A smile from him made me swoon back in the day. Don't get me wrong, he still has a gorgeous smile, but it doesn't have quite the same effect on me that it used to. Only one man had been able to make me swoon as of late.

"Life has been fine," I answer. "Just fine."

"You've never been much of a just fine kind of girl though."

"Maybe, you're right. But right now, I'm trying to figure out what it is that will actually make me happy."

He leans back in his chair. "Any idea what that may be?"

"I'm working on it."

"Does it happen to be tall, dark, and handsome?" He asks, clearly referring to Alexander.

"Mark, this isn't about him. This is about me finding out what's missing in *my* life...besides a man. Something has been missing since long before I met Alexander. I just want to enjoy life every single day."

"Did you enjoy it when we were doing Doctors Without Borders?" He asks.

I nod. "Yes, but I was also in a whole other place in my life. I would say that I am ready to really put down roots. And I guess I have put down some the past few years, but I'm ready to put down roots that make me happy. Living that life with you was great and exhilarating, but it couldn't last forever. Not for me anyways."

"Mark, be honest. Why'd you come back?"

He sighs. "I guess I feel a little bit like you. Like maybe something is missing. I've felt like that ever since you left. Putting two and two together makes me think that maybe you have something to do with that. And like you said, it's hard to put down roots in the middle of the jungle. I'm ready for the whole picture…wife and kids and all that."

I twinge when he says the word 'kids'. I consider telling him that I have no interest in having any, but I decide that's a conversation for another time. After all, we are just supposed to be having an innocent dinner as friends.

We talk about work for awhile and laugh over different antics going on around the hospital. We catch each other up on our families, and I tell him all about Lilah and Abby.

In a word, it's fun. I'd forgotten how being around Mark was just so easy. We were so similar and had a lot of overlapping interests, so fighting was never an issue for us. Hell, I can't even pinpoint a single fight we ever had.

Alexander, on the other hand, was capable of pushing every button I had, and I know he felt the same way about me.

Trying my best to push him from my mind, I truly enjoy my time with Mark. It really is great to see him again. After all these years, it's like some things haven't changed at all.

And on the other hand, it feels like everything has.

When we finish our meal, he takes me back to my apartment. I invite him to come upstairs for a drink but assure him that I'm not inviting him to bed.

He smiles and agrees to just the drink.

Always the gentleman.

Once we are in my apartment, there is a comfortable silence between us, but I can't shake this nagging feeling I have inside me.

I walk over to him. "Okay, I am going to do something just to see what happens."

"Okay?" He replies.

Pulling him in, I wrap my arms around his neck and press my lips to his. Automatically, he realizes what I'm doing and follows suit. His arms wrap around my waist as his tongue delves into my mouth.

We stay in that moment, kissing each other like our lives depend on it. Finally, we break apart.

"Hmm." I mutter. "Was it just me, or did you feel…"

"Absolutely nothing?" He asks.

"Oh, thank God it wasn't just me," I say, my hand covering my chest.

"Nope. Not just you." He shoves his hands in his pockets looking a little disheartened.

"Well, guess that solves that mystery."

"Guess so. I just don't get it. We were so great back then," he says.

"We were so different back then, Mark. We were young and in the middle of a war zone with our adrenaline pumping like crazy. Maybe too much time has passed, or maybe we are just too different now. Whatever it is, we always have those memories."

"Yeah, I guess you're right. Hey, you mind if I take a raincheck on that drink?" He asks.

"Not at all. I'll see you at work?"

He nods and gives me a quick hug before heading out the door.

As great of a guy as Mark is, that kiss told me we will never be anything more than friends.

No butterflies.

In fact, there was no heat or passion at all. It was just a kiss without any feelings behind it.

What I wouldn't give to have one more kiss with Alexander. Maybe enough time has passed that the heat between us would have died too. If there is nothing there, maybe I can get my closure and move on.

If only we could have one more kiss...

Chapter Forty-seven
ALEXANDER

The night is finally here. The opening of Gino's. The place looks amazing, if I do say so myself. Of course, I might be a little bias.

The last week, I have spent every spare moment putting the finishing touches on this place. Despite originally doing it so that I could keep my mind free of Tess, it actually paid off in a really great way.

That night at Club Rock, I couldn't go through with anything with Tracy. The moment she got on her knees and looked up at me, I knew I couldn't do it. I'm sure once I get my head out of the Tess fog, I will kick myself for that decision. But I just didn't feel right going any further with her while my mind was on someone else.

Would you look at that? Maybe I'm starting to gain a soul after all.

I make my way over to Nancy who is grazing over all of the appetizers I have set up. After all the marketing I did for this place, I knew we would have a huge turnout, and it wasn't equipped to handle that many sit down diners at once. Instead, I opted for smaller portions of some of the restaurants most popular dishes.

Nancy spots me and comes over to give me a hug. "You did good, kid. Again."

"Thanks, Nance. And thank you for all that you have done for me over the years. I wouldn't be here without you."

She waves her hand as if brushing me off. "You would have still found a way. But you're welcome all the same. How did things go with that other matter we talked about?" She asks, referring to Tess.

I simply shake my head.

"I'm sorry, dear. Things will get better."

I change the subject and show her around the place. It's crazy that ten years ago, she was showing me around her restaurant for the first time, and now, I'm showing her one of mine.

After Nancy says her goodbyes, I continue to make my way around the room, mingling with people. Chet arrives a few minutes later and makes his way straight to the food.

"Looking good, Boss," he says, and I know he's slightly irritated with how much of an asshole I've been lately.

"Okay, Chet. Gino's is open, and I'm ready to hear about this wonderful business proposition you have for me."

"Really?" His eyes widen.

"Really. Be at the office at Club Rock tomorrow at 10 AM and you can lay it all out for me."

His smile widens. "Great! You won't be sorry!"

We'll see.

The son of a bitch is lucky I'm in such a good mood.

The rest of the night goes swimmingly. Food bloggers and journalists come and try all of the offerings. Some of my other restaurant owners even stop by to show their support.

When things finally begin to wind down, everyone slowly begins to shuffle out, and I begin to clean up. The wait and kitchen staff come over to help.

"Go home, guys. I will take care of what I can and anything else can wait until tomorrow. Thanks for all your wonderful work tonight."

They all thank me and grab their stuff to head home. Once

they are out the door, I turn to head toward the kitchen, but I hear the door chime once more.

"Someone forget something?" I ask while turning around.

Tess Wendell stands in front of me. "Are you still open? I'm sorry I'm late."

"You came…" is all I manage to get out.

"I made you a promise I would be here. I wasn't about to break that," she smiles.

"Are you hungry?" I ask.

She shakes her head.

"How are you?" Good lord, I sound like an idiot. I can barely put together a coherent thought.

"I'm okay. Been busy trying to get some things in order."

Without thinking if I want to really know the answer, I ask, "How's Mark?"

She shrugs. "He's fine, I guess. But Mark and I are just friends. There's nothing there."

A wave of relief comes crashing over me. You would think someone just told me I won the lottery.

"It's really good seeing you," I say.

"It's good to see you, too." She walks toward me. "I just have to do something."

Leaning up, she presses her lips to mine. What starts as soft, soon grows needy. I run my fingers through her hair, pulling her as close as possible while I taste her addicting kiss.

When she pulls away, our breaths are both ragged. She looks up at me with tears beginning to streak her cheeks.

Her eyes gaze into mine, and I wonder what she's thinking.

"Damnit," she says quietly.

"What?" I ask.

"I felt the damn butterflies when I kissed you. I felt everything."

"What's wrong with that?"

Her lip quivers as she answers. "Because it means that I'm still in love with you."

Chapter Forty-eight

TESS

I turn around to leave, unable to look at Alexander a moment longer as my heart breaks more and more with every second that passes.

I'm almost to the door when Alexander steps in front of it.

"Wait," he says.

"Why? There's nothing more to say. You clearly don't want me. Or you do want me, and you don't want more than casual, but I've got news for you, buddy, this has gone way past casual for me. I can't just be your fuck buddy anymore. I want more, and I'm not trying to give you an ultimatum, so I am just making this very easy on both of us and walking away…"

My rambling comes to a screeching halt when he takes my face in his and kisses me once more. This time, his tongue takes its time exploring my mouth, and I open for him without so much as a second thought. I let myself get lost for a moment before realizing what was happening and pull away.

"What are you doing?" I ask, wondering if he gets some twisted pleasure out of making this harder for me.

His blue eyes lock onto mine, and without missing a beat, he says, "I'm kissing the woman I'm in love with."

"What?" My mouth practically falls open.

Gently, he takes my hands in his. "I'm so sorry I couldn't say it before. No, I'm sorry I couldn't *show* it before. Not having you around has made me realize how important you are to me, and I'll do anything to make it right. I've wasted so much time pushing you away when we could have been moving toward our future.

"Tess, I have always been okay with being a loner. I've never needed anyone, nor wanted anyone. Turns out I was just waiting for the right woman to come along and change my mind. I'm so sorry I was such an idiot and didn't see it before. I just worried that I wouldn't be worthy of a woman as amazing as you. Hell, I was ready to let you go be with Mark when I saw you at the hospital together just to make sure you were happy."

I interrupt him. "Wait, you saw Mark and I together at the hospital? When?"

"About a week ago. When I finally pulled my head out of my ass and realized I'd made a huge mistake, I went to the hospital to talk to you. I waited out front when you got off, and then I saw you two together. You were laughing, and you looked happy."

Of course, he managed to see me the one time in the past month that I had actually looked like I was having a good time.

I rub my thumb along his cheek, which now has the stubble on it that I had mentioned I loved. "Like I told you, there's nothing with Mark. Not anymore. The second you walked into my life, the door shut on anyone else being able to get to my heart."

The smile that spreads across his face is the largest one I've ever seen on him. "Be my girl?" He asks.

"You know, I am still going to drive you crazy. I'm not going to stop being independent and a pain in your ass."

He laughs. "I never thought differently. And I wouldn't want it any other way. And for the record, I'm not going to stop being protective and bossy."

"I know," I smile. "I'll just have you put you in your place."

"Guess so," he says, but before he can get the words out, I

kiss him once more.

It starts sweet, but it doesn't take long for it to turn into something carnal. We *need* each other. All of each other. I run one hand through his hair and wrap the other around his neck pulling him as close as possible.

He holds the nape of my neck with one hand while his other palms my ass. Every touch he is giving sends heat directly between my legs, and I'm practically panting like a dog.

He stops our kiss and looks at me. "Sweetheart, as much as I love this place, this is not where I want to lay you down tonight. I need somewhere that I can take my time with you. Do you want to go to your place?"

"Your place is closer," I say with a sigh.

"You're right. Let's go."

He calls Barry to pull the car around, and we are out the door. We make out the whole way to his place, and we don't even wait for the elevator doors to close before we are at it again. He has me pinned against the wall, kissing me once more. His rock hard body pressed against mine reminds me of just how strong he is. I'll never get tired of feeling his muscular form against mine.

When we finally get into his apartment, he wastes no time in picking me up and carrying me straight to the bedroom. He lays me on the bed, and I watch as he stands and undresses. His body is perfection, and I can't wait to have it on top of me again.

His knees sink into the foot of the mattress as he begins to pull my clothes from my body. Every move he makes is teasingly slow, and my body practically quivers with anticipation.

"God, I've missed you, sweetheart," he says while his eyes rake up and down my now naked body.

'Show me how much," I whisper.

Granting my wish, he trails kisses along every inch of my body while his fingers lightly caress every sensitive spot. I about jump off the bed when I feel his warm breath on my pussy. He flattens his tongue and licks up and down the length of my slit as I writhe beneath him.

"I'd forgotten how sweet this pussy tastes," he says against the hyper-sensitive flesh.

As if settling in for his last meal, he gets comfortable between my legs and takes his time getting me off. Every time he quickens the pace, and I get close, he slows down the pace again, and draws out every single drop of ecstasy.

My legs begin to shake, and he knows I won't last much longer no matter what his tempo is. He sits up and says, "Although I love going down on you, I want to be inside you when you come."

With one long thrust, he sheathes himself inside me, and I cry out in pleasure. I have missed this feeling of him inside me, and I know, now that I am getting another taste, no one else will ever compare.

It will only ever be Alexander.

He leans down and gently tugs my bottom lip between his teeth before his mouth shifts its focus to my nipples. One hand goes between us as the pad of his thumb circles my clit, and I'm done. My nails dig into his shoulders, and my legs wrap around his hips so hard that I feel like I'm going to leave marks. As my body quakes around him, I hold him as tightly as possible, not wanting the moment to ever end.

When my body finally loosens, his lips find mine once more as he slows his pace. Leaning back, he looks at me. "I love you," he says, and the look in his eyes confirms his words.

"I love you too," I moan.

We spend the rest of the night wrapped in each other's arms. Whether it's making love or just lying with each other. The familiar scent of him makes me feel entirely at home…like I am finally at peace.

I came to Gino's tonight looking for some type of closure, but instead, I got exactly what I have been hoping for all along. I got Alexander. I got him to finally see that he is worth loving, and that maybe us two crazy kids belong together in this big old world.

Maybe the two half of our souls finally found the missing

pieces they've been searching for.

Chapter Forty-nine
ALEXANDER

My eyes open to Tess lying next to me. I blink a few times just to make sure it isn't the dream I have had so many times over the past month. But as I trail my fingers along her silky skin. I made sure to kiss every square inch of that skin all night long.

"Morning, Ace," she grumbles and begins to open her eyes. Her hand reaches up to rub my chin. "Did you grow this out for me? Because I said I liked it?"

"No. My other girlfriend said she liked it," I joke, and she playfully slaps the same spot she was just rubbing.

"Don't test me, Ace," she quips.

"Or what?" I ask, pinning her beneath me and kissing her neck.

My length presses into her stomach and she moans. "As much as I would love to do that again right now, I'm going to need some food. You wore me out last night."

"I didn't hear you complaining," I whisper against her neck.

"Oh, I would never complain about that. But I do need some food, or I will die of starvation."

Sighing overdramatically, I say, "Okay, let's get you some

food. But you're going to have to watch me cook with a hard-on because it's not going away any time soon."

A wicked smile crosses her face. "Get some food in me, and I'll let you do whatever you want with that thing."

"Not helping matters," I say, glancing down at my steel cock.

We get out of bed and I fix french toast, which she eats more of than I do. Her appetite will never cease to amaze me.

When she is filling her mouth with the last couple bites, she says, "So, can we just stay in bed and have sex all day?"

"That sounds amazing, but…oh shit, I have to go Club Rock and meet Chet for a meeting. I've been promising to hear him out for weeks now on this new business venture he wants me to invest in, and I've been blowing him off. I'd feel awful canceling on him again. Oh well, he'll just have to deal with it."

"No, you should go. Don't cancel on my account. You made a commitment, and I'm sure you won't be gone long. I can be naked and waiting when you get back," she grins.

"As wonderful as that sounds, why don't you come with me?" I ask.

"Really?"

"Of course. I just got you back, and there's no way I want to let you go for even a moment today."

The excitement is palpable from her grin. "Okay, that sounds nice, but first, we have to take care of your little problem." She walks toward me and puts her hand on the bulge in the front of my sweat pants.

"Let's," I reply. "Chet doesn't need to see this."

Without another word, I fuck her right there on my kitchen table.

An hour later, we are walking into Club Rock. I hold Tess's hand while we walk, and her fingers intertwined with mine feels like the most natural thing on Earth. Despite us being apart for weeks, we are back together and closer than ever.

"Where's Lars?" She asks.

"Lars?"

"Big guy who sits here who looks like he should be in the CIA."

"Vince?"

She rolls her eyes. "Yeah, him. I like Lars better."

"Lars does have a nice ring to it. He is probably upstairs. He coordinates security for some of my properties, so he has his own office up there. Believe it or not, he isn't just a bouncer."

"Hmm," is all she says.

"So, what do you want to do tonight, gorgeous?" I ask as we begin to climb the stairs to my office.

"Sex. More sex. Followed by some sex. And dinner. But let's get it to-go so we can get back to my first few suggestions."

I lean in and whisper, "Behave or I'm going to have to bend you over my desk."

"How many times do I have to tell you, Ace? Don't threaten me with a good time."

A chuckle rumbles in my chest.

As I open the door, she says, "Remind me later, I have a surprise for you."

My eyebrow raises. "Oh, really?"

"Really," she giggles.

Chet has his back to us but immediately turns when he hears Tess laugh. Immediately, the air in the room shifts as Tess stops in her tracks.

"Tess? Sweetheart?" I say, but she doesn't look at me. Her feet are planted as though they are stuck in cement, and her eyes are locked forward.

"Tess!" This time, I say it louder. "What the hell is wrong?"

"Him," she whispers. "That's the guy who attacked me outside the hospital."

Ice runs cold in my veins, and I figure she has to be mistaken...until I see the look on Chet's face. The look that said he'd just been caught.

"I really wish you hadn't brought her here, Alexander," he says. Without warning, he reaches behind his back and pulls out a gun from his waistband.

"Chet, what the fuck?!" I scream.

"Do you know how hard it is to work for a prick who doesn't take anything you say seriously? Do you know how hard it is to get you to stop acting like an infant long enough to listen to me? I say something, and you do the exact opposite. And then, finally, I have you beginning to listen, and then, this walks through the door." He waves the gun in the direction of Tess.

He continues. "She walks in, and you focus even less than before. Her pussy must be damn good for you to put everything we have worked so hard for on hold."

"Watch it," I snap.

"No, Rockford, *you* watch it. Who's the one with the gun? I thought that if I got your little girlfriend out of the way, you would finally start taking business seriously again. No one told me she was trained in some self-defense bullshit they probably teach in Feminism 101."

I try to stifle my laugh at the fact my girl beat this little piece of shit up.

"I thought you were done with this whore, yet here she is. Let me break it down for you. You're so busy being such an idiot that you didn't even realize I put myself as your beneficiary in most of your holdings. I'm done being under your thumb. I'm going to finish this now and sneak out the back. When I show up for our meeting, *oh no, something awful has happened!* And I take control of everything.

"And just for shits and giggles, I'm going to shoot you first and shove my gun in your girl's mouth while I fuck her before I kill her."

My blood is pumping so loudly in my ears that I can barely hear a word Chet is saying anymore. All I can focus on is trying to find a way out of this. There is a gun in the bottom drawer of my desk, but I am nowhere near it. He will instantly sense if I'm going for it.

I can try just tackling him, but I know he will put up a fight, and I know exactly how that will end.

"Any last words, prick?" Chet asks.

He cocks the gun, and I brace for impact. If he hits anywhere aside my head or heart, maybe I will have enough strength to knock him over. I begin to move my body toward him, but before I can get very far, Tess uses the entire weight of her body to knock me just off balance enough to move out of the way.

I hear the loud roar of the gun, and I watch the bullet connect with Tess.

As if in slow motion, she looks at me before her eyes close, and she falls to the ground. As if my body has a mind of its own now, I lunge at Chet. His gun goes off again, but somehow, he completely misses me.

My fist connects with his face so hard he falls backward into the bookshelf, and I use the opportunity to pry the gun from his hand.

Vince must have heard the commotion because he comes flying through the door. "Boss!" He screams when he sees me.

"Call 911! Police and ambulance," I say, crawling over to Tess. There's blood everywhere, and it's hard to see where all of it's coming from.

"Tess! Baby!" I scream as my eyes begin to fill with tears. "Tess, I need you to listen to me. I need you to be okay. I need you to pull through this. We just found our way back to each other, and I can't lose you. This thing we've got going on deserves a real chance."

She doesn't answer me, and she's slipping in and out of consciousness. "Oh, sweetheart. Why did you do that? Why did you get in the way? You stubborn, crazy, fearless woman."

I pull her close to me, uncaring that blood is now soaking my clothing.

As we wait for the cops, I find myself calling out to whatever higher power will listen to me. I rock back and forth silently muttering, "Please be okay. Please be okay."

Please God...let her be okay.

Chapter Fifty
TESS

"Ouuuuch," I groan as my eyes begin to flutter open.

"Sweetheart?"

Alexander.

I feel his thumb stroking the back of my hand, and I keep trying to open my eyes.

When I finally let the bright light in, it burns. Blinking a few times, I slowly begin to adjust.

I turn my head toward where I know he sits, so that he is the first thing I see when I finally open my eyes.

His worried face looks back at me. "Tess? Are you with me?"

"Hi," I whisper.

"Thank fucking God," he says, letting out a deep breath.

My eyes leave his and go to where my pain is radiating from. My shoulder is bandaged all to hell, and I can't see any of what's underneath.

"They had to do surgery to go in and get the bullet. Said if it was a couple inches over, it would have hit your heart."

"Guess I got lucky," I force a small smile. "Still hurts like a bitch though."

When I look back at him, his face is stern. "Tess, what the

fuck were you thinking? You should have never jumped in front of that bullet."

"You're welcome," I reply sarcastically.

"Tess, I'm serious. I know that you are scared of literally nothing, but I can't lose you."

Averting my eyes from his, I look down at my hands. "I might be scared of almost nothing, but the one thing that scared me was knowing that bullet was heading for you. The thought of the world not having Alexander Rockford scared the shit out of me. I couldn't let that happen."

When I look back at him, tears are falling down his cheeks. "How about we both just try really hard not to be in this position again because neither one of us are going to take a chance on losing the other."

"You mean you don't think we will anger another maniac at gunpoint any time soon?" I ask.

He chuckles. "Well, I don't have any plans on it, and if you do, I'll bend you over my knee and spank that little ass of yours."

"Sounds fun," I say with a weak smile. Looking around the room, I notice that every surface is covered in bouquets of flowers. And in the extra chair sits a giant teddy bear that is probably as big as I am.

"Alexander, it looks like the gift shop threw up in here. Did you do all this?"

"No...Tyler sent some."

"Which ones did Tyler send?"

He points to one tiny arrangement among all the larger ones. My eyes roll. "Ace, you didn't have to do all this."

He shrugs. "I wanted you to wake up to something beautiful. When I was trying to pick one out, I couldn't decide which was the prettiest, so I bought them all."

I smile. "I love them, but really, it was unnecessary. I got to wake up looking at you, and you're way better looking than any flower," I wink.

"Well, I've never bought flowers for a woman before. Figured I had some lost time to make up for."

I begin to giggle but wince in pain instead.

"Do you need some pain medicine?" He asks.

I shake my head. "I'm fine. Just tell me when I get to go home."

"Tomorrow probably as long as everything looks okay. When they discharge you, we can go back to my place to stay indefinitely."

My head snaps to him. "I'm sorry. Did you just ask me to move in with you by commanding me? I like my apartment, Ace."

He shrugs. "Okay, fine, we will live at your apartment although you have to admit mine has more space. But us staying together is non-negotiable. I want you by my side every night from now on. I don't care where that is."

Leaning forward, he plants a tender kiss on my lips. The magnitude of everything the past couple days has brought suddenly begins to catch up with me, and my eyes grow heavy.

"I love you, Ace," I whisper.

"I love you too, Tess."

"And Ace? I think I'm ready for that pain medicine now."

Chapter Fifty-one
ALEXANDER

The next day after Tess is released from the hospital, we end up back at my apartment. Getting her to agree to mine instead of hers wasn't an easy feat, but when I reminded her about my oversized bathtub, she caved.

Damn, she's stubborn. But I wouldn't have her any other way.

I enlist Chris to go pick up some essentials for Tess to make her as comfortable as possible. He stops by her apartment and grabs some of her favorite clothes and toiletries and then hits the grocery store to get some snacks that she loves.

Everything is waiting when we get home, and there's a note from Chris sitting on the counter.

Hope you get feeling better, Baby Girl! Dinner and drinks when you feel up to it. Love you!

She smiles as she reads it, and I remind myself to give Chris a raise for being such a good friend to her.

Not comfortable with soaking in bath water just yet, Tess asks me to help her take a shower just to get the funk of the hospital off of her. I oblige, and I take my time cleaning every inch of her and washing her hair.

As much as I am usually turned on by my sexy woman, I

know me pawing at her is the last thing she needs right now, so I keep my libido in check.

Once I have her out of the shower, dried off, and in her favorite pajamas, I lead her back to the living room. After she is settled comfortably on the couch, I hand her the remote, but she just sets it down beside her.

"Thanks for taking such good care of me," she says with a smile.

"No thank you necessary. You better get used to being taken care of because it's not going anywhere anytime soon."

She rolls her eyes. "I don't mind being taken care of, but I need you not to be crazy overbearing."

Laying my hand on top of hers, I say, "How about I stop being so overbearing when you stop being so stubborn."

"Looks like we are at a crossroads, Ace," she says.

"Looks that way."

She sighs. "Guess we should just call it quits now."

I lean forward and kiss her. "Too late, sweetheart. You're stuck with me now."

She smiles. "Promise?"

"Swear. But I do have a question."

She raises her eyebrows waiting for me to ask.

"Well, when I called the hospital to tell them you weren't going to be coming in for a while, they informed me you are no longer an employee there."

My jaw about hit the floor when I had made that phone call. They said she had quit about a week ago but wouldn't give me any more details than that.

Her hands travel to her hands again. "Remember that surprise I told you about the other day?"

I nod.

"That was it. I quit my job. No more working at the hospital in the unsafe part of town," she says with a soft smile.

"As relieved as I am to hear you say that, I don't want you doing this for me. If you really want to keep your job, I will find a way to deal with it." I just got her back, and I don't want her to re-sent me for anything.

Her head shakes back and forth. "No, it's not you. The past month, I have really been trying to examine my life, and I realized I just wasn't happy. The reason I liked working in Doctors Without Borders so much was that it had one simple concept: save lives. It didn't matter who had the best insurance or who could pay the most money. There was no bureaucratic bullshit to navigate through. I miss that part of being a doctor. So, I have decided to open up my own low-cost clinic to try to see all those people that the hospital doesn't really care about."

That's my girl. Always with the big heart.

"I think that is amazing, sweetheart. Now, don't get mad when I ask you this, but do you have the money you need to get things started?"

She nods. "Being a doctor has always paid well, so I have most of my trust fund left which I have always invested wisely. Plus, my parents are selling their company, and my mom told me that all of us kids will get a share since we are technically part share-holders. And even though I should be set for a while, I will still try to get some grants to keep things running smoothly. Maybe someone who is pretty savvy in business could help me navigate the waters a bit," she winks at me.

"I will do absolutely anything I can to help. And if you ever need another investor, count me in."

She gives me a big grin. "I'm very excited about it. So, in a few days when I am feeling a bit better, I'll move forward with everything."

"But for now, you rest," I command.

"Okay, Dad," she scoffs.

We spend the rest of our night talking and laughing. Even injured, she lights up an entire room. I can't believe I lived without her for a whole year. She's like my fucking oxygen, and I can finally breathe again.

"Marry me," I blurt out in the middle of our laugh fest.

Her laughter immediately stops. "What?"

"Marry me," I repeat.

"Are you being serious?"

"Of course. I told you that I was stupid for not wanting any kind of commitment, and now, I don't want to ever be without you."

She pauses for a moment to really think about what I said. "Ace, I love you, and I don't want to be without you either. As much as I want to one day marry you, I am not saying yes right now."

"Why not now?"

"Because we just went through the wonderful experience of getting back together as well as the traumatic experience of me getting shot. I don't think that we need to make any life-altering decisions right now. Let's wait until the dust settles."

I know she's right, but it doesn't make it sting any less. I must admit it was a bit impulsive though. Hell, I don't even have a ring to slide on her finger.

"Believe me, I am going to ask again," I say, pointing my finger at her.

She smiles. "I will be anxiously waiting. But I think I need to tell you something first."

My stomach drops.

"Just so you know what you are fully getting into. I know I have told you this before, but I don't think I ever want kids. It's not that I don't like kids, but I feel like it's never been on my list of things I want to accomplish. I am more than okay being the cool aunt. I know this can be a deal-breaker, so I just wanted to let you know before we go any further."

I take her hand in mine. "Sweetheart, I've always felt the same way. I've never really pictured myself as a dad. As long as I have you by my side, that's all I need."

"You're the sweetest. Do you know that?"

"Don't tell anyone. I have a reputation to uphold," I smile.

"It'll be our little secret."

Chapter Fifty-two
TESS

"Oh God! Alexander!" I cry out as I find my release. Alexander isn't far behind me. His face contorts as he spills into me.

"Wow," I whisper once he's finished.

"No joke," he agrees.

"Perfect way to start my birthday. Countless orgasms with my man," I giggle.

"Well, come on, sweetheart. We have to hurry up and get ready. I have a big day planned and didn't think we would be in bed so long." With a quick slap to my ass, he gets up and heads for the shower.

It has been over month since the whole Chet incident. My shoulder has healed nicely, and I'm pretty much back to normal. We've gotten started on plans for the new clinic, and I am enjoying every minute of it. I am thrilled to have this place be *mine* and not having to answer to anyone.

Today is my birthday, and although I have no idea what Alexander has planned, I know it will be good. Hell, he already topped my wildest expectations with the amazing orgasms he just gave me.

But I know that's just the tip of the iceberg with him.

Once we are showered and dressed, we are on the road. When I see the direction we are heading, I have a pretty good idea of where we are going.

"Hey Ace, are we going to ride some roller coasters today?" I ask.

"Maybe. Can't you just be patient and find out?" He teases.

He should already know the answer to that is no. But I try to behave and wait until we get there.

When we finally pull into the parking lot, I am practically buzzing with excitement. When we get to the entrance, I get even more giddy when I see Tyler and Sam, Chris, and my parents.

"Happy Birthday!" They all yell in unison.

"You guys!" I cry.

After a quick round of hugs, we all head inside. The second I hit the front gates, I'm in heaven. This place will always be my home away from home. I love everything about it.

"Lead the way, sweetheart," Alexander says.

Happy to oblige, I begin making my way to my favorite. I don't know why I always pick the biggest, baddest rollercoaster to start with. You'd think I would work my way up to it, but I love that strong shot of adrenaline first thing in the day.

"You don't have to ride if you don't want to," I say to Alexander as we stand in line.

"I wouldn't miss this for the world, beautiful."

I wish there were words for how much this man has worked his way into my heart. The man who seemed so cold and distant to start has a heart of gold that can't be matched.

I sold my apartment, and we moved into his. For now. We both agree that we should find another apartment of both of our choosing. But finding a place in New York City that we both love is proving to be difficult.

The one thing we do agree on is we prefer the city over the suburbs. No white picket fences for us.

Chet went to jail…not only for the shooting but also for all the fraud he committed within Alexander's company. He's going to rot in there for a very long time.

Finally, the ride attendant tells us it's our turn to step onto the coaster. We get all buckled in, and I smile at Alexander who looks surprisingly calm.

Maybe he's finally getting over his fear of heights?

As we begin to slowly travel up the first hill, Alexander starts to talk loudly enough so I can hear him over the metal chain being pulled beneath us.

"Tess, you know I love you, right?"

"Of course!"

"And you know I want to spend the rest of my life with you. So, will you make me the happiest man in the world and marry me?"

My eyes grow as wide as saucers, and when I glance over at him, he's holding he most beautiful diamond ring I've ever seen.

I sit mute for a moment in complete and utter shock.

"Sweetheart, I need your answer because we are getting closer to the top of this hill, and there's a strong possibility I'm going to get scared and lose this ring."

"Yes!" I say, blinking back tears. I hold out my hand for him to slip it on my finger.

My family cheers from the seats behind us, clearly knowing about his master plan.

I give him a quick kiss as we reach the top of the hill, and the excitement builds in my stomach. Being with Alexander is a lot like this rollercoaster.

A little scary yet totally exciting. But no matter what happens, I know it's going to be one hell of a ride.

Epilogue

"Are you nervous, big guy?" The tiny voice beside me asks.

I look down into the eyes of Abby and Lilah who are wearing the cutest little dresses to be our flower girls.

"A little. Do I look okay?" I ask.

I kneel in front of them, and they spend a moment looking me over to make sure I'm presentable.

"Perfect," Abby finally replies.

"Whew!" I say with a mock wave of relief. "Does Aunt Tess look good too?"

They both smile and nod. "Like a princess!" Lilah says.

It has been close to a year and half since I asked Tess to marry me. Although both of us were anxious to get our lives together started, we were busy trying to get her clinic up and running, so we didn't rush.

Since then, we have found an apartment that we both love and has plenty of space. That space comes in handy when Lilah and Abby come to stay the night. We seem to be taking them more and more now because Tyler and Sam had a son, Jonathan, a few months back, so we help out as much as we can.

Since we don't plan on having any kids, we will always be

the best aunt and uncle in the whole world. At least, that's what the girls call us.

Tyler pokes his head in, "It's time. Come on girls, you need to go with Mommy."

I walk to the front of the small chapel and wait. Tyler stands next to me and watches his wife push their son in the stroller while escorting the two girls who are throwing flower petals everywhere.

When the music starts, my heart thumps in my chest.

This is it.

When I see Tess, my mouth drops. She's wearing a sleek white dress that shows off her amazing figure and sparkles in the light. Her hair is down and in loose curls hanging down her shoulders and her back.

And those brown eyes of hers meet mine, and I melt. How the fuck did I get a woman as perfect as her?

When she reaches me, she lets go of her father's hand and grabs onto mine. We face each other, and the preacher begins.

When it comes time for the vows, he pauses, letting us each exchange what we have written for each other.

I go first. Smiling, I say, "Tess, from the moment, I met you, you have been absolutely fearless. I, on the other hand, seem to be scared of a lot of things. But nothing has ever scared me more than realizing I might have lost you. Somehow, when you're around, you make all my fears seem small and inconsequential. Even when we are about to fly down a terrifying rollercoaster, or when we are about to jump off a cliff just to get closer to a waterfall, I know that my fears aren't nearly as big or as powerful as the love that you and I share. And I promise to always put our love first and remind you of how amazing you are every day for the rest of our lives."

Tears are glinting in her eyes at my words, and I know I am not far behind.

She clears her throat as she begins to speak. "Alexander, you once asked me why I call you Ace. And back then, I told you it was because in Blackjack, an Ace can make or break you. Back then, I told you I hadn't decided on where you landed yet. But over time, I realize you're not my Ace in Blackjack at all. Instead, being with you is like playing poker. And in that game of poker, the Aces are wild. Because I have realized in our time together that you have molded to be whatever I need you to be. My friend. My lover. My confidant. Hell, even my business advisor as of late. In poker, when the Aces are wild, you can play them as anything. That's why you're my Ace. Because you are always whatever I need you to be. And sometimes, you know what that is better than I do. I love you so damn much, and I am so excited to be your wife."

I choke back a surge of emotion and just get lost in her eyes. The eyes of the woman that saved my soul. My soul that I was convinced was a lost cause.

The preacher says a few more things, but I don't hear a single one of them until he tells me I can kiss my bride.

The rest of the evening passes in a blur. We dance, we eat, we mingle, but all I want to do is get my woman home and take her to bed. Our flight for our honeymoon doesn't leave until tomorrow, so I plan on having her in our bed tonight.

When we finally get done with all of the festivities, I carry her across the threshold of our apartment. I can barely contain myself as my mouth crashes against hers.

Her lets her hands tangle in my hair and lets my tongue open her up. She moans into my kiss before pulling away.

"I have a surprise for you, Ace," she whispers.

"Oh, really?"

"Really. Wait here, and I'll tell you when I'm ready." She hurries off into the bedroom, and I can barely sit still.

It seems like an eternity before she finally calls my name, and when I walk in, I can hardly believe my eyes.

She wears absolutely nothing at all as she lays spread out on the bed. Next to her, sits a blindfold. And there are restraints tied to each of the four corners of the bed.

"Sweetheart?" I ask.

"I know how much you like being in control, so I'm here to

satisfy your every desire."

Little does she know, she already *is* my every desire.

She throws in, "Don't get me wrong, I'll be back battling you for control tomorrow, but tonight, I'm at your mercy."

Knowing how much Tess loves control, this means the world to me. I begin to strip out of my tux preparing to give her just as much pleasure as she's given me.

And I plan to do it every single night for the rest of our lives.

Want more Tess and Alexander?

What happens when Tess and Alexander play house for a week and babysit three little kids? Find out in my holiday novella, Christmas Aces.
It's an exclusive to my newsletter subscribers, so sign up on my website to get your free copy!

https://www.stephaniereneeauthor.com/

Books by Stephanie Renee

The Constant Series
A Constant Surprise
A Constant Reminder
A Constant Love
A Constant Christmas (holiday novella)

Spinoff Standalones
Seeing Red
Aces Wild

Grady Romances (steamy small-town romance)
All the Right
All the Right Reasons

About The Author

Stephanie Renee

Stephanie is a born and raised Midwestern girl living in Indiana with her husband, their two sons, and two giant fur babies. She's addicted to strong coffee and cheap wine.

When she isn't writing stories that will make you swoon, she holds down a full-time job and loves to spend any spare time reading and supporting other Indie authors.

Acknowledgements

I said in the beginning, but a huge thank you goes to my husband who is always supportive of my writing. He's always there to listen when I have good news or hold my hand when I need him to. Hell, he came up with the name for Aces Wild when I was completely stuck. I couldn't ask for a better partner to share my life with.

Thank you to Hannah who is the best editor a girl could ask for...and even better best friend. She's my ride or die, and I'm sure we annoy absolutely everyone with our constant texting (spoiler alert: I don't care). Thanks for being my main bitch through it all.

Thank you to my parents who have always been supportive no matter what I decide to do in life. And to my mom who is a best friend to me and reads all my books as soon as I finish them.

And most of all, thank you as the reader for taking a chance on the works of this Midwestern girl that no one has heard of. I am forever humbled you took the time to read.

Made in the USA
Columbia, SC
21 June 2025